P9-DJL-677

A Map of the Known World

ALSO BY LISA ANN SANDELL

THE WEIGHT OF THE SKY

SONG OF THE SPARROW

A Map of the Known World

LISA ANN SANDELL

SCHOLASTIC PRESS • *New York*

 Published by Scholastic Press, an imprint of Scholastic Inc.,
Publishers since 1920. SCHOLASTIC, SCHOLASTIC PRESS, and associated logos are trademarks and/or registered trademarks of Scholastic Inc.

Library of Congress Cataloging-in-Publication Data Available
ISBN-13: 978-0-545-06970-0
ISBN-10: 0-545-06970-X
10 9 8 7 6 5 4 3 2 1 09 10 11 12 13
Printed in the U.S.A. 23
First edition, April 2009

For Meredith

and

In loving memory of my grandmother

Bessie Sandell

A Map of the Known World

Chapter One

Somewhere, things must be beautiful and vivid. Somewhere else, life has to be beautiful and vivid and rich. Not like this muted palette — a pale blue bedroom, washed out sunny sky, dull green yellow brown of the fields. Here, I know every twist of every road, every blade of grass, every face in this town, and I am suffocating.

So, I stay in. I don't have to leave the house to trace the picture of this town. I know it all by heart. I can map all of these houses that look so similar, practically identical to my own, with their dusty aluminum siding, sagging porches, and buckled sidewalks; the curves and lines of town and county roads curling between homes and farmsteads; the straight-as-an-arrow line of the highway heading straight out of town; Union Street with its bank and bakery and video store, weathered wood slats and dark windows. I can also see the slippery bank of the creek, the water lower than usual; the wide gray rocks populated by turtles and singing frogs; the gnarled old weeping willow tree, her branches yellow and soft, skimming the surface of the stream.

All of these things that I have seen countless times in my life will be there. All of it known and certain.

I sit in my bedroom, on the pale blue-and-white braided carpet, and sigh. If a sigh had a shape, a taste, a color, it would be a salty yellow triangle. And sitting here, in the triangle patch of weak sunlight falling through the window onto my rug, is summery enough for me. I could leave the house, go to the tennis camp at the middle school around the block, but I don't. Because I know that if I go, tennis racket in my hand, the ordinary *thwack* of racket on ball, the *screakk* of sneakers scratching across courts would quickly grind to a halt. Silence. And a dozen pairs of eyes would focus on me, follow every swing and every serve, every missed volley. Stares would hold me captive, paralyzing me. Pitying me. No thanks, I do not want that.

I could put on my swimsuit, bike to the town swimming pool, and carefully spread out my towel on the poolside grass. I might ready myself to dive off the board into the cool, blue ten feet of chlorine-and-pee filled water, submerging myself, becoming a blurred streak, watching dozens of legs kicking above me. The thought of all those goggled eyes watching me with their hard, plastic stares makes my head swim, my legs feel leaden, and my fingers too tired to open the door. And I'm sitting here in the air-conditioning.

I could step out, but I don't.

I do have a window onto escape, though. Onto that somewhere else, where colors and smells and winds are fresh and delicate, vibrant and new.

A free map of the world arrived in an envelope of junk mail at the start of summer, and I rescued it from the trash and pinned it up on the wall over my desk. I look at that map every day, as if my life depends on it. It very well might.

I like places with lots of vowels in their names, like Ulaanbaatar. The Isle of Man sounds like an important place, a place for adults. And the "stan" countries are fascinating — Kyrgyzstan, with all its consonants, is smaller than South Dakota, but contains the largest walnut forest in the world. A walnut forest must be a very romantic kind of forest.

Basically, what all of this map studying amounts to is a belief . . . no, a certainty that the world — well, the world outside of Lincoln Grove — is an exotic and alluring place. And it beckons to me. So, for the eighty-one days of summer vacation, during which I've stayed at home, stayed indoors, I pore over this map and push little green bubble-topped pins into the country and city names that catch my eye, catch my fancy. I know there is no chance my father, who once would have had a small coronary at the sight of all these pins stuck in the wall — "Do you know how much it will cost to fix that wall!" he would have barked — will ever even open the door to my bedroom, let alone set foot in it now. I'm safe.

For each bubble-marked spot, I imagine a whole vista, letting the sounds of the names and the topographies suggest a scene. I like to go online and look at the Web sites for different countries or cities. It's amazing how even the most remote countries have their own Web sites. But thanks to the World Wide Web, I learned that *Bhutan* means Land of the Thunder Dragon, and the Himalayas intersect with the northern portion of the country, and from this I can imagine a picture of a cold snowy land of fierce mountains and dusty rock, ancient temples with curving horns perched on the steepest ledges. Perhaps a sleeping dragon lies in the most remote of craggy caves.

Now enter my pad and pencils. I draw pretty well, I think. As I take careful crosshatch strokes, brushing the lead over the brown paper, following the silhouette of borders and natural boundaries, cityscapes and mountainscapes and roiling seas, within and without the lines of each map, slowly emerge. A cobblestone alleyway slick with rain, lined by sidewalk cafés and shops, a flower seller, the flutter of a red scarf on a beautiful lady, and a bustling newsstand caught up in the unfurling snail's shell shape of the city — this is Paris. I can practically smell the bread baking, the rich scent of coffee. I want to be there so badly.

Day after day, while the heat and all that is known festers outside, threatening to choke me, I make my escape into the unknown as I draw my maps of the world.

But time is fleeting. Time is fleeing. School begins in just four days.

• • •

When dusk comes, my parents come with it. First my dad arrives, the tires of his Volkswagen squealing in the garage. He enters the house, depositing his rumpled jacket and tie on the nearest living room chair, and without a call of greeting, proceeds immediately to the refrigerator. I can hear the freezer door swing open, and the *clink, clink, clink* of three ice cubes dropping into a glass, the squirt of gas from the tonic water bottle, as my father mixes his first gin and tonic. Silently, he retreats into the den, from which I can hear the low hum of television babble.

Then my mother gets home, and the door flies open, slamming loudly into the wall behind it. She calls out to me, "I'm home! Cora? Where are you?" her voice cracking with concern, as if she's scared I won't be here to answer her. Every single time. She flings her jacket and worn leather purse on the same chair as my dad. And as I join her in the kitchen, she inquires about what I've done today.

Once, dinnertime in our home was warm, important, ordinary. My mom used to take pleasure in cooking and trying new dishes. Duck confit, chicken tikka masala — I think she had the soul of an explorer, too, once. She would light candles, her hazel eyes catching the firelight and reflecting a radiance and gladness that suffused the room. I would help my father choose a record — yes, my dad's the last man on earth to listen to *records* — to play softly in the background.

He would run his thumb across the spines of every album in his massive collection, pulling them out and holding them up for me to judge. Crosby, Stills, Nash & Young's *Déjà Vu* merited a nose wrinkle, head shake, and a *come on* eye roll. Next, Earth Wind & Fire's *Greatest Hits*. "Dad!" I would squeal with a giggle. "That's so lame! No way!"

He'd give an exaggeratedly aggrieved sigh, "Ah, youth. What has it all come to? Okay, Rabbit, how about this one?" Then, the Beatles' *White Album*. I'd nod vigorously. "Blackbird" was one of our favorite songs to sing together.

Music chosen, dishes steaming on ivy-leaf trivets, our whole family would sit around the big oak dining table and take turns recounting the events of our day. I took those dinners for granted.

Now, though, I just look on as my mom prepares a frozen meal, microwaved for five and a half minutes on high, and, peering at her taut face, I try to think quickly of an answer to the question of what I've done today that won't make her cry. I've taken to lying. Sometimes I tell her that I played tennis or I went swimming — never mind the fact that I never have a bathing suit hanging to dry over my bathtub or sweaty smelly shorts and T-shirts in the laundry. She doesn't notice those missing details.

We sit down at the kitchen counter to eat our microwaved

peas and chicken, while my father takes his on a tray into the den, the only sound the clinking of ice cubes.

When my dad comes back into the kitchen to fix himself a second drink, I scrutinize my parents' faces, taking in their matching gray pallor, pinched foreheads, and deadened eyes, his hair gray and thinning, hers limp and greasy. They both look as though they have been broken into a thousand pieces and never properly mended. My mother's face is sewn too tight, while my father's face has become fuzzy in outline, like a cloud, with all of these little particles loosely holding on, floating, floating. But when he pours himself a tall glass of gin, those pieces come back together, just momentarily, again.

I wonder how my parents look at work, if they shed their brokenness outside the house. My own skin, the walls of this house, the *clink* of ice cubes, are all a prison. I must look broken, too.

• • •

Everything fell apart because of Nate. I try and try not to think about him, but as the start of school looms near, he keeps trespassing into my head. He always trespassed.

It happened six months and twenty-three days ago. Eight things went wrong on that eighth of February. Eight things that started out small. First, I slept straight through my alarm, so I was running late. Then, when I couldn't open the orange juice carton and punched a misshapen hole through the container, juice dribbled down the side, spilling all over the counter and floor and the front of my jeans. Next, I missed the bus as a direct result of the orange juice incident. The series of eight continued as I forgot my Spanish homework and flubbed a math quiz; my favorite pen broke and leaked all over the bottom of my backpack; I got into a screaming match with my older brother, Nate; and then he died. Yup. There it is. Number eight. It's a big one. My big brother got killed when he stormed out of the house that night, the night of February 8, drove his black Honda Civic in the dark without the headlights on, skidded around an icy curve in the county road, and wrapped this Honda Civic around a tree.

And the last words Nate said to me were, "See ya, wouldn't want to be ya, loser!" to which I very maturely responded, "Up yours, jerk!"

I had the last word.

But those words banged around and echoed in my head as the screen door banged shut. When the hospital or police, or whoever it was, called, those words thrashed around and rang in my head some more. In fact, they haven't stopped knocking and pounding in my head these last six months and twenty-three days. If there is one thing besides the certainty of all the houses and trees and creeks and streets that lie right outside the front door, I am certain of the fact that I cannot forget those angry, careless words.

In four days' time, I'm supposed to start at Lincoln Grove High, where my brother should have been entering his senior year. Nate Bradley made sure that every student, teacher, and administrator at LGH knew who he was. He was the Juvie D of LG. Always getting in trouble, getting detentions, getting arrested for stealing and trashing and tagging and generally being where he shouldn't. Nate never did anything really terrible, but he sealed his seat in infamy by sneaking into the teachers' lounge and spray painting the walls with the postulates and theorems of geometry. He picked up all of the fallen street signs along a two-mile length of the county road that were knocked over during a storm, and kept them. He pried the placard off the principal's office door and rehung it on one of the stalls in the second-floor boys' restroom. He talked back to teachers, forgot homework, flunked quizzes, sped in his car, violated his probation, and then started all over again.

I had grown used to the constant fighting between Nate and our parents. But I couldn't get used to the terrible anger that seemed to have taken hold of him after his fourteenth birthday. From then on, he was a stranger to me, to all of us, I think. I never really figured out where the older brother whom I used to follow dutifully on bike trips across town to the Wyatt cornfields where we would play spies, or whom I would trail to the creek, watching in awe as Nate hopped from stepping-stone to stone, sweeping up minnows and toads in his mesh butterfly net, went.

So I must start high school, where Nate's friends and teachers and ex-girlfriends will all be. If he had still been alive, I might have had a fighting chance at being able to distance myself from him, but now there is no escape — I will be known as Nathaniel Bradley's little sister. It's bad enough being the daughter of parents whose son died, every single minute of every single day, trapped in the house with their overpowering sadness. Now I'll be the girl whose brother died.

Chapter Two

"Should I wear my pink sundress or the lavender mini-skirt with the white ruffly tuxedo shirt?" Rachel's voice pours through the phone. Her intonation seems to have acquired a twang, a sort of valley girl twang to it, and I have no idea where it's come from. Rachel spent the summer with her family in Michigan, as she always does. Do they talk like valley girls in northern Michigan? Wherever it comes from, I am beginning to find it grating. Very grating.

"Why are you talking like that?" I interrupt.

"What?"

"Why do you have this stupid accent all of a sudden?" I demand.

"I have no idea what you're talking about," Rachel snaps defensively.

"Yeah," I snarl. "Whatever."

"What's your problem, Cora?" Bolts of hurt shoot through her voice.

"Nothing, Rach. Look, I should go," I say lamely.

"Well, okay. But, wait, tell me what I should wear!"

"The skirt."

"Really? Because I was thinking the sundress." Rachel sighs.

"So wear the sundress." I shake my head. Rachel and I have been best friends since first grade and never, in the last nine years, has Rachel ever seemed so completely possessed by frivolity. Yet, something about the very inanity of the conversation is also comforting, a glint of ordinary life.

"You don't have to bite my head off," Rachel retorts.

"I'm sorry. I didn't mean to," I say, trying to placate her and regretting my stupid temper — it's new . . . since The Accident. "I'm just nervous about starting school."

"I know, me too! I mean, I want this year to be perfect! It's *high school*! It's our chance!" I imagine every sentence out of Rachel's mouth as punctuated by exclamation points with little bubble-heart dots.

"Our chance for what?" I have a bad feeling I know where this is heading. South. I just can't get excited.

"Our chance to be popular, to be *in* —"

"In with the Nasties?" I ask disbelievingly, accusingly.

"I'm just saying *in* with everyone. I want to go out on a date, Cora, I want to be kissed, I want high school to be *fun*. Everyone says it's the best years of our lives. Don't you —" She doesn't get to finish as I cut in.

"I don't think it's the best years for *everyone*," I sneer. It is cruel. I know. I just can't help it.

"I'm sorry, Cor," Rachel immediately apologizes, contrite as a puppy.

"No. No, I'm sorry, Rach," I say. "I know what you mean. It'll be great." I try to sound cheerful, but even to my ears, my voice sounds hollow.

"So, what are you going to wear?" Rachel asks after a brief pause, as if nothing has happened. Pretending.

"Um, not sure. I haven't really thought about it. What do you think?" I'm desperate for normalcy to return, but I realize I don't know how to feel *normal.* Dread begins to churn in my stomach; is this what the entire year will be like?

We stay on the phone for another five minutes, as Rachel launches into a detailed analysis of my wardrobe, while I only half-listen. The conversation finally comes to a close, and I welcome it with relief.

Since The Accident, I get the sense that Rachel doesn't know how to talk to me anymore. She has taken to babbling. Now, I appreciate that having a best friend with a dead brother might be awkward for her and that she probably doesn't know what to say. Most people don't. But, aren't best friends supposed to know how to find the words?

Rachel did stand by my side at the funeral, wreathed in black as we three remaining Bradleys were, and she hugged me, and hugged my mother. She helped trolley out the platters of fruit salad and cold cuts, gather the dozens of flower arrangements, and clean up the mess after the funeral. She was quiet, afraid. She was there, and not.

Now, though, I'm sensing a deeper change in Rachel. The valley girl drawl and the pronouncement that she wants a boyfriend are new. We used to mock the girls who lived to find boyfriends. We called them "pathetic" and we even pinkie-swore to despise the Nasties for life. Now, though, I suspect that Rachel might be backing out of our pact. Or maybe she's growing out of it?

Rachel and I had named Kellie Gibbon, Macie Jax, and Pearl O'Riley the Nasties, because for as long as we have been in school together — which is basically our whole lives — this trio has lorded their popularity over the rest of the class, meting out kindness and cruelty among the other kids unevenly, randomly.

In fourth grade, they were fixing their lip gloss in the mirror of the girls' room and deciding who was cool, and by fifth grade, they dictated who was *so* not. In the sixth, seventh, and eighth grades, the Nasties solidified their clique and labeled the rest, the jocks, the nerds, the goths, the losers. Rachel and I have always sort of floated outside of clique boundaries. We were never subjected to the worst of the terrible Nasties torment — although they weren't kind to us — but we never really fit in anywhere, either. Now Rachel wants to be "in" with them?

Great. School is going to be just great.

I stop pacing in front of my dresser mirror and take a look.

Long frizzy waves of brown hair, vampire pale skin, freckles on my nose, and big muddy brown eyes that are so dull, I would fall asleep if I had to look into them. Nate had the same hair, the same brown eyes, but his eyes glinted with a ferocity that never looked boring.

• • •

The bleating of the alarm clock pulls me abruptly from sleep. It isn't difficult; these days I don't sleep so well, restless with anxiety. My eyes are open, but it takes a few minutes before I can bring myself to sit up. Then, as I plant unsteady feet, the floor crackles and slides away. Startled, I look down and smile. A pile of pencil sketches is scattered across the floor. I had gotten up in the middle of the night to draw — a map of Edinburgh. Dark lines molding the shape of a city, finer strokes of gray for the castle and moody fall sky.

Quickly, I wash and dress and make my way down to the kitchen. My father is already gone, without a farewell, of course. I can feel the tension practically smothering all of the air from the room with my mom's nervous pacing. She flits around here and there as she waits for me. The kitchen is filled with early morning sunlight, the yellow gingham curtains and seat covers adding to the cheery effect. *A false front,* I think. The smell of cooking oil lingers, and there are pans and plates strewn across the counter.

"Oh, good, you're ready," my mother says breathlessly.

"Hey, Mom," I reply, dropping my backpack on a chair.

"Sweetie, did you sleep well? You look a bit tired. Here, I made you breakfast; look, scrambled eggs, toast. Have some orange juice." She is talking a mile a minute, practically doing a jig as she dances from one side of the kitchen to the other. "High school! I can't believe my baby is starting high school. Take a vitamin!"

"Wow. Okay, you can stop hovering, Mom. It's just the first day of school. I've already been through eight of them before this."

"But it's the first day of *high* school! You're all grown up. I can't believe it," my mother repeats. She pauses and her forehead tightens. "You'll come home immediately after school, right, Cora?" she asks.

"Yes, Mom," I answer. I can feel the irritation inching into my voice. I try to push it down, but I need to get out of the house. *Now.*

"I don't want you hanging around anywhere," my mother warns. "And you'll watch out for traffic?"

"I understand, Mom. I'll come straight home and I'll be careful. Promise."

"All right. I love you. Be careful, and have a good day. I can't believe it's your first day. . . ."

"I love you, too, Mom." I wave good-bye as my mother gathers her belongings and moves into the garage. I scoop a couple of forkfuls of runny eggs into my mouth and take a hurried bite of toast, then throw the rest in the trash, toss my dishes in the sink, and get ready to dash out of the house without drinking any orange juice or taking my vitamin pill. Very rebellious.

Suddenly, my mother pops her head back in through the door to the garage. "You'll come home straight after —"

"Yes, Mom!" A flash of ire rises into my throat, onto my tongue. It tastes bitter. "I promise!" I pull my backpack onto my shoulder and move past her, stalking through the garage, then, guilt getting the better of me, turn and tell her again, "I love you."

When will she get off my back? And when will I stop worrying that an angry word to her will . . . make her fall apart?

My mother just raises her hand and gets into her car.

My ten-speed bicycle is a smoky, silvery blue, and it's beautiful. I caress the frame, lovingly squeeze the tires. They are both soft. Quickly, I grab the pump. I am so stupid for not checking the air pressure last night. Ugh. My hands are covered in grease, but I at least manage to avoid getting it on my clothes. And then I am on my way, and as I cruise down the street, my legs pumping hard to regain familiarity with the pedals, I can just about forget to feel anxious. The scenery is a blur and I hardly remember to notice it, to resent it. My mind is as blissfully blank as the wind.

Not for long.

As I pull up to the high school, with its tan brick facade, and dull, darkened windows that peer back at me like listless aliens, the churning in my stomach returns.

Quickly, I wheel my bike over to the crowded bike rack and chain it up. The parking lot is filled mostly with dusty older cars that look like hand-me-downs, probably from parents to kids or from older siblings to younger ones. The last part of that thought is accompanied by a twitch in my gut.

My gut. I never felt like I had a gut before The Accident. I'd gotten stomachaches — or tummy aches as my mom calls them — but my gut hadn't ever been a part of my anatomy I was aware of. Now I know just what that metaphor, to feel like you've been punched or kicked or any other manner of battering in the gut, means.

Anyway, I had better snap out of it. I can't just hang around here staring at the cars all day. People will really think I'm weird.

I steel myself, take a deep breath, and walk toward the front doors. The doors swing shut after each body that passes through them, beating the air as if to say, *There's no coming back out.* Dozens of kids are pouring past me, like salmon swimming upstream. Everyone is pushing to get in here, and I'll bet no one even actually wants to be here. As I look all around, the urge to turn and run is strong. Very strong. Oh my gosh, I *so* don't want to be here.

Well, tough.

The corridors of the school are narrow and dimly lit. The walls are painted mustard yellow, and the linoleum floor tiles are a grayish white like dirty dishwater. So different from the cheery hallways of my middle school. Even the classrooms in Lincoln Grove Middle School had been painted in bright, happy colors: sky blue and buttercup yellow, with encouraging posters and artwork welcoming the students. By the time I'd started the eighth grade at LGMS, coming to school felt like being enveloped in a warm, fleecy blanket. If not the most fun place to be, it was familiar and safe. But this, Lincoln Grove High School, is just foreboding. It's cold and scary.

I stop in the middle of the hallway, trying to get my bearings. I came in here once during the summer for freshman orientation and a pair of bored-looking seniors showed me, and a group of other kids whose last names started with the letters A–F, around. I can't remember where any of the classrooms are, where these hallways go. Kids stream by me, swiftly dodging and moving past in circling eddies, like a river will wash around a tall rock or log. The tide of faces shows worry and excitement, eagerness and despondency. Upperclassmen find their friends and younger kids wander alone, searching.

Most of the kids look old. The girls have chests, actual chests, and bouncy, movie-star hair. I look down. It's a flat slope all the way, and I can feel my blue jeans hanging loose at my waist, gathering at my ankles, pooling over the tops of my sneakers. I still look like a little kid. I don't feel any different, no more grown up. But I'm in high school now. Shouldn't I feel older? Shouldn't I have good hair and curves and a boyfriend? Instead, I'm still flat and straight and hopelessly single. No one wants to date the dead guy's sister. And probably, no one ever will. I glance around again and feel my stomach clench. This is it. I'm really here.

Yet, I can't shake this awful sense that the next four years will be another kind of prison. I just have to get through this. Four years and then I'll be free.

I feel myself floating adrift in the whirlpool of bodies, but in a strange way, I find the sea of the hallway almost reassuring. Maybe if I see the others as this muddled, huddled mass, maybe no one will notice me at all.

I shuffle along, letting the current pull me, and I have the sense that I am like a rat caught in a maze of tunnels, moving endlessly toward some promise of . . . of what? Light? Life? Cheese?

The thought tiptoes idly through my mind, when suddenly I see something that makes me stop abruptly. That blonde hair. I know it. It's Julie. Julie Castor, Nate's ex-girlfriend. More specifically, the girlfriend who dumped him the night he died. The girlfriend whose ex-ness triggered Nate's nighttime automotive antics. She is talking to some scruffy-looking guy with saggy jeans.

Julie glances up; her heavily lined green eyes meet my own and widen slightly. Then she looks away. I bow my head, afraid to look up and meet her hard green glare again. I was not prepared to see Julie. Well, I guess this is how it is . . . *high school*. I'd better get used to seeing people from Nate's life, here, every day.

I finally find my locker in the next hallway and put a combination lock on it. Then I move along to my homeroom. As I enter into the classroom, a gradual hush descends, and twenty-nine heads swivel toward the door. I feel dizzy, and for a second, just a second, I think I might be sick. But Rachel is there, waving to me, and as I gratefully make my way to sit down beside her, the buzz of chatter and gossip resumes.

"You'd think no one ever saw a girl with a dead brother before," I say softly.

Rachel puts her hand on my arm and squeezes. "Ignore them," she whispers. "Hey, guess what's happening this weekend?"

"What?"

"The LGH Bonfire! We have to go. *Have to.* Everyone who's anyone will be there. *Everyone.*" Rachel still has the funny valley girl twang, and she has actually said the words "everyone who's anyone." *What?*

I shake my head as vigorously as I can without totally messing up my already messy ponytail. "Uh-uh, no way, lady. Not in a million years. Besides, my mom will never let me go." For once, I am thankful for my mother's crazy, overbearing rules.

My Mom's Rules:

1. No drugs (fine, makes sense)
2. No alcohol (also reasonable)
3. No riding in cars unless a parent is driving (a little bit overprotective)

4. No going out without a parent at night — ever (kind of crazy, right?)
5. Permission to go out without said parent on daytime outings will be given on rare occasions only (seemingly very, *very* crazy)

"What do you mean?" Rachel whines. "You *have* to come with me! I can't go alone. Puh-leeeese!"

"I'm telling you, my mom won't let me. I'm not allowed out after dark, remember? I might turn into a pumpkin or something."

"No, seriously, you cannot miss this. And I can't go without you. Please, just ask her. If you don't, I will," Rachel threatens.

"Yeah, good luck with that." I smirk. "Anyway, I don't even want to go."

"What do you mean? How could you possibly mean that?" Rachel squeals.

"I don't know. I'm just not . . ." My voice trails off as the teacher begins to call roll.

"Just ask your mom, okay?" Rachel wheedles.

"Fine, I'll ask! Jeez."

Rachel shoots me a wide smile, and I can't help but return it.

After homeroom, Rachel and I split up and head to our first classes. I edge into the surge of students, bodies pressing tightly together, pushing and fighting through the halls. I have geometry. When I arrive in the classroom, the teacher, Mr.

Lane, announces that everyone will be sitting in alphabetical order.

His voice drones on as he calls the names, "Allan, Andrews, Ballans, Belson, Bradley —" He looks up, looks around. "Bradley? Any relation to . . ." He doesn't finish. I had begun to raise my hand, and I drop it too quickly, so that it slaps the wooden desk with a resounding clap. I can tell that he had been about to say something smart-alecky about my brother, but stopped himself when he remembered. My face is hot, and the nausea has returned. I stare at the ground. *Really?* Did this *really* just happen?

The class shifts uncomfortably, and the silence stretches on.

"Uh, sorry, Miss Bradley, for your loss. Your brother was quite a character — a, uh, fine young fellow."

I can't even begin to find my voice. I just nod my head and feel my ears catch fire. Seriously? *A fine young fellow?* I cannot believe this is happening.

The rest of the morning passes relatively smoothly — relative to the humiliating debacle of geometry class. My classes will be challenging, and there is sure to be a serious load of homework for each one. But I can't shake the feeling that my teachers are examining me, looking for signs of — I don't know — grief, similarity to Nate, craziness. Who knows? But I can sense that they're treating me carefully. So are the other kids. A few girls I used to be friendly with B.T.A. (Before The Accident), like Callie Rountree and Carolyn Wright, have said hello to me, but I can tell they want to run away from me as fast and far as possible. Like I have leprosy or something. I pat my nose. Still there. No crumbling body parts.

At lunch, Rachel and I sit together as we have done since the first day of first grade. I bought the hot lunch and I cast around the tray for something edible. The chicken is simultaneously stringy and rubbery and strangely gray. The green beans are cold and rubbery, and the rice pudding is stringy and also gray. To be expected from a school-issue lunch. While we sit at our end of the lunch table, next to a wide window, Rachel keeps darting looks across the cafeteria at Josh Mills, one of the boys in our grade. We've known Josh for as long as I can remember — that's how it is with most of the kids in our class, we've been together since we were babies — but we've never counted him as a friend. I mean, he is probably decent enough, but he's definitely more interested in soccer than in girls. His hair is shaved close to the scalp, and his ears stick out like half moons on either side of his head.

He is laterally friendly with the Nasties, meaning his friends are friends with the Nasties, and he is allowed to sit at their lunch table. Important fact: He has never participated in the Nasties' merciless shredding of other classmates. He's never stuck up for any of their victims, either. (Well, neither have I, for that matter.) Still, I figure the fact that he's never joined in the Nasty choral renditions of calling Rachel "McFattie" — her last name is McFadden — is a plus.

"So, I just have art left this afternoon. Thank goodness," I remark.

"Mmm," Rachel mumbles distractedly.

"They put me in Advanced Art, you know, with mostly upperclassmen. They hardly ever let freshmen into the advanced classes," I tell her.

"Cool," she mutters, clearly not interested even a little bit in what I'm saying.

"So, what do you have after lunch? History?" I ask, trying. Really trying.

"Don't you think Josh got cute over the summer?" Rachel finally asks in a hushed voice. "Like, supercute?"

"Supercute? Really?" I repeat stupidly.

"Oh my gosh, yes! Are you not seeing?" Rachel continues. "I think I have the biggest crush on him!"

"Josh?" I ask. I am dumbfounded. I can't see past the big ears and the Nasties.

"Yeah! Don't you think?" Rachel carries on, not waiting to hear my opinion. "I mean, he must have grown like three inches."

"Hmm," I murmur.

"Do you think he'll be at the bonfire?" Rachel asks.

"Well, you said everyone who's anyone will be there," I snicker.

"You're right. He'll definitely be there," Rachel agrees, not noticing my tone. "You have to call me as soon as you ask your mom, okay?"

"Uh-huh," I answer without really paying attention to the question. I stare out the window at the cars in the parking lot and the broken glass glittering on the sidewalk like diamonds. It's funny how a blown-out windshield can look beautiful.

• • •

Nervously, I make my way to the back of the high school, where the art studio is tucked away in a light-filled corner hallway. I enter the classroom and peer around. The walls are covered with a messy flood of color, cutouts from magazines and books, all kinds of images, paintings and drawings and photographs of sculptures, some of which I recognize, many more that I do not. Easels people the room, draped with canvases and drawing tablets. Students are perched on rickety stools stained with paint and dotted with spots of glue.

I settle down in the far corner of the room, near the windows, which are filthy and tall, reminding me of some neglected cathedral. Then I hang my smock, one of my dad's old work shirts, on a hook at the back of the room.

There are fifteen other students in the class, mostly a mix of sophomores and juniors. Including me, there are eleven girls and only four guys. The teacher, Ms. Calico, looks young. She is wearing khaki bell-bottoms and a flowery blouse with a long silver chain and a thick wooden pendant hanging down by her belly. Her brown hair is messy — like mine, I think — short and tucked behind her ears. She is standing by her desk at the front of the room, flipping through a magazine.

Suddenly, a shadow fills the doorway. Ms. Calico looks up, then smiles. "Just in time," she says.

I look up to see who's come in with the bell. And I feel my stomach plummet into my feet. I stand up quickly, knocking my stool over. I'm frozen and I look away from the dark gray eyes that are now staring at me curiously. *Work, feet,* I plead silently. I bend down and pick up my stool, then sit and huddle behind my easel.

It's a strange sensation, feeling all the color drain away from my face. The blood runs away slowly, leaving a sickening shiver in its wake.

Damian Archer. I glance up, and see him still standing in place, staring at the floor, a queasy grimace on his face. *Good,* I think, *I hope he feels worse than I do. Maybe he'll feel so bad, he'll leave.*

How can I be in a class with Damian? I can't sit here in the same room as him. I just can't.

Damian was in the car with Nate that night. The night of February 8. Nate died. Damian walked away. *Walked away.* My mom said it was Damian's fault, his influence that made Nate do such a terrible and foolish thing. And looking at Damian in his black combat boots, black jeans, black trench coat, I'm inclined to believe it, too.

"Okay, everyone!" Ms. Calico's voice cuts through my nausea, and I glimpse Damian taking a stool at the front of the room, as far from me as possible. Thank goodness.

"Welcome to Advanced Art. I have a couple of announcements to start with," Ms. Calico continues. "First, there will be a school-wide art show at the beginning of February, and while it's not mandatory that my students participate, I highly encourage all of you to think about submitting pieces to the show. The second piece of business is that I have information for a couple of summer art programs at my desk. The applications are due in mid-November for most of them. If you are interested in more information, please see me at the end of class."

Summer art programs. An art show. Oh my gosh. I look around and all of the other kids in the class look so much older than I am, so much more . . . capable. Even if they're only a year or two older, they just seem more confident than I feel. I don't have the nerve to ask about the art show or the summer programs. Anyway, Ms. Calico was probably talking to the upperclassmen, not to me.

I glance up and catch my breath when I catch Damian peeking at me around his easel. How am I going to share art class with Damian? It was the one class I was excited to take. Now, though . . . *Does he hate me as much as I hate him?* I wonder. *He must hate my whole family.*

• • •

I go straight home, just as my mother had commanded me to do. I have at least three hours before my parents get back, so rather than starting on the homework I seriously cannot believe the teachers had the gall to assign on the first day of school, and rather than think about the first day of high school at all, I go straight to my bedroom. I move to turn on my computer, but I stop to consider the map of the world.

This map is a little — or a lot — out-of-date. The shapes and borders of many of the nations have changed . . . entire pieces of the world have switched hands, been broken apart and put back together differently since this piece of paper was printed. All of it, the world, home, life, just keeps shifting, keeps on moving.

Idly, I let my fingers run over continents and mountain ranges and oceans. There is so much. There is no land that remains to be discovered, no continent left unexplored. Still, the whole world is out there, waiting, just waiting for me.

Oh, I want to do things — I want to walk the rain-soaked streets of London, and drink mint tea in Casablanca; I want to wander the wastelands of the Gobi desert and see a yak. I think my life's ambition is to see a yak. There is just so much, so much to see, to touch and taste and explore. And above all, I want to *do* things, things that will mean something, that will matter. More than anything else, I am terrified I won't have that chance.

So, I do what I always do when the fear of being trapped

here in Lincoln Grove for the rest of my life wells up in my throat and threatens to choke me. I escape to my refuge.

I take out a tablet of drawing paper and cradle it in my lap. As I stare up at the continent of Asia, I let the soft graphite follow the lines of China and Mongolia, Russia, then move south, to Burma, Thailand, Laos, Cambodia, and Vietnam, Malaya, Sumatra (I told you the map was outdated), Borneo. I look north again and study the vastness of Siberia. I know the Russians used to exile criminals — revolutionaries — at various points in the country's history to Siberia. I imagine an empty ice field, barren and cheerless, inhabited by a solitary woman in a sable fur cap and coat, a countess, marching by herself to a looming, frozen doom. How dreadful. Lines meet and capture the bent shape of a cold and lonely woman as my pencil flies over the paper, tracing this scene inside the boundaries of Siberian tundra.

I move back down the map again, pausing at Sumatra, which I think is a part of Indonesia now. I picture lush green jungles, dense with shiny leaves and vines, rich black soil, and eyes of varying colors peering out from among the trees. My pencils scratch across the page, the paper wrinkling finely. I don't mind when the paper looks crumpled — it gives the drawing an old map quality. I love watching the supple gray line chase the point of the pencil. Strokes and strokes giving shape to a great, wild, jungle life, monkeys and frogs peeping from between leaves.

The sudden grumbling of the garage door opening pulls me

back, back to Lincoln Grove and my bedroom and the sound of tire wheels squeaking on the smooth concrete of the garage floor. My dad is home. I feel my whole body tense up as I wait for him to enter the kitchen, as I wait for the greeting I know won't come, and as I wait for the inevitable clink of ice cubes.

The door slams, footsteps. Then I hear the cupboard bang shut, a glass slams onto the countertop, the refrigerator opens and closes, the freezer door swings open . . . pause, *clink, clink, clink,* and close. Then footsteps into the den, and silence. My fingernails have been digging into my palms.

When I was in middle school, B.T.A., my dad would come home, race up the stairs — the thudding of his footsteps like a happy waltz — and he'd knock, saying, "Shave and a haircut," to which I'd answer with a shouted "Two bits!"

"Hey, Rabbit, how's the homework coming? I know I'm old, but need any help?" he would ask. It was like a dance that we'd performed over and over, so many times for all thirteen years of my life. Till now.

I leave the pencils and paper and map behind, pull my textbooks and notebooks from my backpack and, sliding onto the bed, begin to do my homework.

Geometry, with its postulates and proofs, theorems and corollaries, will be hard. American history might not be too bad, but biology will surely be. For English class, I'm going to have to read a ton, but honestly, I'm kind of looking forward to reading some of the books, like *The Odyssey, Wuthering*

Heights, *Romeo and Juliet*, and *Invisible Man*. And then there is art class. Ms. Calico explained that we will start with sketching still lifes, then painting them, and then we'll each have to find an independent project to focus on. I wonder if I could make something of my map drawings. How much freedom to explore will Ms. Calico allow us? Just thinking about it starts a tingle of excitement in my stomach. Or my gut. Even if I have to face Damian Archer, there is a glimmer of promise yet.

The door to the garage suddenly crashes shut, and my mother's voice rings out. "Daniel, Cora, I'm home! Cora, are you here?" she calls shrilly.

I run down the stairs and meet her in the kitchen. "Here, let me help," I say, bending to assist her in hauling in and putting away the bags of groceries that now cover every inch of floor space between the stove and dishwasher.

"How was school, Cor?" my mother asks, eyeing me keenly and ignoring the fact that my dad still has not answered her call.

"Fine," I reply.

"Fine? Just fine? How were your classes? Are you in many with Rachel?" she peppers me with questions. I'm not in the mood to be grilled, but it looks like it will be unavoidable.

"My classes were fine. I only have homeroom with Rachel, and we had lunch together today."

"I see," Mom says, sighing, looking tired and downcast.

My mom used to look pretty young — younger than most of the other kids' mothers, at any rate — for her age with her short, light-brown hair and once-bright hazel eyes. But the dark, puffy circles beneath them cast a shadow over her face. Now she looks old and tired beyond her years.

"Art class seems cool," I add, feeling sorry for her. If only there was something I could say that would make her feel better, less worried about me falling into an abyss, which would pull her back from her own black hole. There's no way I'm telling her about Damian.

"That's nice," she murmurs, her voice, her gaze far away. Where does she go when she grows distant like this? Is she thinking of Nate? Of how our family used to be? Is she traveling through time? Or does she get caught in some quicksand pit of despair?

"Well, what's for dinner?" I ask, trying to stir her, bring her back to the present.

"Meat loaf," my mom replies absently, then she sort of shakes herself and sets about making the preparations.

"Can I help?" I offer.

"No, it's okay. Go do your homework."

"Um, Mom, could I ask you something?" I begin.

"Sure, what is it?" she answers, coming back to me.

"There's this thing, the LGH Bonfire. They have it every year. It's an official school thing, like a pep rally, only it's at night. Could I go? Mom? I'd go with Rachel, and it'd be really safe." I know I am talking way too fast, but I don't know how else to ask this. Just bringing it up feels like an act of contrition. If I seem normal, maybe she'll feel better.

"Oh. I — I don't know."

"Please, Mom? You can't — I — It's a school thing. Teachers will be there, and tons of kids. It'll be safe. I promise." I think about how I don't even want to go, but as I speak, I realize this is a battle I have to win. For both our sakes.

"But you'll be roaming around at night, and I know how these things are — I remember —" Her voice breaks. But she clears her throat and presses on. "There will be drinking there. And I don't want you out on the roads at night."

"Mom, I can't drive, remember? Can't I go if *you* drive me? Or Rachel's mom?" I can see that she is considering this.

"Well . . ." She drifts away again.

"Mom?" I try. "Mom!"

"All right." She snaps back to life. "You can go. But I'll drive you there, and pick you up at nine thirty, no later."

"Mom, it only starts at eight. Can't you pick me up at ten thirty?" I plead.

"Ten o'clock. No later, Cora. I mean it. If you're not in my car by ten, I'll come and get you," she warns.

"Fine!" I snarl, contrition and guilt and concern to the wind. I stomp upstairs to call Rachel and wait for the awkward dinner that is bound to follow.

Chapter Three

The air is thick with falling ash, black-and-gray snow. As the sun slowly sinks, the sky turns as orange as the bonfire itself. All around, kids, their faces painted red and black with the school initials, whoop and dance around the fire. Voices rise in a crescendo, chanting, "LGH! LGH! LGH!"

Rachel and I arrived early, and until more people came, we hovered several feet away from the pyramid of sticks, looking on as a teacher, Mr. Cross, flicked match after match, trying to start the fire. He kneaded his brow with soot-stained fingers and wiped away the sweat. Finally the match caught, and the bits of grass and paper lit, and the flames grew and billowed. We watched as students trickled onto the field, and dusk fell, bringing with it the chirping song of crickets and the blinking flickers of fireflies. Cliques seem to gather their members, the way a magnet will draw filings of iron. Soccer guys find soccer guys, drama kids find drama kids, and even though I don't know all of these people, each group is pretty much distinguishable on sight. The football players shuffle their feet and stand in a crooked line, uniform in their black leather team jackets with the red sleeves and the fighting badger on the back. The stoners stand off to one side, baggy pants and dreadlocks their own kind of uniform. The cool kids are easy to spot, the girls dabbing at their sparkling lip gloss, fluffing their manes of hair, dressed perfectly, while hangers-on orbit around them like they are caught in a gravitational pull. These kids glow.

I cannot figure out for the life of me how to put together an outfit like these girls do. I can never seem to find that adorable top or the perfect pair of jeans. And even if I do have the "right" clothes, forget about wearing them the way these girls do. I simply cannot carry it off. Rachel says it's about attitude. Clearly I have an attitude problem.

I study them, each and every group in turn, and wonder, how do these kids find one another? How does someone decide, I'm going to be a stoner or a goth or a princess or a jock? Why haven't I found a place, a definition? Would being a part of the group chase the loneliness away? Or does everyone feel as scared as I do?

A part of me aches to be in one of those cliques, laughing easily, knowing exactly where I'm supposed to be, knowing exactly who I am. Categorizing, classifying is so easy, so certain. Yet, I'm here on the fringe, on the outside, a watcher.

Soon the field is crowded with students from all four classes, and the chanting, singing, shouting is echoed by the rattle of waving grasses and chirruping crickets.

Rachel squeezes my arm tightly, her fingernails like a hawk's talons. "There he is! He's here! How do I look?" she squeaks. I follow Rachel's gaze to see Josh with his baggy jeans and unlaced sneakers shuffling up to the fire.

"You look fine," I tell her, shaking my head, feeling lame.

"Just fine?" Rachel asks, her eyes filled with panic. "Do I look fat?" She really looks scared now.

"You look great," I say. I smile and nudge Rachel's shoulder. "You should go talk to him."

"Really? You really think so?"

"Yeah, why not?"

"I don't know. . . ." Rachel looks down. She seems so vulnerable, so frightened. And I see her, really see her, probably for the first time since school started, and I realize — sort of surprised by my own surprise — that she looks *good*. Rachel has always been a little bit plump, but the suntan she cultivated over the summer and the blond streaks in her hair give her a pretty glow. "I just want this year to be great, you know?" she says softly.

"Yeah. I know. Just go on!"

"What if . . . He's so cute. He probably won't want to talk to me. Don't you think?" Rachel says doubtfully.

"Rach, *you're* cute! I bet he'll be happy if you go over to him!" I am trying to sound cheerfully confident.

"Well . . ." Rachel pauses. "All right. Will you be okay here by yourself?"

"I'm fine," I reply. "Just flash him your gorgeous smile."

"'Kay, wish me luck!" Rachel sings out and starts off toward her target.

I watch Rachel blend into the thickening crowd. As she disappears, I wonder if I'm weird for not liking any of the boys in our class. If Nate hadn't died, would I be as carefree as Rachel and all the rest of them? Would I be able to jump into the fray and dance and laugh and be happy? Why does this thing mark me, anyway? It's like the other kids can sense it — well, I figure most of them know, anyway. But it's not just that they treat me strangely. It's me, too. Acting different. Feeling different. Nate hardly even talked to me anymore. . . . Why has his absence, his death changed *everything*?

I keep to the edge of the crowd, listening to the jocks singing fight songs and the murmur of conversations and the crackling of the flames. Suddenly, a tingle creeps down my spine, and I look up. Like I've been shocked, my eyes meet another pair, across the field. In the graying light, I can just make out who it is. And as the realization sets in, I step back in surprise. *Damian.* He lifts his chin slowly in greeting and begins to move toward me, deliberately weaving through the throngs of students. My knees quiver and my stomach takes a turn. I look around, as if help was going to arrive (which it's not), but I can't stir from my spot.

Feet, let's go, I plead with myself. They won't move, though; they are firmly rooted to the grassy field. Why does Damian do this to me?

When he reaches me, I can't help but stare down at the ground awkwardly. When I glance up to meet his eyes, I find him studying me carefully, tensed as though afraid I might run away — which I very much want to do, if only it weren't for my stupid, stubborn, mutinous feet.

"Hi, Cora," he says softly.

"Hi," I reply, my voice barely a whisper, my stomach still roiling.

"How are you? How's —" He stops and clears his throat. "How's your family?"

"Everyone is fine. We're all fine," I say, my voice pitched in that hard, shaky tone I get when I lie.

"That's good," he replies, gazing at me closely.

"Huh," I grunt.

"What?" he asks.

"Like you care," I mutter darkly.

Damian takes a step back, recoiling as if I've slapped him. His eyes fill with a look of hurt that pricks me down to my soul. There's so much hurt to go around.

I feel like I'm melting. I wish I were melting. "I'm sorry," I whisper. "It's just . . ." I shake my head and focus on the ground. "Anyway, how about you?" I ask.

"What about me?" Damian replies, uncertain.

"How *are* you?"

His shoulders had been hunched, and they relax a bit now. "Oh, okay. You know." He shifts his weight and looks up at me. "So, uh, how do you like art class so far?"

My stomach lurches. It feels wrong to share something — anything — with Damian. Even something as harmless and unavoidable as art class. But his face is open, and somehow I can't muster my rage just now.

"It seems like it'll be okay, right?" I ask.

"Yeah, I think so." Damian gives a small laugh. When he smiles, his eyes go all squinty. His strange gray eyes look almost silver in the twilight. And when he smiles the straight angles and high planes of his cheekbones and jaw seem softer.

He is handsome, if a little unusual-looking, with his crooked nose, broad cheeks, smooth coffee-and-milk complexion, and short curly hair. I never really noticed that before. And he looks older. Older, but lost a little bit, too.

Stupid stomach doing gymnastics.

"Well, we'll see." I stare into his face, while my mind turns circles trying to understand what Damian is doing here, talking to me. Why did he cross the field to speak to me when in all the years he was Nate's best friend, he practically ignored me? And when, now, I see him standing in front of me, I can't help but hate him just for being able to stand here.

We are both silent. I wonder if he knows what I'm thinking. I peer down at my watch; I have to squint to make out the numbers in the dying light. Quarter to ten. "Look, I should go. My mom is probably waiting for me," I tell Damian. Without waiting for a response, I walk away, silently chastising myself. What am I doing talking to him? He's bad news.

Somehow, though, thinking of him as a monster has now become just a little bit harder.

I suppose I should find Rachel. But the number of students has grown, and as I push through the crowd, everything starts to feel crooked, as if the earth is tilted and I'm in a fun house. I'm dizzy and all the kids I pass seem to be laughing at me, turning leering faces with twisted grimaces on me. I spin around, vainly looking for Rachel. Then I stop. *Get ahold of yourself.* I take a deep breath and sweep my eyes over the crowd.

There she is, standing off to the side of a narrow circle of bodies near the fire. She is smiling, but I can tell that it is pasted on. Her hair has flattened in the warm, humid air, and she holds her hands clasped in front of her. I can sense her sadness and I feel sad *for* her. Rachel is on the outside, too.

The Nasties are busily ignoring Rachel, leaning on each other's shoulders and giggling and talking to Josh and three other boys. And clearly, the boys are eating up the attention like starving cubs. Macie, as always, is at the center, a sun for the others to revolve around. Rachel and Elizabeth Tillson hover at the outskirts of the circle, like distant planets, while

Pearl and Kellie, Josh, Matt James, and Evan Miller compose the rest of the Nasty solar system.

I remember when Macie first moved to town; we were in the fourth grade. This odd-looking girl with a big puff of hair and mismatched socks and electric pink sneakers stood hunched at the front of our classroom as the teacher introduced her as the new girl. I remember Pearl and Kellie scorning her outrageous outfit and ridiculous hair. One week later, however, Macie had turned the tables on the other two and installed herself as Queen Bee, the barometer by which every measure of cool was measured. And the Nastiest trio was cemented.

I hate watching the Nasties treat Rachel like this now. I hate seeing her just standing there, being purposefully ignored, seeing her watching Josh flirt and be flirted with. I can feel their Nasty intentions spreading out like rotten roots curling beneath the ground; I know they are perfectly aware of Rachel standing beside them. I can feel their cruelty curdling the soil. It makes me so mad.

I walk over to Rachel and tap her on the shoulder. As she spins around, I say, "Hey, I have to go. Are you coming?"

"What? Is it already ten?" Rachel looks annoyed and glances around at Josh and the Nasties. "Uh, I think I'll hang around here. Is that okay? I can get a ride from someone else." She avoids my gaze, kicking at the straw on the ground.

"Are you sure?" I ask almost pleadingly. *Why?* I add silently. *Why do this to yourself?*

"Yesss," Rachel hisses.

"Fine." I turn on my heel and snake my way out of there and head for the parking lot. Sure enough, my mother is there, waiting. As I near the car, I can see that she is anxiously tapping her fingers on the steering wheel.

"Hey, Mom," I say casually as I climb into the passenger seat.

"Where's Rachel?" she asks.

"She's staying," I tell her, my voice wavering.

"Well, how was it, honey?" my mother asks, quickly putting the car in drive.

She looks so tired. I'd bet all of my best drawing pencils that I look the same.

"It was fine," I reply.

• • •

Except everything isn't fine. I sit on my bed, staring across the room at the map pinned to the wall. Nothing is fine at all, actually. I am mad. Mad at Rachel for being different from how she's always been and for being obsessed with "everyone who's anyone" and for wanting to be accepted by the Nasties when they won't even open their circle to her. How could she ditch me at the bonfire, leaving me by myself to talk to Damian? How could she make me walk out of that field alone? I'm mad at her for her stupid valley girl voice and her tight miniskirt and her green eyeshadow and her dumb crush on Josh. *Josh!* Whom she's never spoken to, who probably doesn't remember her name, who probably has never read a book in his whole stupid life.

"Auggghhh!" I cry and pound my fists against the comforter. "I hate her!" And I burst into tears. Fat, hot, angry tears that course down my cheeks in a very satisfying way, while snot leaks from my nose. I sob like this until I can't catch my breath and can only gasp.

I cry like this a lot. It's like someone has hooked up my tear ducts to the county water line. Ever since the funeral.

Funeral.

Damian was at the funeral, in a dark gray suit. His eyes were dark, dull as lead. Dead. But not dead like Nate's. I remember my mother had walked up to Damian after the service and asked him to leave. She had sounded so cold. So furious and hateful. And Damian had looked as though he'd been struck. Stunned, he'd blinked and stared back at her, his mouth opening and closing like a fish, before he turned and left the cemetery.

It's so easy to blame Damian for that night — for Nate getting so angry over Julie breaking up with him that he jumped in his car, picked up Damian, then flew off into the darkness without his headlights like a demon. It's so easy to think that Damian should have made Nate stop, turn on the headlights, hand over the keys.

I wish I could stop thinking about this, thinking about

Nate. It's constant, and it leaves me feeling dead myself. Or dying. Yet in these moments of silence and loneliness, it's as though I've stuck my toe in the cold, cold ocean. And I get caught, turned upside down in a riptide as my mind skips over to him all of its own volition. Then comes the instant when I lose my breath and feel the freezing water tumbling, battering, covering me, and it's the most painful tug of my heart, an aching hollowness that never stops, as I remember over and over, like the never-ending waves of the ocean, that I won't ever see him again. He's gone.

But Damian . . . this is something different. Somehow, at the bonfire, he seemed thoughtful, subdued. He looked so serious, so different from the laughing, easygoing guy I remember, the delinquent bad boy who had been my brother's partner in crime, in detention and suspension.

More than that, though, tonight, in all his earnestness — well, he looked kind of cute. Really cute, actually. Intense. I get a shiver as I recall his face and those haunting, haunted gray eyes.

This is ridiculous. He is nothing but trouble, and that is all there is to it.

The tears have dried, and I've finally stopped gasping and croaking like an asthmatic bullfrog, so I reach over and turn off the night table light. I try to will myself to sleep before any more absurd notions can creep into my brain.

• • •

Now that the first couple of weeks of school have passed, the days begin to feel routine, and I find I don't have to double-check the schedule I taped to the inside of my locker anymore. I think I can even almost forget about the funny looks from other kids in the hallways and classrooms, the hesitant, awkward intonations of my teacher's voices when they address me, when I imagine they see Nate's face instead of my own.

The linoleum and cinder-block gloom of the place is the perfect backdrop to the callous shouts and raucous laughter that seem to perpetually fill the halls, muting everything. It suits my mood very well.

As I jog into homeroom one sunny late September morning, a second ahead of the late bell, I see Rachel bent over her desk, her shoulders shaking and her knees drawn up to her chest. Carolyn Wright, Callie Rountree, and Susan Meredith are sitting at their desks, glancing at her, and laughing softly, covering their mouths as though they don't want her to see they are laughing at her. I don't know if Rachel is laughing or crying. So I race over to her and throw my bag down on the ground, my arm around her shoulder, and a glare at these girls who used to be my friends. B.T.A.

"What's wrong? Rach, are you okay?" I ask.

Rachel looks up and then I can see that she has been laughing. Small drops of moisture leak from the corners of her eyes. She is shaking helplessly. The other girls are laughing out loud, too, now.

"What is it?" I begin to smile in that *I don't know what's going on but you all look pretty freaking funny and I'll laugh because you are* way. Rachel is trying — and failing miserably — to gain control. She just keeps giggling. "Oh my gosh, tell me! What happened?"

"Oh —" Rachel gasps, and hugs her knees tighter.

"Seriously! Tell me!" I can feel my chest getting tight with the giggles, too. "What!"

Rachel just shakes her head and points to her feet, which are tucked up on her chair. I bend down and look at her feet. "So?" I ask, confused.

"Look!" Rachel pushes her chair back and holds her legs straight out. She is wearing dainty ballet flats with bows on the tops of her toes. Ah. She is wearing dainty ballet flats with bows on the toes, and they are two different colors. She has on a navy shoe on the left foot and a black one on the right. In the light, the difference is plain to see.

Callie, Carolyn, Susan, Rachel, and I launch into fresh gales of laughter.

"Oh, you're such a dork! How did you do that?" I ask, trying to snatch a breath.

"I-It was dark when I got dressed," Rachel manages to explain. "What am I going to do?" she howls. "I can't walk around like this all day! I'll never live it down!" She lets out a loud guffaw.

"I can't believe you own the same pair of shoes in two colors!" Callie says.

Rachel shakes her head helplessly. I tell her, "I think I have an extra pair of flip-flops in my locker. Come with me after the bell."

"Cora," Rachel says with a gulp of air. "What would I do without you?" She squeezes my arm and I smile broadly at her. It feels like the first real smile I've smiled in ages. My mouth muscles hurt but they're enjoying the exercise.

Rachel follows me to my locker, where she quickly switches shoes and continues to chortle. I watch her affectionately. This is how it used to be between us. How it should be.

Suddenly, a shadow falls across us. I look up; Rachel is still bent over, wriggling her foot into one of my flip-flops. *Damian.* He has stopped in front of me, his forehead crinkled. A long black trench coat waving around him, brushing the tops of heavy black combat boots. I've been carefully ignoring him in art class. It's not too hard; mostly Damian buries himself behind his easel, and we might as well be in different rooms. On different planets.

"Hey," he says uncertainly. Rachel shoots up at the sound of a boy's voice. "Hey," he repeats, to Rachel this time.

I am frozen.

"Um, hi," Rachel says, scowling.

The three of us stand there awkwardly in front of my locker, Damian's hands shoved inside his pockets, I'm stone-still, with my history book in hand, not at all sure what to say next.

"Well, I'll see you in class," Damian says, his voice cool as ice.

"Yeah, um, see you," I reply. I sound like such a dolt.

"Whoa, what was that?" Rachel asks, turning to face me as Damian takes off, long loping strides carrying him down the hall.

"He was just saying hi, you know," I stammer. "We have art class together."

"You *do*?" Rachel asks, her eyes huge. "Why didn't you tell me?"

"Well, it's not a big deal or anything."

"It's a *huge* deal!" Rachel exclaims. "He's a total waster. And your mom will freak!"

"I know. Look, it's nothing. He just said hi, is all," I say weakly.

"Hmmm . . . well, just be careful." Rachel warns, then she kisses my cheek. "Thanks for the flip-flops! I'll bring them back tomorrow." And she bounces down the hallway.

I let out a breath I didn't know I'd been holding. That was weird. I wonder what Damian's deal is and why he won't leave me alone.

• • •

During geometry, as Mr. Lane drones on and on about planes and postulates, I start to think about the strange incident in the hall. Had Damian been looking for me? He's never once passed my locker since school began. No, it has to have just been a coincidence. Right?

When the bell finally rings, I quickly head to my locker. As I am exchanging the notebooks and textbooks in my bag for the ones I need to take home, I spot Damian, in his long trench coat that flutters about him, gliding down the hall like some large black bird. He looks over at me and nods his head solemnly.

Again I wonder if he's been looking for me.

"Hi," I say, and suddenly a major case of nerves descends on me, as he comes up alongside my locker.

He straightens and grins. "Hey."

I wait for him to say more, but Damian just stares at me, giving no indication that he is going to speak again. I suddenly feel a bit unsteady. The moment stretches out, interminable, uncomfortable. I shift my bag from one shoulder to the other and shuffle my feet.

"How are your classes?" Damian finally asks, breaking the silence.

"My classes?" I repeat. I must admit, the mundanity of this conversation is breathtaking. "They're fine. Well, except for math. Geometry kind of sucks but, yeah, they're fine." I pause. "How about yours?"

"They're okay," he responds. Then, silence.

"What are you taking?" I ask.

"You know, the usual," he starts casually. "Art, of course, English, calc; AP physics is kicking my butt —"

"AP physics?" I ask, cringing at the note of astonishment in my voice.

"Don't sound so surprised." Damian smirks.

"No, I just didn't know," I try to explain lamely. Dolt. Dolt. Dolt.

"I know. Don't worry about it." He looks at me, and his harsh smile softens. He pulls a silver cell phone out of his coat pocket and checks the time. "I should get home." He looks up at me. "Um, want a ride?"

My breath catches. *What?* "Oh, no, it's okay. I have my bike." Damian glances away. "Look. Why are you following me?" I am taken aback by my own directness.

"Sorry. Didn't mean to bother you," Damian mumbles. Then he is gone.

I fall back against my locker. What is going on? Does he really think I'm going to get in a car with him? Is he nuts?

He is so odd. Kind of sweet, I guess. Maybe I was too harsh? A pinprick of guilt jabs at me. Well, nevertheless, Damian is going to stay a mystery for another day. I gather my belongings and head outside to get on my bike.

As I coast down the streets, I think of Damian as a raven, his black coat flapping like feathers around him. Strange and fierce and hard.

We'll see what this is about.

Chapter Four

Autumn has come, crowning the fields and woods with red golden leaves, and the wind carries with it a sharpness, the crisp hint of apple cider and wood-burning stoves. There is a buzzing, a tingling of anticipation in the air. Girls chatter back and forth in the hallways about the costumes they are going to wear for Halloween. The sad yellow walls are festooned with paper cutouts of jack-o'-lanterns and black cats alongside posters calling on kids to come out and vote in the student elections and to sign up for various committees.

I have avoided getting involved in any after-school activities. I am having a hard enough time keeping up with my classes, especially geometry. There is so much memorization, and for some reason, none of it makes any sense to me, no matter how many times I read and reread the same chapter. How did someone figure out, for instance, that $a^2 + b^2 = c^2$? Who has a brain that works like that? Who looks at a triangle and thinks, I will figure out a way to understand how the lines and angles relate to one another? When I look at a triangle, I see the shape of a cheek or the space below a jawbone. I see the silhouette of the Arabian Peninsula.

I do not get involved. But it isn't just because I have too much homework. It's just that . . . I still feel like the girl whose brother died. I still feel the teachers holding their breath, waiting to see if I am going to turn out like Nate, if I'm going to slip up and cut class or pull a prank or talk back. I feel the other kids waiting to see if I'm going to lose it, if I'll shatter, if whatever peculiarity I seem to embody will come exploding out of me in a terrific show of fireworks and freakdom. Nobody says anything outright; it's just this subtle tension that sits beneath the surface.

Art class, though, is different. There, I feel like I'm really learning. There I feel unburdened. Ms. Calico is new, so she never knew Nate. And just for that I feel freer in her class. Ms. Calico has introduced us to charcoal and pastels. They can be unruly, especially the oil pastels, but I've grown to love the challenge of keeping my lines in line. When I leave class, my fingertips smudged black or all different colors, my cheeks streaked with green and blue and yellow, I wear those colors proudly. I might be a weirdo, but I am a weirdo who can make stuff.

I have brought all of this color home with me and I've introduced it into my map drawings. Suddenly, the French countryside is blanketed with yellow and violet wildflowers, the sage green of olive trees. And the rain forests of the Amazon are ablaze with a lush green vibrance.

In art class, I sit on my stool next to the window, listening to an angry rain pelt the glass with a thrumming tattoo, as I nibble on the tip of a charcoal pencil. I stare at the basket of jelly jars and fruit posed at the front of the room. There is never much talking in this cavernous studio but for the hushed murmur of Ms. Calico's voice as she moves from easel to easel, guiding each of us, her flock. Sometimes she lectures or demonstrates a new technique, but mostly the class remains swathed in silence.

I glance around the classroom. Damian is tucked away behind his easel and a huge drawing tablet at the front of the room. Quickly, I look away, then turn to watch as my nearest neighbor, a sophomore named Helena, who has blonde curly hair that she always keeps clipped in a messy twist, runs broad strokes across her paper with a scarlet pastel stick. The lines grow heavy and thick, livid. I love to watch Helena's dainty hands gripping the pastel and dragging it so furiously, her plastic bangle bracelets banging and clacking boisterously. What drives this tiny girl into such a fury of motion?

Helena looks up and catches me studying her. I feel myself blushing, but she shoots me a wide smile and nods her head. "It's therapeutic," she says.

"Really?" I ask. When Helena nods vigorously, I add, "Maybe I should try it."

Helena grins and replies, "Maybe you should." Then she returns her attention to her easel. With green and black, she evokes the shapes of the fruit and jars. I am spellbound. I've never seen anything like it. I have seen prints of some of Picasso's paintings in the Cubist style, and while Helena's piece looks like some distant cousin of that, it's a method and a look all its own.

"I'm sorry to keep spying on you, but that's really amazing," I tell Helena.

"You think so?" Helena takes a step back from her easel and scrutinizes her drawing. "I don't know. Maybe it's a little too angry?"

"Why's that a bad thing?" I ask as Helena returns to her stool.

Whatever Helena was about to answer in response is drowned out by a very loud buzzing sound. It sounds like someone is fiddling with the school's PA system, which is only supposed to come on in the morning during homeroom, or in an emergency.

"Hey, everybody," a voice filters through. "Here's a little senior surprise for the semester. Some might call it a prank, call it what you will, but I present to you my bud, DJ Ben Maxwell! Everybody, I want you out in the halls, dancing and putting your hands together for this rhymin' fiend. Now, Benny-boy, rap!"

For a second, everyone is frozen. Nobody laughs or speaks or moves. We just stare at one another, then all eyes come to rest on Ms. Calico. A beat starts to pulse through the PA speakers.

"Well, who am I to stop you? You heard what the man said." Ms. Calico steps back and opens the studio door.

I look at Helena, who just shrugs in return and slides off her stool. She peels off her smock and beckons for me to follow her out into the hall. The nearby classrooms are emptying into the hallway and most of the kids are standing around awkwardly, hands shoved in pockets, toes scuffing the linoleum tiles. Then, a brave few begin to dance. Now, the doors to all of the classrooms up and down the corridor are flung open, and more students are writhing and twisting to the rhythm of the PA beat. I can't believe what is going on — it's a dance party. Suddenly, someone touches my arm. I start and spin around. It's Ms. Calico and she waves me back into the art room.

"Cora, before you jump into the crush, I wonder if I might have a brief word with you?" she asks.

"Um, sure," I reply. Uh-oh. A *brief word* never seems like a good thing; it's what cops and principals always had to ask my parents for when Nate was alive, after he had gotten into one kind of trouble or another.

"Your work in this class is quite impressive, Cora," Ms. Calico states as more people brush past us to get out of the classroom and into the hall. "I can see so much potential in your line, in your forms. And I've seen your maps when you've turned in your sketch pad. They are fascinating, Cora." She looks at me closely as she continues, "You remember I spoke about some summer art programs at the beginning of the semester?" I nod, my gut buzzing like it's filled with a bee's nest and the inmates have just escaped. "Good. I'd like to recommend you for one of them. Would you like that?" Ms. Calico's gaze is piercing, as if she is searching me for some kind of answer or information, and meanwhile my heart might just swell so big it'll pop out of my chest. She thinks *my* work is impressive?

"Really?" I ask. "Yeah, I would *definitely* be interested. That would be incredible!" My mind is whirring so fast. *Can this be real?* I study Ms. Calico's face. "You really think I'm good?"

"I wouldn't stand here and say it if I didn't mean it. And this particular program has a cartography class that I think you'd really enjoy."

"Wow," I say softly.

"Yes, well, I will bring the application forms to you tomorrow. The program is in London, so you'll have to cover the airfare, but beyond that, all expenses would be covered."

"London?" I repeat in amazement. For a moment, I feel like I'm taking off, leaping into glorious flight. *Finally,* I will *go* somewhere. Then, reality thumps me over the head, as it always seems to do. My mother is never going to allow me to go to London for a summer. Never. "Oh, I — I don't know. . . ." I whisper.

"Well, how about you just fill out the application, and let's see? All right?" Ms. Calico prods.

I can only nod my head mutely.

"Okay, go party with the rest of them," Ms. Calico says, lightly steering me back through the door. "And remember, the application is due November fifteenth."

Words are fumbling through my mind. *Impressive. Potential. London.* I know I'm walking a tightrope. I could let go and allow myself to believe in this fantasy that my art has potential, that I have talent, and that I could go to London to explore it. But, it's too dangerous. This is something I want so badly, too badly, and I can only crash and fall flat on my disappointed face.

I walk out into the tangle of swaying bodies, my mouth hanging open as I take in the mass of wriggling dancers, the teachers standing silently, smilingly in their classroom doorways. Mr. Halpern, the assistant principal, is wading through the sea of students, helplessly flapping his arms, anxiously tugging at his greasy hair and wiping at his brow, as he tries heedlessly to shepherd everyone back to class. He makes an absurd and lonely picture in the midst of all the jollity. Actually, the whole affair makes a pretty absurd picture — a dance party in the high school hallway at two o'clock in the afternoon. But

I feel lonely and removed from it all. Funny, how I am more in sync with Mr. Halpern than anyone else at this moment. I continue moving through the crowd, feeling gangly and wooden, aware of my arms hanging limply at my sides — they feel too long and stiff.

Suddenly, I walk into something. Hard.

"Ouch." I look up. "Oh."

Damian. He is standing in front of me, rubbing his arm. "Hey," he says.

"Um, hi," I reply. "Sorry about that. I was distracted." Was he waiting for me again?

"Yeah, I could tell," Damian says, smiling. "What's going on? You're not partaking in the senior prank?"

"Senior prank?" I echo.

"It's a tradition, the senior class stages a prank sometime during the semester before Homecoming." I suppose my face looks blank, because Damian grins, and says, "You know, big football game, fancy dance? Homecoming?"

"Oh, right . . . I heard about it . . . from . . . Nate." We both look down, and I'll bet my face looks as twisted with confusion and discomfort as his does. "Wait, Homecoming? When is it?" I ask, my mind starting to reel. I am so not clued into anything going on at school, I haven't even thought about the dance once. I am pretty sure Rachel has mentioned it at some point or another, but I really can't recall any details.

"Seriously? You must be the only girl in school who doesn't know when the dance is," Damian replies, laughing. "It's the second weekend in November. Sound familiar?"

"Oh," I murmur. A dance? What do I do? Do I go? Would my mother even let me go? I don't have a dress, a date. Oh my gosh, I'm not ready for this. Images of girls in poofy Pepto-Bismol pink dresses and high heels, boys with their hair slicked back, waltz through my mind. Not to mention the game . . .

"Hey, do you want a ride home?" Damian asks, startling me from my train wreck of thought. He shrugs, smiling. "I thought I'd try again."

I feel my eyelids stretching to blink over my bug-eyes. Hold on a minute, what? "Um . . . okay." I answer. Wait a second; what have I just agreed to? Getting into a car with Damian Archer? I must really be losing it. My mom would have a conniption if she knew that I was riding in a car with anyone under the age of forty (Rule #3), not to mention the one person in the world she hates most and trusts least. Not to mention the fact that he's . . . Damian Archer!

Little beads of sweat break out on my forehead, but I follow Damian, threading through the still-dancing students, to my locker, where he waits for me to grab my coat and books.

"You don't need to go to your locker?" I ask.

"Nope," he answers. I cock an eyebrow. Does he ever do homework? But I continue after him toward the parking lot.

He drives a gorgeous, carefully painted 1971 cobalt blue El Camino with a silver racing stripe down the middle.

"My lady," he says, opening the passenger-side door for me.

"Why, thank you, good sir." My voice sounds tight; this playacting at normalcy feels false. My stomach is going spastic, and suddenly I realize, I'm scared. *What am I doing? What am I doing?*

"Nervous?" Damian asks. He looks at me closely and climbs into the driver's seat.

I pause before answering him. That's a big fat yes. "Ah, a little bit."

He nods and turns the ignition. The car roars; it is a lion of an automobile. I jump.

"Don't worry. I'll drive carefully," Damian tells me. He grins cheekily, but true to his word, Damian drives as slowly and deliberately as my mother. We sit in silence for a while, until Damian speaks. "Hey, do you mind if I show you something before I take you home?"

"What is it?"

"Well, it's hard to explain. I'd rather just show you."

I can't imagine what he could possibly want to show me. An insatiable curiosity grips me. "All right, I guess." Those bees start kicking around in my gut again, like they're trying to sting me back to reason and out of this really stupid haze of pliancy.

"Good," he says, and smiles again.

Soon, Damian crosses the county road and turns right onto Union Street. He's heading east, away from my neighborhood and out toward the fields of the Wright farm. *Oh, where are we going?* I wonder. This is likely the stupidest thing I've ever done. There is a racket of bees buzzing in my ears, pricking my stomach with angry stings. Two minutes later, we're pulling off the road and onto a gravel track. Damian slows before stopping altogether in front of a tall gray barn.

"We're here," Damian announces with that same cheeky grin as we get out of the car. He heads down an overgrown path and takes hold of one of the barn's massive double doors. Damian waves me over. "Come on!"

I hover at the entryway to the dim, yawning space. Motes of dust flicker in the single shaft of sunlight that penetrates the crack between the doors. Damian flicks a light switch, and I can make out a host of bulky shapes standing at attention, but I can't tell what they are. I start to feel nervous again. What am I doing here, with *him?*

Despite my trepidation, I follow Damian into the barn. I step gingerly, cringing as the wooden floorboards creak and groan beneath me. Damian treads lightly as a cat, carefully placing his feet to avoid the complaining planks.

"Look, what are we doing here?" I ask.

"You'll see," he answers. "The Wrights let Nate and me use their barn in exchange for help with some chores around the farm," Damian explains.

"You and Nate worked on the farm?" My voice cracks with disbelief.

"You'll see," Damian repeats.

When we reach the back of the barn, Damian strikes another switch, and golden light floods the space. I suck in a sharp breath. "Oh my."

There, before us, lay a jungle of sculptures, hulking pieces of twisted metal and torn wood, jumbles of wire and slabs of stone. Giant canvases covered with thick, violent slabs of oil paint, and other *things* hang on the walls.

"What is all this?"

"This is my studio. It was, ah, Nate's and mine," Damian says in answer.

"Yours and Nate's?" I ask. "You *made* all of this?"

"We both worked here," Damian explains nervously.

"When — how — how did you make all this?" I stutter.

"Well, I have a welding workshop in here; it's over there, around in the corner, behind those sculptures. And, you know, we, uh, collected all this stuff to use, and —"

I interrupt, "You're telling me that you and my brother made all of this?"

"Yes. I just told you —"

"I know what you told me, but how come . . ." My voice trails off as I gaze around the room, my eyes crawling over each piece. I can barely process any of it.

"Cora?" Damian asks.

I turn to look at him. "How come I never knew Nate was an artist?" A towering dam of tears is piling up, burning behind my eyes, threatening to spill over my cheeks.

"He didn't . . . No one knew but him and me," Damian responds softly. "He didn't want to tell anyone."

A vision of Nate, at ten or eleven, racing into the living room, a sheet of paper flapping in his hand, pops into my head.

"Look!" my brother cried, holding out the page to our grandfather, our dad's father, who was visiting for the day. It was a drawing of a dog.

Grandpa drew a breath, his cheeks caving in and his lips puckering. "Did you trace this, son?" he'd asked. He'd lifted me from his lap, where we'd been reading a story together.

Nate solemnly shook his head. "No, sir," he'd replied. "I drew it."

My grandfather held up the drawing close, close, and lifted his glasses and peered at it. I stood up on tiptoe, straining to see the page, but my grandfather would not lower it. "Are you telling the truth?" Grandpa growled. At Nate's vehement nod, he said, "Son, if you truly drew this, well, then I'd say you have a mighty fine talent. Mighty fine." And Nate had grown pink, a proud flush.

That's the only time I can recall seeing Nate show any interest in art. I knew he doodled, but nothing like this.

"How long have you guys been working on all this?" I ask Damian, and silently curse the quiver in my voice.

"I guess it's been, like, three years."

"I can't believe it." I wipe away the traitorous tears, hating myself for appearing so weak, for feeling so weak.

I turn my back on Damian and begin to wander among the pieces. "Here's that yield sign he got in trouble for stealing." I sniff and stop in front of a mammoth statue that has the shape of a man's silhouette, constructed of gnarled metal rods, with the triangular traffic sign for a head.

"Basically," Damian starts with a chuckle, "everything Nate was ever accused of 'taking without permission' is down here. In one of these pieces."

"And the paintings?" I ask.

"I made the paintings," Damian admits abashedly.

"They are amazing," I whisper. The canvases look like bruised flesh with slashes of violet and black pigment, metal parts sticking out of small hills of oil paint. I walk closer and see that there are all sorts of objects concealed in the canvases: buttons, nails and bolts, a small wrench, computer keyboard letters.

We stand together and survey the cluttered, chaotic gallery. There are car parts that look like they came from Nate's first car, which he also wrecked; broken bits of furniture; scraps of fabric. I'm pretty sure I recognize a pattern from an old set of my mother's sheets. Everything precarious and wild. Yet there is a rhythm to the pieces, a poetry and a logic.

"I always thought that one day he would grow up and stop destroying everything," I say quietly. "And it turns out, he already had." I turn to Damian. "Why did you bring me here, show me all of this?" I ask.

Maybe if I stare at him long enough, hard enough, I'll be able to pierce his brittle exterior and learn some truth. Some kind of truth. There has to be a meaning to all of it, a secret that he will reveal to me. Because I never, never believed that Nate — or Damian — might be capable of creating such . . . such beauty.

None of it makes any sense. All the time everyone thought they were just out to destroy and take everything apart, they were creating and building this wonder. My chest hurts. My chest hurts and I think my heart might be breaking. Again.

"I don't know why," Damian replies. "Ever since I saw you in school, I've been thinking about it. That's why I was following you. I mean, your mom made it pretty clear at the funeral that I wasn't welcome anymore, and I didn't think you'd want to see me, either. I didn't know how else to tell you about this, except to bring you here to see it." Damian pauses, averting his eyes. "And I think — I think Nate would have wanted you to know." The words fall between us like a thousand raindrops.

"Well. Thank you."

Silently, I weave between the sculptures and pass all around the barn walls one more time, as Damian stands by, watching.

"What is this one?" I've stopped in front of a large round stone with a tall metal pole poking from its flat top. Several two-by-six boards have been nailed together, and are leaning against the wall behind the pole and stone.

"Oh, that was . . . well, that was Nate's last piece. He never finished it. . . . Obviously." Damian has come to stand next to me. "I think he was going to mount those boards onto the rod when he was done, but I'm not sure what he was going to do with the wood itself."

I circle the stone base, and kneel down to study the boards, which are marked with soft gray swirls and dots and lines and smudges.

"His last piece, huh?" I turn to look at Damian. He nods. I look back at the pieces of wood. I wonder what it is, what Nate was going to do with them. I will never know.

Finally, I rise and realize that I've made an illegal stop after school with the Bradleys' Number One Most Undesirable. I pull out my cell phone and check the time. It's just after four. "I should go home, before my parents get there first. Would you take me?" I ask Damian.

"Sure. Let's go. But, first —" Damian grabs the phone out of my hand and punches some buttons. He hands it back to me with a grin and says, "Just in case." Then he leads me through the barn, out into the fresh air, and back to his car. And the whole time my ears feel like they've ignited and my heart is racing. *Did he just give me his number? Oh my gosh . . .*

Damian drives slowly through town, crossing back over Union Street. I watch the ramshackle houses trickle past. Then the houses begin to grow nicer and the lawns better kept when we near my neighborhood. I can't think of a thing to say. I'm still flabbergasted.

But the silence between us is comfortable. When I'm sure he's concentrating on driving, I turn to study him. His gray eyes are focused intently on the road. They are light against his caramel skin. He looks lonely, terribly lonely. And then it occurs to me that he is bereft, too, in a way. He lost his best friend. I haven't seen him hanging around with anyone at school, certainly no one from his and Nate's old gang.

I don't actually know *anything* about Damian, who his friends are, what his family is like.

Turns out I hardly knew my brother, either.

As all these thoughts are passing through my mind, I'm not paying attention when we finally pull up in front of my house. So, I don't notice my mother's car in the open garage, or my mother pacing back and forth on the front porch.

"Uh, Cora?" Damian mumbles as he comes to a stop. "Cora," he repeats, snatching me back to planet Earth.

"What?" I reply, then, "Oh, no," as I notice my mom noticing Damian's car and me in it.

My mother freezes, her eyes popping wide open with shock then narrowing with anger. She starts to stride toward the car, then stops, and begins waving her arm, motioning for me to get out of the car — Right That Instant.

I nod at her, and turn to Damian. "I guess I'd better go."

"Yeah, it looks like it," he says with a rueful smile. "Well, see you at school."

"Bye, Damian." I swing around and start to open the door, then look back at him. "And thank you. Really."

I brace myself for the onslaught, straightening as I come face-to-face with my mom, who is marching agitatedly across the lawn.

"What were you thinking?" As she approaches, I can see that her face is drawn and white. "Please. Tell me what were you thinking?" she shouts.

"I —" I start; she won't let me speak.

"Do you know what that boy — what he did?"

"Yes, Mother. It's kind of hard to forget. So, why don't you spare me?" I answer, cool as a cucumber.

"He was in the car with your brother that night, and now *you* get into a *car* with *him*? Into a *car*! I just can't believe it." Then, abruptly, she switches tacks. "Where have you been all afternoon? You had a dentist appointment! And you aren't supposed to go anywhere after school; you're supposed to come straight home. And you skip your appointment to go gallivanting around with that — that . . ." All of a sudden, she runs out of steam.

The dentist. I forgot all about it. Too late — I'm not apologizing now, not when she is treating me like this, like a child. Like a prisoner.

"That *what?*" I yell. "What is he, Mom? Because I'm pretty sure he isn't some monster. You know, I think Nate took care of messing up everything all by himself!" I am really shaking now. "And you know what, you can't keep me locked up in the house all the time, like Rapunzel! You can't!" All of the heat that has crept up my neck and into my cheeks blooms into a hot fountain of tears that now courses over my face, spilling around my collar and down the front of my jacket. Hot, then cold.

At that moment, my father's car pulls into the driveway, and he gets out of the car. Great, perfect timing.

"What's going on here?" he asks in an empty voice, drained of life, as he slowly walks over to us. Family huddle.

Mom whirls around, rallying for his sake. "I was home early to take Cora to her dentist appointment, only she never came home. Then, she shows up almost two hours late in Damian Archer's car."

My father stares at me mutely.

"Well, what do you have to say to her, Daniel?" My mother's voice has risen to a decibel that would deafen bats. Still, he just stares without speaking. "Would you say something?" she screams.

"Cora, your mother told you to come home directly after

school," he mutters halfheartedly, then turns away. Seriously? That's all he can muster? "Go inside," he says, not directing the last part to anyone in particular.

I feel like spitting. "Wow, this is your united front? Well done!" And without looking at either of them, I run into the house, slamming the front door behind me. I let out a shriek, releasing some of the frustration and fury and fly up the stairs, into my bedroom, slamming that door, as well. I wrap my earphones around my head, and begin to play my most pissed-off playlist.

How dare she! How can she even think that locking me up in the house is okay? That I'll just take it?

For so long she filled me up with so much hatred for Damian. She taught me to blame him for Nate's accident, and it was easy to do. But now I'm not so sure. Nate was behind the wheel that night, after all.

Oh my gosh, how can she be so wrong about everything? My mind is spinning furiously, but suddenly, with a pause in the music, I feel as though all the clouds in my mind have suddenly cleared, letting a shaft of pure light in. All of us were wrong. None of us knew Nate — not Mom or Dad, or even me.

I pull off the headphones and tiptoe to the door. I do not want to see either of them. I turn the knob as slowly as I can so as not to make a sound. I check both ways down the hall, making sure neither of my parents is about. The dull murmur of the television travels up the corridor from the den. I can hear my mother bumping around in the kitchen, slamming pots and pans onto the countertop. It is safe.

I slink out of my room and down the hall until I am standing before Nate's door. I haven't been inside since the night he died. I take a deep breath, as though steeling myself. Then I start to turn the knob. It is cool to the touch.

Suddenly, I snap my hand back. No, I can't do it, can't go into his room and remember. I've had enough of Nate and the memories and all the emotions he always dredges up. I don't want to think about this, about him anymore.

I run back to my room, and with relief, replace my earphones. I've learned enough for one night. Discovering that I've never known Nate at all, learning that he was an artist who made beautiful things and then was lost to me — it is too much. I let the music carry me off. I'll never let that happen with anyone else. I will know the ones I love.

Chapter Five

"Puh-leeese, Cora! You *have* to go with me!"

Just two weeks away, the Homecoming dance is on the tips of everybody's tongues and at the fore of Rachel's mind. I don't have a date or a dress or a desire to attend. Rachel has a dress, but no date, and she fully expects me to go to the dance with her. She hounds me about it relentlessly. She has made begging a daily habit in homeroom, pleading with me to come to the dance with her. She has given up on my company at any other school events, especially the sporty kind. I've told her that there was no way, no how I would ever subject myself to sitting in the freezing cold, watching a bunch of guys beat up on one another. Rachel just shrugs her shoulders helplessly, shaking her head, unable to comprehend my complete lack of school spirit or interest, probably unable to understand how she got saddled with such a lame best friend.

But I am really trying to be a better friend, trying to restore some semblance of normalcy to our friendship. So I've made a decision.

"Okay, Rach, I'll go to the dance with you," I tell her, not quite prepared for the explosion of hysterics.

"What!" Rachel shrieks. "You will?" She looks so happy, I have to smile with her. "Oh my gosh, we have to go shopping! We have to get you a dress! Oh, thank you thank you thank you!" She throws her arms around my neck and hugs me way too tight.

"There're two conditions, though," I caution.

"What?" Rachel looks unfazed.

"I'm not going to the game," I say.

"But —" Rachel begins.

"No. I'm sorry."

"Okay," she answers. "What's the second condition?"

"*You* have to get my mom to agree. She is all about keeping me locked up in the house at night. Like I'm Rapunzel or something. So, that's the condition. If you can get her to say okay, I'm all yours."

"No problem!" Rachel crows. "I have a way with your mother. It'll be easy."

And true to her word, Rachel calls my house that night to convince my mother to let me go to the dance.

"I *promise*," Rachel swears, "my mom will drive us both ways." She's so excited, her voice pours through the receiver with all the subtlety of a locomotive.

"Will there be adults at the dance?" my mother asks.

"Oh, yes," Rachel answers. "The dance is in the school, so there'll be tons of teachers there. And the principal."

"No funny business," my mom warns.

"Of course not!" Rachel promises.

And that's that. I tell Rachel that I'll meet her at the mall on Saturday to go shopping, as Rachel has assumed responsibility for finding an appropriate dress and shoes for me to wear.

Now, as I walk through the halls at school and sit in class, where I can't get away from the chatter about dresses and corsages, hairstyles and shoe styles, I feel I am a part of it. For the first time since school began, I feel like a piece of the whole.

The rest of the week flies by, and I am buoyed by Ms. Calico's praise and encouragement and by Rachel's cheerful banter. The spectre of Damian and the studio seems to have faded. I put both from my mind. Maybe life, maybe high school isn't doomed to suck after all. There is only one dark spot in my week: when I open my locker and spy the application to the London art program just sitting there at the bottom, peeping out from beneath a stack of papers, a daily reminder that I'm too chicken to show it to my mom. Maybe this weekend. I have to make a move soon; the application is due in a couple of weeks. With a sigh, I excavate it from the mess on the floor of my locker and stuff the packet into my backpack.

• • •

The mall is buzzing with families and pairs of teenagers. I am trailing behind Rachel, letting her sweep me from one store to the next as we search for the "perfect dress." I have some money saved up from my last birthday, and my mom gave me a bit more, so I should be able to get a nice dress and a pair of shoes. I've also agreed to go with Rachel to the tanning salon, where we're going to get spray-on tans — a test run for the dance, Rachel says.

We finally end up in the department store at the far end of the mall, where Rachel is tearing through the racks with a ferocity and intensity I don't think I've seen in her before. This is good, right? Girl bonding? We're supposed to chat and gossip and talk about life in this sort of situation, right?

"So," I oh-so-casually attempt, "um, what's up with you and the Nasties?"

"What do you mean?" Rachel asks blandly.

"I mean, you hang around with them a lot now, and, well, I just wondered . . ." No, I don't think this is going well at all. My face is growing warm.

"You know, they're not *so* bad," Rachel says coolly.

Uh-huh. I shoot her a look, cross my eyes, and waggle my eyebrows. Rachel chuckles.

"Well, I think Macie is supercool. I mean, she's so mature," Rachel tells me. Her face is screwed up in a look of serious concentration as she pushes aside several hangers.

"How so?" I ask halfheartedly.

"She hooked up with Matt James over the summer. She said it was amazing." A look of wistfulness has replaced the bossy squint of her eyes and crinkle in her nose.

"Ew," I say, hardly able to believe that Rachel thinks this is a good thing.

"Oh, Cora, you're such a baby."

"Yeah? Well, in that case, I guess I'll stay a baby for a while longer."

"Suit yourself," Rachel snorts.

"Well, what about you?" I ask her.

"If Josh wanted to hook up with me, I'd do it," she says enthusiastically. My insides are melting. I cringe and feel like I might throw up.

"Seriously?"

"Of course," Rachel says matter-of-factly. "I mean, Macie said that guys only hook up with girls they think are cool. So, you know, it'd mean he was really into me."

"Ew," I say again. Her explanation hardly even makes sense. One would hope that if a guy wanted to hook up with a girl, he'd be into her, right? Isn't that how it works? "Rach, don't do it if you don't feel totally ready. I mean, don't let them pressure you into anything. They *are* the Nasties," I remind her.

"Yeah, well, it's just that the guys worship them like they're goddesses, and Josh is always hanging around them, and I just . . . I'm sick of being a loser, you know?" Rachel says, avoiding my eyes.

Oh, Rach. "You were never a loser," I say softly.

"You know what I mean, though, don't you? I'm tired of being the girl the guys never see, never notice, never talk to. I want this year to be different." Rachel speaks quietly but with force. "High school should be fun and about boys and parties."

"Yeah, but it's about other stuff, too. Like figuring out what you like to do and what you want to do, and what you're good at and who your friends are."

"I know *you're* my friend," Rachel replies.

"Well, duh." I grab a black halter dress off the rack and walk over to her, holding it up. "What do you think of this?" I wait for Rachel to nod her approval, then continue, "I just don't want you to get hurt, is all. Because they're still the Nasties."

"I know," Rachel answers shortly. "It's fine. Let's just concentrate on the shopping, okay?"

"Okay," I say, and turn back to the racks. I can't seem to say anything right. When did it become so hard to be a friend to Rachel?

When our arms are piled high with dresses in all kinds of colors — my one stipulation was that I will not wear red — we move into the dressing room. Rachel stands outside the booth issuing orders like a drill sergeant, directing me from one dress to the next.

"I don't think you should go the mermaid route," Rachel tells me after I come out in a blue dress that is weirdly wide at the waist and tapered as it falls to my ankles. "Also, *no one* will be wearing a long dress!"

"Rach, I don't know if I can hold out much longer. This is torture," I whine through the dressing room door.

"Well, you need a dress, Cor. Come on, suck it up!"

Finally, *finally,* I try on an emerald green silk gown that hugs my body in just the right places and falls to my knees in a sweeping skirt. It even looks nice against my pasty skin. Rachel utters her approval: "Oh, Cor, it's beautiful. It's like it was made for you."

It's pretty. I twirl and watch with satisfaction as the skirt spins out. Every Christmas I used to watch the *Nutcracker* on TV and covet Clara's dress. When she would spin into a pirouette and her skirt would bloom around her in a perfect circle, I didn't think anything could look more elegant. I sigh with relief as I peel off the dress and carefully replace it on its hanger. I really, really like this dress.

The hunt for shoes is, thankfully, much easier and quicker, and I find a pair of strappy gold heels. Soon we're on our way to the spa.

A woman wearing what looks like a pink nurse's uniform ushers us into a changing room, where we don fluffy white terry robes. Then we are led into separate areas that look like showers. There is a heavy, cloying stink in the air, and I feel like I could maybe faint. But I step into the shower anyway and let the noxious spray fall over my body. When I step out again, I can't help but marvel at the golden tan I'm now sporting.

Everything looks brighter — my dull brown hair, my brown eyes, even my smile. I stare at myself in the mirror for a long while, watching as all the pieces of my face seem to fall apart and come back together.

It is still my face, but I look so different somehow. Older, maybe.

I find Rachel in the changing room and, as I'm getting dressed, Rachel suddenly lets out a piercing shriek.

"Oh my gosh!" she screams, peering at herself in the mirror, pulling back her bangs from her forehead. "Oh my gosh," she repeats.

"What? What happened?" I call, racing over to her.

"Look what happened!" Rachel moans. She turns to face me, and when I see what has Rachel so upset, I try very unsuccessfully to stifle a laugh.

Right in the middle of Rachel's forehead is a big bronze streak. A stain.

"Did you rub it in?" I ask.

"Oh . . . I thought I did," Rachel says tearfully. "I guess I missed a spot." She sniffs and turns back to the mirror. "I look ridiculous!"

"No, it's fine . . . your bangs cover it up." I reach over to try and brush her bangs down across her forehead.

"No, they don't!" Rachel argues. "I look so stupid!"

"You can barely notice it, Rach," I say, straining to keep the grin from my face.

We both examine Rachel's forehead in the mirror. The bangs do cover a little bit of the stain, but a substantial part of the zigzag line still shows. As we stare at Rachel's reflection, our eyes meet and I can't hold it in any longer. I burst out laughing and, holding up my hand as I double over, I manage to squeal, "I'm sorry, Rach! I'm sorry . . . it's just so — you look like —"

"Harry Potter!" we both finish at the same time.

I help her rub at the streak with a wet paper towel, until Rachel's forehead is red and raw. We're still giggling when we get on our bikes, with the green dress folded carefully into my backpack. We wave good-bye, and pedal our separate ways home.

I can't remember feeling so light in ages. As I ride back to my house, the wind rakes over my face and through my hair, making my eyes water. I pump my legs faster and faster, then stand up on the pedals and coast, and with the trees and fields whizzing past, I feel like I might take flight. I am free, unburdened, and it is the most wondrous sensation. I ride, the sun behind me, and decide it is time to tell my mom about London. If she agreed to let me go to the dance, maybe she is lightening up.

I pull into the driveway and lean my bike up against the

garage. I burst into the house, calling, "Mom! Hey, Mom, I'm home! Where are you?"

"Cora? Hi, I'm here, in the kitchen," my mother answers.

I run down the hall and find her washing dishes at the sink.

"Did you get a dress?" she asks.

"Yup. Want to see?"

My mom nods, and I pull the bag out of my backpack, carefully releasing it from the plastic. I feel a little bit giddy. I hold it up against me, once again admiring the rich grassy green of the silk and the way the fabric catches the light. I sway, letting the gown fan out at my knees. Happy. Hopeful. That's what I feel.

"It's really beautiful, Cor," my mom says. "You look so grown up." She pauses, and I swear she looks a little misty around the eyes. "I can hardly believe it," she murmurs, then shakes herself. "Anyway, what about shoes?" She wipes her hands on a dish towel and comes closer to rub her fingers against the smooth silky material.

"Got them, too," I tell her, marveling at how normal our conversation is. How good it feels to be talking with her like this, peacefully. I reach into the bag and grab the shoe box, sliding it out, and opening it to show my mother the gold slingbacks with the tiny heels and slender straps. I slip them on and suddenly feel very grown-up.

"You'll look gorgeous, Cor," my mom says softly. "So mature."

This is it, I decide. Things are going so well; it is time.

"Hey, uh, Mom, could I ask you something?" I begin as I slide my feet out of the shoes.

"Sure," she responds distractedly. She is holding up one of the pumps.

My heart pounds like a jackhammer. "So, my art teacher, Ms. Calico, told me that she thinks my work is really good," I say hesitantly.

"Really?" she replies. "That's nice."

"Yeah, well, she thinks it's really, *really* good; she said she thinks I have a lot of potential." My mother is paying attention now, looking closely at me, wondering where this is leading. I continue, "And, um, she wants me to apply for this summer art school that has a mapmaking course."

"That sounds great, Cor. That is really nice of her. Is it at the high school?"

"Well, no, that's the thing," I hedge. "It's kind of — well, it's in London. But all the expenses are covered, everything but airfare, and I figured that I could use some of the money that Grandma and Grandpa gave me, and —"

"London?" my mother interrupts.

"Uh-huh."

"Is she kidding? Who does she think she is?" my mom

thunders. "Trying to send *my* kid so far away, off to some *foreign* country?" Her face is growing red, and the crease between her brows has deepened.

All of the lightness and joy drains out of me, as quick as a flash of lightning, leaving me burnt, empty, and hard.

"What is wrong with you?" I hiss. "Why can't you let me do something fun, something that's good for me?"

"It's not safe for a girl your age to travel so far by herself," she hollers. "And I will not have you talking to me like this. Watch your tone, Cora!" she warns.

"You don't want anything good to happen to me. You just want to control me!" A momentum to my rage is building. "You thought you could control Nate, but you didn't know the first thing about him." My voice has grown cold and quiet. "You're wrong about everything. Everything." Now I feel I am losing control, and my chest burns and tears are pricking my eyes. I can't stop. "You didn't know Nate at all, and you rode him so hard; you pushed and pushed him. He was an artist, he *made* things, and I bet you didn't even know that! You just yelled at him all the time, and now you're doing the same to me!" I scream.

"You little brat!" My mom has her hands on her hips and her face is twisted into the angriest grimace I have ever seen. Like some ferocious creature, her eyes flash. "You don't know a thing, not one single thing about your brother! How dare you! How dare you speak to me this way, and about your brother, when you don't know a single thing! Get out of my sight!" she rages. "Get out! I don't want to see you!"

"With pleasure!" I spin around and run up the stairs to my room, which is starting to feel like a well-trod racecourse. I fall onto my bed in a flood of blistering tears. I don't know where all this anger, this vitriol comes from. You'd think that after Nate died, Mom and I would have grown closer, that we'd have come together. But, no, we've dug a moat between us, and it goes deeper every day.

"I hate her!" I scream into my pillow. I kick and ball my hands into fists, punching the mattress. I keep shrieking and crying into the pillow, possessed by a fit of temper stronger than the fiercest wind or the highest wave. I weep and rage until I am empty. Hollow. "I hate her," I whisper over and over. Yet, I know it's not true. We're both marked, ravaged by this thing that happened to us.

It seems to run in the family. I remember a few months before Nate died, he and my parents had gotten into a screaming match, their voices flared like those little explosions that happen on the surface of the sun. A letter had arrived from the school saying that Nate had missed twenty-three days of school since the start of the semester, and my mom wanted to know what Nate was doing.

"What do you think will happen to you once you're kicked out of school? How are you going to live?" she'd shrieked shrilly. "Because I promise you, you will not be welcome in this house anymore."

"Good, I look forward to that day!" Nate had yelled back. "Then I won't have to waste my time with so much useless crap!" As I spied on them from behind the railings at the top of the stairs, I saw tears streaming down Nate's cheeks. Back then, I couldn't imagine what my brother was doing during those twenty-three days of illicit freedom. Now, I would bet anything that he was in the barn, working.

"You think you're so smart," my father had snarled.

"No, Dad, but I know that school is a waste of time for me!" Nate had cried. Then he'd pushed past my parents and raced up the stairs, passing me without seeing me. I heard him stomping and rummaging around in his bedroom. I followed him, then stood in the doorway of his room.

"Enjoy the show, Squirt?" Nate had asked, looking up at me with a scowl.

I shook my head no. "Why didn't you go to school, Nate?"

"Sometimes the same things aren't right for everybody, you know?" When I shook my head a second time, Nate closed his eyes and sighed. "Forget it. Just go to bed or something."

And later that night I'd heard Nate's door open, his familiar stomping gait tamped down to be nearly silent; he'd headed down the hall toward my room, and then he'd knocked softly on my door.

"Hey, Squirt, you up?" he'd whispered through the door.

"Uh-huh," I'd mumbled. My door opened, and Nate came in, dressed to go out.

"I'll be back. Don't tell Mom and Dad, okay?"

"Where are you going?" I'd asked.

"Nowhere. Don't worry about it. I'll be back before they wake up." Then Nate had opened my window and pushed his legs, then his body, then his head through it. As he crouched on the roof, he stuck his head back inside the window. "Don't worry about me, Squirt. And close the window behind me, okay?" Then he disappeared.

I sigh and remember how afraid I'd felt. And how sad — sad for Nate, for our family, for myself. When there is no more poison left inside of me, I sit up and rub my eyes. My mother's voice echoes in my head: *You don't know a thing, not one single thing about your brother!*

Who knew what? Did my parents know about his art? I was convinced after seeing the studio in the barn that I finally knew the real Nate. And now my mother has made me doubt it all over again. There is only one thing to do. I rise and move out into the hallway.

I glance about furtively, and hear only the buzz of the television. I make my way down to Nate's bedroom and stop in front of it. Gently, I push the door open and step inside, quickly, quietly shutting it behind me. I take a deep breath, then look around. Most everything seems the same, but there is an air of emptiness that leaves the room feeling cold and wrong. His bed is made, and his closet door is shut, all of the clothes and books and CDs and other assorted junk that had covered his floor and desk and chair and every available surface is gone. The place is too clean.

But the dozens of posters still cover the walls. They're posters of bands I've never listened to, movies I have never watched — bands and movies I am pretty sure most people have never heard of, but that look angry and alienating. I sit down on his bed, then flip onto my stomach, hanging my head over the edge, and pull up the bedskirt to peer underneath. There is some sort of flat black case; it looks kind of like a skinny briefcase. I stretch my arm to try to slide it out from under the bed. Finally, I manage to pull it free and up onto the bed. Crossing my legs, I turn over the case and squeeze the clasp. Inside is a pile of papers tied together with a strip of black ribbon. I gasp. It is a collection of pencil sketches by my brother, and they are beautiful. At once delicate and strong, there are scenes of a mother and her son resting beneath a tree, a cat balancing on a fence post, a gang of little kids playing soccer in the street. So many tiny, ordinary pieces of life. I spread them out across the bedspread and study each one. Nate rendered these moments so intimately, so truthfully. The lines of his pencil brushed across the pages with sensitivity, with empathy. I can see that. Feel it.

I imagine I can hear Nate's raspy voice snarling, "Hey,

Squirt, what do you think you're doing in my room? Get lost and stay out of my stuff!"

I shiver, then get up and approach his desk. The computer was moved into my room, and there is a square space slightly darker than the rest of the wood where it used to rest. Again, the emptiness, the disuse gnaws at me. I begin to pull at the drawers, tearing at the contents with trembling fingers. In the first two there are CDs — *The Velvet Underground & Nico,* The Who's *My Generation,* Miles Davis's *Kind of Blue* — pens and rubber bands. In the next one is a battered copy of James Joyce's *A Portrait of the Artist as a Young Man,* and a small wooden box. I pull it out and slide the flat top open to reveal a set of drawing pencils and a gummy eraser. I place the box on top of the desk; I will adopt its contents. I pull open the last drawer and find it empty but for a single, narrow strip of white paper.

I pick it up and flip it over to find a row of photographs, the kind you could take in the booth in the mall. And there are Nate and Julie, making faces and kissing and smiling so broadly, I guess they must have been laughing uncontrollably. I trace my fingernail over their faces. He looked so happy. So filled with laughter and unburdened by the darkness that seemed to come over him at home, that had driven him out of the house and into his car that night. So many nights.

How could Julie look so cheerful in these photos, so in love with Nate? They dated for almost a year. What had brought them together in the first place? And why did Julie break up with him? Did she know about his art? Did she know him better than we did?

Why didn't Nate tell us — tell *me* about it? Did Mom and Dad give him such a hard time that he felt he had to hide it? And how could he be so intent on destruction when he was creating such amazing art all the while?

I move toward his closet and begin to rifle through it, pushing the clothing aside. The smell of him is overpowering, sweet, like gingersnaps mixed with patchouli and deodorant. I can't believe that after so many months, his scent still lingers.

One summer Nate and I — we must have been eight and twelve or so — set off for the Wyatt cornfields, where we liked to play hide-and-seek. We headed over there on our bikes, and it was late in the afternoon, maybe early evening. The sun was well on its way to meeting the horizon in a ball of pink-and-crimson fire, the sky still light in that dusky half-glow, in which colors seem richer, subtler.

A group of neighborhood kids had gathered in the fields, and Benji Tuckerson was "It." He closed his eyes and counted to fifty as we spread out and burrowed beneath the cornstalks, which were fully grown, sprouting a jungle of leafy foliage to camouflage us. I waited, crouched beneath the corn at the most distant corner of the field. I waited and waited. I listened to the shrieking yelps of laughter as other kids were discovered. I felt smug, congratulating myself for finding such a good hiding spot. I heard the singing of crickets. Still, I waited. Twilight was descending, and the sky turned indigo; I could see the evening star. Soon, the cries of other kids faded, and my chest began to feel tight with panic. Where had everyone gone? I wondered. Why hadn't Benji found me? Why hadn't I heard the game called? I stood up, and my legs shook from kneeling for so long. I started walking, but shortly realized that I wasn't moving toward the barn. I became disoriented and frightened. The cornfield went on for acres, and I couldn't see in the gathering darkness any longer. Tears began to fall from my eyes, and I couldn't catch my breath. I was so scared, I began to run. Suddenly, Nate was there.

"Hey, Squirt! Are you okay?" he asked, his eyes scrunched with worry. "I've been looking for you forever." I just shook my head, sobbing now, and Nate picked me up, even though I was too old and far too big to be picked up. Then he carried me out of the maze of corn. "It's okay, I found you," he said. I buried my head in his neck and cried and breathed in his scent, suddenly relishing how safe I felt. How loved.

Now, I sink to the floor, holding up one of Nate's T-shirts to my face, clasping it to my mouth and nose. It was almost five years ago when I first started to miss him, when he first went away from me, when he marched off to eighth grade, grew some hair on his lip, and became a giant jerk. When Nate stopped being the brother I had always known and worshipped, the brother who used to take me down to the creek, balanced on the handlebars of his bike. The brother I used to follow bravely, happily, anywhere.

Squirt, which he had always called me with affection, became a weapon, inflicted with a spike of malice. "Get out of my way, Squirt," came to be the best I could expect from him. That turned into "Get out of my way, *loser*." Then just "Move."

When he died, I felt like someone had taken a softball and punched it through my stomach — my gut — because I knew then that the older brother I used to idolize would never, ever come back.

I set the T-shirt down on the floor beside me and begin to dig deeper, moving boots and sneakers, which do not smell nice, out of the way. At the back is a cardboard tube. I draw the plastic cap from one end and crawl out of the closet. I hold the tube up to the light, peering into it, trying to see what its contents are. There are several papers rolled up inside it. Probably more posters, but I snake two fingers down into the tube, tapping on the other end, to try to shake them out, anyway.

Finally, I manage to snag them, and slide them out slowly. The paper is grainy and rough, not poster material. With shaking fingers, I unroll them and let out a low whistle when I see the delicate blush of pigment. Subtle splashes of color and fine black lines. It is a series of watercolor paintings, of tree branches, birds, flowers. And Nate's spidery signature marks the lower corner of each piece.

Not in a million years, not in ten million years, would I ever have expected this. He was great. He could have been truly great.

I gather all of the drawings and the watercolors and the wooden box of pencils in my arms and move to the door. The knob is warm and cool at once. I pause and look around the room. Could it be? Could he be here with me? Not since he died have I ever had the sense that he was nearby. I don't know if I believe in heaven or any kind of afterlife. But I do know it makes me very sad to think Nate is just lying in the ground, being eaten by worms and maggots. But not sensing his presence makes me sad, too, and so usually I try not to think about it. Yet, with a doorknob feeling hot and cold at the same time, I start to wonder if maybe Nate is here and, if he's here, maybe he's glad I've found his artwork, glad his secret is finally out in the open, and that I can finally know who he really was.

As I poke my head out into the hallway, I can hear my mom's voice coming from the den. She is probably yelling at my dad about me. And my father is probably just sitting there, taking it. Silent. Absent.

I smuggle all of Nate's things into my room, hide the drawings and paintings under my bed, and tuck the pencil box away into one of my desk drawers. I pull out my history book and get ready to do the assigned reading before I go to bed. The Civil War. It used to feel like a civil war was being waged inside the walls of this house when Nate was alive. At first, my parents tried to cajole Nate into behaving. As he grew more reckless, more angry, more defiant, finally, they took to screaming at him, doing battle with him every chance they had. And Nate almost seemed to relish in fighting back. Their sparring would usually drive me into my bedroom, to take cover under my covers. It was bloody. And it was awful.

Now, my mother ceaselessly tries to engage my father, but he is unwilling to be drawn into a fight. The house is much quieter, but the silence is worse.

I snap the book closed. I can't concentrate. All I can think of is Nate and how angry at him and at my parents I am. How sick of all this anger I am. It's poison. My body feels like it is humming; I can't sit here any longer. For the second time tonight, I check to see if either of my parents is up and moving around the house. The hallway is silent and empty. Suddenly, I feel possessed by a wild recklessness. I don't care if they do catch me. I am going out, and no one is going to stop me.

I fling open the garage door and run outside. The air is cool and clean. I hop on my bike and start pedaling fast. Faster. I am soaring down the streets of Lincoln Grove, onto the county road, and letting my body lean into each curve, I make my way in the growing darkness to the creek. When I reach the spot, I throw my bicycle on the ground and sprint to the weeping willow tree. There, I fall down, hugging the tree's broad trunk for support.

"I can't do this." Sobs are filling my throat, filling the night. "I can't do this anymore. I can't."

What a waste. What a terrible waste. He died and I never really got to know him. I never got to know what he did, what he could do. He will never get to show everybody what he could do. I don't even think *he* knew what he could have done. My gut burns with the same fiery pain I felt on the night he died.

A tempest is raging inside of me, outside of me, and I feel the sky might fall down, come crashing about my head. The ache inside of me keeps me rooted to the ground, to the base of the willow tree.

What was the point of your dying when the rest of the world keeps going? We have to keep living without you, Nate! We have to live and go to school and eat breakfast and live *without you. Julie is making out with other guys, and this stupid world keeps spinning, even without you in it! What is the point? What is the point of any of it?* I want to scream at the heavens.

No meaning, no point.

And if the whole world can crumble to pieces at any moment, why should we struggle to make it through the days and months? Why should we pour our hearts into paintings and stories and families and love if the sky could fall down at any moment? Terrifying, terrifying.

The sun is setting, and the sky is a milky violet, the first star twinkling in the eastern horizon.

What is the point?

As if in response, a strange silvery light falls across the ground where I lie. When I glance up, the moon has risen and hangs low in the heavens. It is a big full moon. As I gaze at it, I can make out the gray eddies of crater and mountain, a whole landscape up there, suspended in the sky. The enormity of the moon sings to me and quells my rage. I feel the singing of the moon in all its hoary beauty like a balm. Yes, I am in the world now.

The singing rings and sings in my ears, and I stare out at the land around me. There, just at the edge of the creek bed, stands a slender white bird. Slender and white like a crane. It seems to have simply appeared, and, oh, what an elegant figure it makes. The neck is long and slim and plunges into a curved back in a single, flowing line. White downy wings are tucked tight to its body, and in the moonlight, the bird seems to glow with an ethereal light.

The bird wades into the water, dipping its pointed orange beak below the surface. Its neck arches and bends in one fluid movement, and lifts, its stark whiteness standing out against the darkening trees and rocks and grass. The bird cocks its head, one eye staring curiously at me. I have never seen such a beautiful creature.

The sweep of its back is subtle and full of grace. I long to sing to it, and my heart longs to sing, too, and all I can do is sit there, transfixed. The bird remains motionless, continuing to watch me, suffering my lingering gaze. Then it turns and bends to stir the water with its beak. All is silent, all is still.

As the warm strength of the tree behind me holds up my back, and I behold the beautiful bird before me, I feel a sudden peace descend. Never have I seen such beauty and felt such peace.

I wish I had my pad and pencils. I want to draw this bird, this perfect wooded spot, with its brown trickling water, cool gray rocks, and bowed and beautiful weeping willow tree. This place I used to share with my brother.

The quiet and beauty of this moment fill my head with a soaring ecstasy. This, *this* is the world. This is life, able to give us such beauty, such love. And the immensity of these gifts is boundless. I can use my pencils and charcoals and pastels and paintbrushes and capture this moment, capture all of this meaning. There is so much beauty to be found in the world, and art . . . *art* is the point.

Chapter Six

I remember the first time I came to the creek by myself, three years ago. My mother had bought blood oranges — another first for me — from the supermarket; they were imported specially from someplace far away, Morocco or Spain, maybe. I had secreted one of the oranges into my pocket as if it were a precious jewel and I a thief, and I'd ridden my bike quickly and directly to the creek. There was no better place to open up the bruise-colored orange-and-violet peel, to open the door to this other world. The creek itself was practically a sacred place for me — for Nate and me, once. As I sat beneath the weeping willow tree and began to tear away the thick skin, exposing the crimson-purple flesh of the fruit, I imagined I was entering some magical, exotic country. A land of dark-haired, black-eyed women, and sand and secret garden courtyards.

Someday I will travel. I have nursed that fantasy and grown it, in my drawings and maps, in my eagerness to get out of the house, this town. Now, though, now I know what to do.

I ease my bike back into the garage and open the door.

There is no light. My parents are not in sight. I tiptoe down the hall and up the stairs to my bedroom. Immediately, I reach for my sketch pad and open the box of Nate's pencils. *Get to work, Squirt,* I imagine Nate saying.

Then I begin to make a list.

The creek
The Wyatt cornfields
The swimming pool
Lincoln Grove Middle School
Lincoln Grove High School
The skating pond
The baseball diamond
The playground
County Road 1, the bend in the road
with the bent oak tree

I will map the world that I know better than anything. The world, the places I've shared with Nate. And I will finish his last, unfinished piece with this map of the known world. I'll draw the places we used to go and the kids we used to be. Then I will mount this map on the pedestal Nate built.

I grab my cell phone and search for Damian's number. For a second, I feel a flutter in my belly as I remember him taking the phone out of my hands and punching in his number. I'm thankful he did it. Then I push aside the butterflies, shoo them out of my system, and dial.

"Hello?" His voice sounds scratchy.

"Hi, did I wake you?"

"No. Cora? Is that you?" He sounds clear now.

"Yeah . . . Well, I was calling because I wanted to ask you something."

"What?"

"Do you think I could come to the barn with you after school on Monday? I want to see your studio again," I tell him.

"Uh, yeah, but are you sure? Won't your mom flip out?" he asks uncertainly.

"Well, I'm not going to tell her. I'll just have to make sure I get home before she does," I answer.

"All right, no problem. See you Monday?" he replies.

"Yes, I'll see you Monday." I hang up feeling happier, lighter than I have in a long time. As I get into bed, my heart is filled with hope.

• • •

When Sunday comes, I leave the house as the sun rises, hastily making myself a peanut butter and jelly sandwich and stuffing it, along with a drawing tablet and my pencils, in my backpack. I grab the list I made last night and jump on my bike. I will make the rounds today, visiting all of the places that had ever meant something to me and to Nate.

First, I ride to the swimming pool. It is vacant, closed up for the winter. The front gate is chained shut with a massive padlock. I lean my bike up against the fence and begin to walk around it, peering through the chain links, looking at the empty pool. I'm able to see for the first time the steep slope of the bottom, as it graduates from the shallow to deep end. I stare at the waterslide, and find myself picturing my eight-year-old self perched nervously at the top of the ladder, scared to let go and slide down the curving rivulet of water. I can see twelve-year-old Nate treading water at the bottom, calling for me to just let go and slide.

"Come on, Squirt! You can do it, Cor. Come on, I'll catch you! Nothing bad will happen, promise!" he had said. He had been so patient, so kind to me back then. The memory prods like a blunt blade.

I settle down on the ground and, facing the swimming area, pull out my sketch pad and pencils. Hastily, I begin to lay out the sweeping expanse of lawn, reimagining the blue-and-white lounge chairs that dot the grass in the summertime, the water rushing down the slide, a gang of teenagers gathered around the diving board, little kids splashing noisily in the shallow end of the pool, and old ladies in swim caps and frilly bathing suits slowly doing doggie-paddle laps. I draw it all. And I add a small girl, myself at the top of the slide, Nate at the bottom, coaxing me to come to him.

When I am finished, I pack my supplies and get back on the bike. Next, I ride to the baseball diamond in a park that is a quarter of a mile from the pool. The park where Nate and I had played freeze tag with a whole crew of kids from the neighborhood. The grass grows tall in this field — it always has — except where a baseball diamond has been cut into it. The stationary plastic bases are anchored into the ground, and the baselines are faded, mostly invisible now. I remember sitting between my parents, squeezed onto the tiny bleachers as we watched Nate play ball with his Little League team. Thermoses of hot chocolate and bags of caramel popcorn were passed between my mom and dad and me, as we cheered for the Lincoln Hawks. Nate had played first base, and when he manned his base, his eyes would scrunch up, and he'd stay crouched like a cat, always at the ready to spring after a ball. I was so proud of him. He used to seem so grown-up and capable.

I quickly sketch a picture of cheering onlookers, the Hawks in their pin-striped uniforms, opponents at bat. Then I pack up again and move away from the baseball field. I head out toward the playground that floats like an island of mulch and plastic and steel in the middle of the sea of grass. I walk through the tangle of swings and monkey bars, give the merry-go-round a shove and watch as it spins and spins. Then I sit down on the tire swing, pushing off the ground with my feet, and lean back as the swing tips and moves jerkily under the uneven weight, then faster and faster. I pump my legs and stand up on the tire, clinging to the chains. They're creaking and groaning, and I really hope that they aren't the same chains that held up the swing when I was a little kid. The tire swings higher and faster. I feel like I'm flying. The joy and lightness of last night returns. I imagine the white bird is above me, circling in the sky. But something tells me I will never see it again. It was a thing of mystery. And actually, in the light of day, I wonder if it was even real. But I don't want to dwell on this question. All I know, all that matters is that I saw it and felt its beauty and let that beauty enter me.

As I rock back and forth on the tire swing, I think about when my dad used to take Nate and me to the playground. We'd crowd onto the tire together, begging our dad to push us. Harder. Harder. As we picked up speed, Nate would throw back his head and laugh wildly, shouting and grinning. I loved his abandon, the way he could just laugh and laugh. Dropping my feet, I drag the swing to a halt. Then, I pull out my pencils and pad. I draw tiny crosshatch strokes, filling in two little children perched on the tire swing, calling up the pure joy in Nate's eight-year-old face, a dad pushing them from behind, his face lit with pleasure, as well, and I feel this twinge of happiness.

I spend the rest of the day visiting the middle school we attended together; the Wyatt cornfields, where we used to play spies; the Wilson Farm, where we would take hayrides in the autumn; the skating pond, where we'd go on the coldest days of winter, bundled into our parkas, skates strapped to our feet, and where Nate would sometimes move so quickly, he skimmed the surface of the pond like a bird on wing.

When I was small, probably six or seven, my parents let Nate take me to the pond, just the two of us, and I remember I was wearing so many layers — undershirt, T-shirt, sweater, sweatshirt, parka, ski pants — that I could hardly move. And down I went in the middle of the pond, too laden with clothes to work my way back onto my feet again. Then Nate, spotting me from the other side, flew to me, grabbed my hands and pulled me upright. Walking me over to the benches at the side of the pond, he helped me peel off my sweatshirt, then, pressing a warm hand to my tearstained cheek, he whispered, "Here you go, Squirt, you're all set."

I draw and sketch and fill my pad with images of all the places we had loved together. And I can feel the pieces of my heart coming back, glued together with a tenderness, as I revisit all these places, as I allow the memories in, as I let myself really see my town the way I used to when Nate and I were little. And I can almost start to love it again. Almost.

When the sun begins to set, I still have one final place to go. The bent tree off of the county road. It marks the spot where Nate was killed. Slowly, I head through the streets of Lincoln Grove to the county road heading east out of town. My feet move reluctantly on the pedals. I ride along the shoulder of the road and soon come to the part of the guardrail that is dented and misshapen, that is bent in the shape of a Honda Civic. I steer off the shoulder, into the grass at the side of the road. As

I near the big oak tree, my knees begin to shake, and I start to feel queasy.

"You can do this," I mutter to myself. I swing my leg over the bike seat and walk it the rest of the way.

Then I crawl beneath the umbrella of tree branches, pausing at the foot of its white-gray trunk. I turn and run my hands over the coarse bark, letting my fingers find the evidence of Nate's accident. There it is. A bumpy seam at about waist height. The tree still bears the scar of his collision. The tree shares my hurt. Once again I bring out my pad and begin to draw. But I don't draw Nate or his Honda. I just sketch the tree without its scar, the road without any cars. It is a scene of peace.

When I am done, I sit at the base of the tree and close my eyes, letting the cool autumn breeze find my face. It is nearly dinnertime, and my parents are probably freaking out. I take a deep breath and dig my fingers into the dirt beside me. The moss and dead leaves that have fallen from the oak are soft and damp. There is a sweet, familiar scent in the air, clinging to the ground. Here, now, I feel close to Nate. Really close to him.

Time to go. I pedal away from the oak tree, the disfigured guardrail, but I do not look back at any of it. I ride home.

The lights are on outside the house. Quickly, I push the kickstand down and go inside. My mom is in the kitchen. She looks up as I enter.

"Where have you been? I was worried sick," she says, her voice bleeding exhaustion and worry.

"Sorry. I should have left a note, I guess," I reply. "I was just riding my bike around." I do feel sorry. Not too sorry, but enough to be contrite.

"Yes, you should have," she says, her voice short and tight. "Go wash up, dinner is almost ready."

Clearly, she isn't going to broach the subject of our fight last night. That is fine by me. I dash upstairs and wash my hands and face, put away my sketch pad and pencils, and repack my book bag with my schoolbooks. Then I return to the kitchen to sit with my mom in silence and eat a tasteless dinner of microwaved carrots and fish sticks.

I can hear the television filtering down from the den, and I feel a flash of anger. Without saying a word, I get up from the table and run up the stairs. I open the door and find my father sitting slumped in a chair, his head in his hands.

"Dad," I mumble.

No response.

"Dad!" I repeat, louder.

"What is it?" He doesn't even turn to look at me.

"Dad, why don't you come to the kitchen and eat dinner with Mom and me?" I try.

"I'm fine here," he states flatly, still not meeting my gaze.

"Well, we're not fine out there. Could you please come?" I hate myself for begging, but a sense of urgency, of desperation has seized me. I feel like if he doesn't meet my eye, doesn't take himself downstairs to sit with us, the whole thing will implode — our family will implode and we'll never be able to put all the pieces back together.

"Cora, shut the door."

"Dad —"

"Get out," he says coldly. "Just go."

I feel like he slapped me. I jerk my head around and step out of the doorway. I can't breathe. I pull the door shut hard behind me, but it's not very satisfying, even when the walls shake around it.

Why does he get to behave that way when the rest of us have to pull it together and move on? He's my freaking father!

I march back to the kitchen, pick up my fork, and finish eating. My mother and I both pretend that nothing happened. She knows, though. She knows our family is falling apart around us.

I finish eating, put my plate in the sink, and go up to my room. I haven't done any homework, and now Sunday night is breathing down my neck. The house seems to shudder under the weight of the silence.

Chapter Seven

Monday stretches on and on. I can barely contain my excitement. I can't wait to get to Damian's studio and begin working on my art project. On Nate's project.

It's only lunchtime. I amble into the cafeteria and look for Rachel in our usual spot by the windows. She isn't there. I must have gotten here first, so I go and sit down. It's awfully surprising when I do find Rachel; she's sitting farther back in the cafeteria at a different table, with Josh and the Nasties and the other Nasty satellite, Elizabeth Tillson. *What?* I try to catch her eye, thinking Rachel will wave me over to join them. But she studiously avoids looking in my direction. And all the time, my stomach is churning, because even if I'm hoping she'll invite me to sit with them, I know she didn't sit at our table — didn't wait for me to get there — on purpose. She didn't want to sit with me at all.

Rachel has totally and completely ditched me. And she's clearly embarrassed of me. I eat my lunch quickly, barely chewing my sandwich, the peanut butter lodging in my throat, against the crybaby lump that's grown there. When I'm done, I gather my things and hurry to the library.

I pull out my history book and pretend to do my homework, but it's useless. My mind won't stop spinning over the image of Rachel sitting at the end of the Nasties' table, not talking to anyone seated near her, and avoiding my eyes. I bet all the other kids from our class, the girls I've known my whole life and was even once friendly with, witnessed the whole humiliating debacle, and now, my loserdom is confirmed. It's probably the lead item in the class gossip broadcast. Not only the girl with the dead brother, but the girl with no friends. This is it.

I feel like I'm drowning at the bottom of the deepest sea. There is nowhere for me to go. Home is just as bad as school.

Art — I have art class for last period. Thank goodness. I draw a shaky breath of gratitude. And when the bell rings, I walk meekly, my head bowed, through the hallways, all the way down to the far end of the school to the art studio. And as I step in and look all around at the brightly mismatched colors and images plastered on the walls, the lonely hulks of canvas on easels, and students spread around the classroom, as isolated and alone as I feel, I become calm. When I reach my stool and easel, I prop up my sketch pad and turn to the drawings I made the day before.

The swimming pool, the park playground, the baseball field, the tree . . . all of it from a time when I didn't know unhappiness. Not *real* unhappiness. These images are from a time when I knew only love. When bad things happening, when people leaving, was unthinkable.

Is it possible to live, to exist in the world without any connection to another person? To not care about other people, to not care if other people care about you?

I look up and find Damian sitting across the room, his forehead crinkled as he chews his lower lip and rubs a stick of charcoal between his fingers. He's staring intensely at the paper on the easel before him. He concentrates with such ferocity, I think. He doesn't look up.

"Hey, whatcha working on?"

I startle and surface from my creepy staring and ridiculously moody thoughts. Helena is standing in front of me, curiously studying the drawing perched on my easel. Her flaxen hair hangs loose today, falling in untidy curls around her shoulders.

"Huh? Oh, um, just some drawings," I mutter.

"Yes, I can see that they're drawings," Helena replies with a friendly smirk. "What are they for?"

I hesitate. Should I tell Helena? Will she think I'm weird, will she laugh at me? Helena looks at me expectantly with wide blue eyes.

"Well, they're drawings of places my brother and I used to go." I step back and scrutinize Helena's expression, waiting for the mockery I'm sure will follow. But Helena nods — of course she knows who Nate was, she was at school here last year when he died — and she looks even more curious. "And, well, I just wanted to, um, I don't know. . . ." I can't finish, unnerved by Helena's unwavering stare.

"You're sort of making, like, a memorial to him?" Helena asks softly.

Another lump grows in my throat, bigger this time. I nod my head. "Um, yeah. I guess so." I look down at my feet, the torn cuffs of my blue jeans. "Do you think it's dumb?" Why do I always cry? Tears have filled my stupid traitor eyes. Almost reflexively, I turn toward Damian. As if he can feel my gaze on him, he glances over, and he lets a tiny half grin find its way to his lips. Then he returns to his work.

"I think it's a brilliant idea." Helena smiles at me then moves back to her own easel.

Something lifts in my chest, the twenty thousand pounds of seawater and sadness. I turn back to my sketches and flip the pages slowly from one drawing to the next. When I reach the last picture, the one of the tree, the empty road, I sit back on the stool and put a finger to my lips. Not comfortable. I rest my elbows on my knees and my chin on my clasped hands. I tilt my head and cross my legs. I crack my knuckles and twirl a stick of charcoal. Can't stop fidgeting.

"What's up, Cora?" I jump in surprise. Ms. Calico has crept up behind me, silent as a panther. "You've been sitting here fidgeting for the past twenty minutes. What's going on?"

Helena shuffles over, reaching back to pull her hair into a bun. "She's making a memorial to her brother," she offers helpfully. She comes to stand next to Ms. Calico, behind my stool.

"Your brother?" Ms. Calico repeats quietly.

"He died last year, and —" I don't know how to finish.

"So, she drew all these places that they used to go to together," Helena finishes for me.

"I see," Ms. Calico says thoughtfully. "Well, what are you going to do with them?" she asks, moving around to face me.

"I'm not sure," I reply, looking down at my hands.

Ms. Calico begins to carefully thumb through the pages, pausing to examine each drawing. Her forehead creases in contemplation. "These are really good, Cora." As I meet her eyes, she repeats, "What do you *think* you will do with them?"

I desperately want to tell Ms. Calico and Helena about the sculptures in Damian's studio, about Nate's artwork, about the unfinished piece, and how I want to show the world what Nate did, who he was. But I don't know how to say the words, how to say them without feeling foolish. What if they scorn me the way my mother did? And besides, Damian is here. This is not my secret to tell. He and I share it. There is a fluttering twist in my gut. Damian and I have a secret to share.

I lean back and study Helena and Ms. Calico, their heads bowed close to the sketch pad, to each other, to me. I like the closeness. It feels good. A sense of warmth floods through my hands and arms and feet and legs and chest. It surrounds my gut, fills in the hollow space.

"I don't know what to do with them. I'm trying to figure it out," I tell them.

"Well, whenever you do figure it out," Helena says pointedly, "you should put the whole thing someplace where everyone can see it. I think a lot of people would like that."

Really? I can only gape at her.

"I think that's a lovely idea," Ms. Calico agrees. "Cora, if you need any help, if you want to talk about anything, you know where to find me," she tells me before moving over to Helena's easel. "Come, Helena, let's see what you've been up to besides counseling Cora."

I watch them talk. Ms. Calico stands with one foot in front of the other, leaning back, as she listens to Helena describe her painting. Helena speaks animatedly, waving her hands, her curls escaping from their makeshift bun and bouncing around her shoulders. Ms. Calico nods a couple of times, then bends forward to confer quietly with Helena. They make an elegant picture.

I turn back to my own work. How will I transfer these sketches to the boards in the barn? What will I *do* with it all?

I sit down again on my stool and stare some more, my thoughts not really touching down. They jump around hazily. I look up once more at Damian, who is hunched over on his stool, one hand gripping the top of his easel, the other furiously slashing at his pad with the charcoal. What does he think about me? Does he think about me? I've been so caught up in learning about Nate, but Damian's talent is remarkable, too. It seems so unlikely, because, whereas I used to know Nate as a sweet kid, Damian has always seemed tougher, harder somehow. My thoughts aren't really making sense, and I'm not paying attention, when suddenly the bell rings.

Oh my gosh, I'm supposed to go to Damian's studio today. I begin to feel nervous again at the prospect of going back there with him. Then, the argument with my mother, the blow of my father's refusal to eat with us come racing back to me, and, with a burst of energy, I say good-bye to Helena and Ms. Calico and dash out of the art room with a nod of acknowledgment to Damian. "I'll meet you by your car," I murmur as I push past him.

I swing through the gloomy corridors, not noticing the other kids also pushing through the halls, racing to get out of school. When I reach my locker, I hastily spin the lock around, watching the numbers. Then, as it pops open, I grab my books and notebooks and jacket and slide the books I don't need onto the shelf, and slam the metal door shut.

"Hey, Cora!" Rachel's voice rings out through the fast-emptying hall.

I don't turn. I freeze.

Heavy footsteps pound the tile floor. I still don't move.

"Hey, Cora!" Rachel is out of breath, her cheeks puffing

heavily. She jogs up to my locker and comes to an abrupt halt. She bends forward a bit, fighting to catch her breath. "Hey, what are you —" She stops talking as she notices the ferocity of my glare.

"Excuse me," I say coldly and push past her.

"Um, is something *wrong*?" Rachel asks. But her heart isn't in the sneer. She has a guilty look.

I spin around. "Why would something be *wrong*, Rach?" I say deridingly. "Oh, maybe because you ditched me at lunch today and then didn't even have the guts to look at me? Or because you totally sold out and sat with the Nasties, who couldn't even be bothered to *look* at you, let alone talk to you? Because you left me out to dry? Hmm . . . could it be *any* of that?"

"Huh. I don't know what you're talking about. I'm *allowed* to sit with other people, Cora," she scoffs. "God, don't be such a baby!"

"You know what, *Rach*, you don't have to worry about having a *baby* bothering you anymore. I'll get out of your way." I am seething, my voice has turned lethally quiet. I march down the hall, leaving Rachel behind to stare at my back. I hope her mouth is hanging open.

"Wait, Cor!" Rachel calls. "Please, wait!"

I stop but I don't turn to look at her.

"I'm sorry, Cora. Really. I am." Rachel says pleadingly. "I should have told you. It's just, Josh asked me if I was going to sit with them, and I didn't know what to say. And I *wanted* to sit with him. But . . ." I turn around and face her. Rachel's chin begins to quiver. "I'm sorry."

I sigh, and my anger fades. "It's fine. Just don't do it again. Okay?"

Rachel nods vigorously.

"Look, I've got to go," I tell her, and without another word, walk away.

When I get outside, I start to breathe again. I feel my hands and legs shaking madly. Tears spring to my eyes for the second — or is it the third? — time today, and the fall breeze blows the scent of fallen leaves and coming rain across my face. I wipe roughly at my eyes. What is wrong with me lately?

I spot Damian's blue El Camino. And there he is, leaning up against the driver's-side door. He is fiddling with his keys, eyes narrow, a lock of his hair lifting gently in the wind.

He looks dangerous. My stomach twists and jumps nervously. Damian looks up and finds my eyes. He gives a small wave and straightens up. There, now he looks more harmless. I wave back and go to join him by his car.

This feels like I'm turning a corner, and once I make this turn, I can't go back. But what exactly am I leaving behind? Nothing good, I think. If this is a turning point, I'll take it.

"Hey," Damian greets me. He moves around the massive blue body of the car to the passenger side and unlocks the door, then holds it open.

"Hi." I am smiling, probably like a big dork, but I am sort of happy to go with him, I realize. "Thanks," I say as he closes the door after me. His gray eyes are warm and they crinkle at the corners when he grins back at me.

"Ready?" he asks.

"Yup," I answer. And we're off.

The drive to the Wright farm feels faster this time. The way is familiar to me now and the houses in their graduating tumbledownedness not as noticeable. The trees are beginning to look naked. Golden leaves carpet the lawns and sidewalks, covering up overgrown grass and cracked cement. The sky is a moody gray. Geese rise in a *V* above us, tilting and wheeling in the wind. Winter is approaching.

As we pull into the pebbly driveway, I think about how my mom would ground me for life if she knew I was here, that I had disobeyed her again. I wonder if Damian has told his mom.

"Hey, Damian?" I start. "Could I ask you something?"

"Yeah," Damian replies, sounding cautious. He parks the car in front of the barn, gravel crunching beneath the tires.

"Where are your parents?" I ask timidly. "I mean, do they know about all of this?"

Damian pauses, stopping awkwardly, half in and half out of his car door. He pulls himself back inside and settles into the seat for a moment. "My dad took off when I was just a baby. I don't talk to him, really." He picks at his thumbnail. "Well, he doesn't talk to *me*, actually. He hasn't tried to talk to me or see me since he left." Damian shrugs his shoulders and tries to look nonchalant. "You know, back when he and my mom were together, it wasn't so cool for a white guy to be with a black woman, and I guess he just wimped out, couldn't hack it, and left."

"I'm sorry," I murmur. My mind is whirring. I sure opened that can of worms all on my own, but I guess I wasn't prepared for the starkness of his answer. It explains his coloring, which can only be called beautiful, with his bright gray eyes and light brown skin. How could I have known Damian all these years and never known any of this about him?

"Nah, don't be. My mom's around. She works a lot, but, well, we're pretty close," he says. He turns, climbs out of the car, and begins to head toward the barn again. I stare at his back, straight and tall and broad.

I hope I haven't made him feel self-conscious. I didn't mean to do that. I just thought, if I'm going to hang out with him, I should know more about him. We're virtually strangers, even though he's spent so much time in my house over the years.

I enter the barn and follow him across the rickety floorboards, again admiring his grace, the ease with which he moves. As he switches on the lights, I walk, almost reflexively, to the boards Nate had nailed together. Then I sit down in front of them. The floor is cold and hard, and Damian brings a blanket over. "Here," he says gruffly.

"Thanks," I say, looking up at him, trying to keep the surprise from my voice. When he is gentle and kind like this, I do not feel prepared for it.

The blanket is plaid and navy blue and scratchy. The scent of horse and hay clings to it. After I am settled on top of the blanket, I pull my pad and pencils from my book bag.

Silently, Damian moves off toward his workshop corner. Beginning is always hard, so I gaze around the barn. The high vaulted ceiling shelters a loft that looks to be filled with odd bits of furniture and farming equipment. Damian's paintings cover every inch of space around the walls of the barn, seeming to jump away from the knotty gray pinewood boards. The topographies of his work range widely, and there are slashes and explosions of color. Nate's sculptures stand like hulking hunchbacks, rusty bits of metal scraps, ragged shards of glass and wood stretching and poking like skeletons. All of the art in this space speaks to volcanoes of fury and rage and heartbreak. Somehow, though, I feel closer to Nate here, and all of the anger he brought home with him begins to make sense.

I tear the used pages out of my sketch pad and spread the drawings around me in a semicircle. My eyes dart quickly back and forth between the white slips of paper and the knotty boards leaning against the wall.

I shift the drawings around, figuring on top is north, right is east, left is west, and closest to me is south. I arrange the pages in a loose layout of the town. The map is like Swiss cheese, full of holes, but I can recognize the unseen order of it. I continue to move and play and plot with the pages. Until a shadow falls across them.

I glance up to see Damian standing over me, gazing thoughtfully at the drawings.

"These are really good," he says, crouching down beside me.

"Thanks." Again, I can't keep the amazement out of my voice.

"What are you thinking?" he asks as he continues to look over the pages on the ground.

"I'm not really sure," I answer slowly. "I'm trying to figure out how to make a map. . . ."

"A map of Lincoln Grove?"

"Yes! You could tell?" Damian bounces on his toes as if his crouch has become uncomfortable. "Here," I say, sliding over, making room on the blanket for him. "Sit."

"Thanks," he replies. "Of course I can tell." He gestures at the drawings. "There's the pool, the park. But, where's that?" Damian points to the sketch of the bent tree, the curved and empty road. He squints at it. "Oh," he finishes, not waiting for my response. I catch the glint of recognition registering in his eyes.

"Yeah . . ." I murmur, not knowing what to say.

"Well, are you thinking of putting this map on Nate's piece?" Damian asks, changing the subject.

I nod. "I just have no idea how to do it. You know, I want it to look like it fits with the base and all the rest of his stuff."

Damian props his chin on his fist. "Well, you could sketch these scenes onto the boards, then paint over them," he offers.

"I was thinking that, but I feel like it needs something more."

"Well, you can look around and see if there are any scraps you want to use."

"Really? Would you help me?" I ask. Multimedia . . . That would be something new.

"Of course," he counters matter-of-factly. Then he stands up in a single fluid movement and returns to his corner. He comes back shortly, carrying a battered-looking cardboard box. "Here," he says, putting the box down on the ground beside me. "Here's some scraps of stuff that Nate and I collected. Take whatever you want." He strides away again, and returns to his corner.

I begin to rifle through the box, picking up slivers of wood, metal nuts, steel rods, shards of plastic, a one-way traffic sign, a pane of glass, a small box filled with buttons and another filled with dried marigold heads. I pull some of the objects from the box and place them to the side. This is cool. There are so many possibilities, I feel as though my veins are throbbing and pulsing with ideas and art. It's like I've been shocked back to life.

I get so caught up in the thousands of thoughts that are whirling through my brain that I forget to keep track of the time. Damian is suddenly beside me again.

"Hey," he says, glancing over my shoulder at the pile of objects I've taken from the box.

"Oh, hey," I reply, smiling up at him.

"Um, I'm not trying to kick you out or anything, but do you have to get back home?" he asks.

"Oh, no! What time is it?"

Damian pulls out his cell phone. "It's almost a quarter to five."

"Oh, no!" I shout. "What should I do with all this stuff?" I ask, turning to him.

"Just leave it here. I'll put your stuff in a separate box." When he sees the worried look on my face, Damian reassures me, "Don't worry, no one ever comes in here, except me. Come on, I'll take you home."

We quickly extinguish the lights and unplug the little electric heater, then race outside into the chill evening air. I jump into the car, and Damian brings the El Camino roaring to life. I know I'm acting like a big freak, twitching nervously in the passenger seat, checking the time on my cell phone display over and over again.

"I can't get caught again," I mutter anxiously. "They'll lock me up for good, if I do."

"I think you're safe," Damian replies with a chuckle. We've pulled into my driveway, and there isn't any sign of my parents.

"Oh my gosh, thank you so much!" I say, turning to him. "For everything."

"Don't worry about it. Same time tomorrow?" He grins wickedly at me.

"Sure," I call as I climb out of the car and begin to trot up the path to the front door. "Thanks again! See ya!"

Damian rockets out of the driveway and speeds off down the street. I turn to watch him go, then open the door, blowing out a relieved breath. I made it. I am really going to have to be much more careful in the future. I cannot risk getting caught.

I sprint up the steps and into my bedroom. I throw all of my belongings down on the floor, and pull out the drawing tablet and begin to sketch, plotting out my approach to the map. My head is bursting with music and colors and ideas. And when I hear my dad come home, the familiar slam of the door, and tinkle of the ice cubes, I do not feel knotted up inside. When my mother gets home, I join her in the kitchen for dinner. In a halfhearted voice, she asks me how my day was, and I answer in an equally halfhearted way. I guess there will be peace between us tonight, an uneasy peace. I am too busy to worry about it, anyway.

Chapter Eight

The week of Homecoming is finally here. The thought of it fills me with a sadness, but the dance, thankfully, strangely, manages to distract me.

Every night for the last week I've had to spend at least an hour on the phone with Rachel, listening to her babble about hairstyles and who is going with whom and flowers and Josh and Josh and Josh.

Rachel had heard that, oh my gosh, Josh doesn't have a date. This is good. The soccer guys are going as a group instead. I am very relieved to hear this news, because the notion of listening to Rachel moan about Josh liking another girl would be just unbearable.

A couple of times, Rachel has asked what I do in the afternoons — poor me, trapped like a prisoner by my mean mom, don't I get bored? I haven't told her about the days at Damian's studio. How we work mostly in comfortable silence, each of us caught up in our own world, in our own work.

I do not tell her about how much I look forward to going to the Wright barn. How those couple of hours in his studio feel like an escape, a refuge. Nor do I tell Rachel that I think Damian has the most beautiful hands I've ever seen, that he walks like a cat, that he has the clearest eyes, which seem able to see absolutely everything about me. That he seems to be the loneliest person I've ever met, and it breaks my heart. All of these things feel private. Precious. And I don't want to share them with Rachel. Not yet, anyway.

I have also neglected to tell Rachel about the application papers for the summer art program that are still lying at the bottom of my backpack. I haven't told anyone about them; I'm trying my best to push them far from my thoughts. But the application is there, and it weighs on my mind like an anchor. I know the deadline for the application is quickly approaching. I am going to have to talk to my mom about it again soon or give it up.

Just another week.

• • •

I'm back in Damian's studio, and I return to the map. I've laid out the board flat on the cement floor of the barn. Using the blue plaid blanket as a pad for my knees, I kneel over it, drawing in outlines of the roads and houses, the pond and farms, our school, the park — the whole town — with my charcoal. For the places on my list, I've added the scenes I sketched and am dabbing spots of paint, gluing bits of fabric or wood, and pasting down various odds and ends to give these scenes texture, life.

Damian comes to sit beside me on the blanket. "This is looking really good," he comments.

"Really?" I ask, glancing up at him.

"Yes, really." He smiles at me, then nudges me with his shoulder. "So, ah, are you going to Homecoming on Saturday?" he asks, rolling his eyes good-naturedly.

Wait — what? Damian Archer has just asked me about the dance? He thinks about dances? I am completely caught off guard. I never would have expected Damian to care about something as school-spirity as Homecoming.

"Oh. Yeah. Just with Rachel. She kind of twisted my arm. Are you?"

"I haven't decided yet." He grins.

"Well, what will help you make up your mind?" I ask, desperately hoping I sound cheeky. I feel like my insides are at war: My brain is screaming out, *What are you playing at?*, while my gut, tingling with hope, whispers, *Maybe he'll ask me to go with him? Maybe?* My heart is beating so fast, and I just know a big, red, embarrassing stain is crawling over my cheeks.

Why do I feel like I'm two different people lately?

"I don't know. . . ." Damian suddenly looks serious. "Probably no one will even want me there anyway."

"What do you mean?" I ask.

"In case you haven't noticed, I'm not exactly the most popular guy at school these days," he says, tracing his finger on the dusty floor. "Guys who help their best friends die in a car wreck and then walk away from it aren't really so sought-after." He looks at me. "I'm sorry. I mean, I shouldn't complain about this stuff. Not to you," he mutters darkly.

"Hey," I say, twisting around to face Damian. "It's okay. I mean, I can't imagine what it's like for you. I know it's got to be hard. He was your best friend." He won't meet my gaze. "I can't imagine what it's like for you," I repeat softly. "But I know it's hard."

"Yeah." Damian stands and brushes off his pants. "Well, thanks, and I'm, uh, sorry." He lopes off to his workshop corner, covers his ears with headphones, and doesn't speak to me for the rest of the afternoon.

When we're back in his car, Damian still won't speak. The drive feels like it lasts for hours. Finally, Damian eases the car into my driveway. What do I do? Is he just never going to speak to me again? Do I want him to? I mean, he's right. Right? Oh, how do I fix this?

"Hey, Damian," I speak up, shattering the thick silence. "I hope you'll come to the dance."

I want the driveway to split open and swallow me. I want to die. I can't get out of this car fast enough. I fumble with the door handle, then finally it opens, and I hop out as quickly as possible. I don't look back as I run up the path to the front door. I hear the El Camino snarling down the street. I cannot believe I said that to him, I can't. My face heats up again as I remember the feel of the words on my tongue. I roll them around. *I hope you'll come.* Do I? Will he?

• • •

In art class the next day, I continue to draw sketches for my map, and try hard not to look at Damian. When I think about what I said to him, my ears heat up. You could cook eggs on them. "So, Cora," Ms. Calico says, suddenly coming up behind me, "have you sent in the application yet?" She is a sneaky one.

"Oh — uh — not yet. I'm almost done, though," I answer nervously.

"The deadline is coming up, isn't it?" Ms. Calico asks pointedly. "I'd hate for you to miss it."

"I know. I'm on it." I'm trying to sound confident. Probably failing miserably.

"Well, if you want me to look at your portfolio before you send it, I'm happy to," she offers.

"Thanks. Yeah, I'll definitely take you up on that," I say. I suck.

I rock back on my stool as Ms. Calico walks away. Why did I just say that? How am I ever going to get out of this mess?

For now, I'll ignore it.

I squint my eyes and peer at the drawing in front of me. I've colored in the park meadow and the playground with oil pastels. The children clambering on the tire swing are practically bursting to life. When that was me, when I was one of those little kids, I thought I could do anything.

"Hey." Helena's voice swims from behind me. I whip around to see her staring at me curiously.

"Hey, what's up?" I respond.

"What was all that about?" Helena asks, gesturing to Ms. Calico, whose back is turned to us as she speaks quietly with another student.

"Oh, nothing," I groan.

"Doesn't sound like nothing," Helena rejoins.

"Well, Ms. Calico asked me to apply to one of those summer art programs she told us about on the first day, and I said I would."

"That's amazing!" Helena exclaims, throwing an arm around my neck.

"Yeah, well, I can't go," I say, wriggling uncomfortably out of her grasp.

"What do you mean? Why not?" Helena asks, puzzled.

"It's in London, and there's no way my mom will *ever* let me go." Something releases in me. It is a relief to finally tell someone about the application.

"Really? Have you asked?"

"Yes, actually. And she flipped out."

"Maybe your mom will change her mind?"

"No, I know she won't. I just know."

"Hmmm . . . This is a tricky one," Helena says sympathetically. "I'll think about it and we'll figure out what you should do."

"Yeah, well, I wouldn't waste too much time thinking about it," I tell her glumly.

"Hey, cheer up." Helena is trying to comfort me. It's futile, but I don't have the heart to tell her that. She points to the drawing on my easel. "This one is going really well, at least."

"I guess so," I say doubtfully. But the truth is, even if I'm too embarrassed to admit it to Helena, I'm pretty happy with how all of the studies I've done so far for the map are turning out. And the map itself is growing more colorful, more alive every day. "How about your painting?" I ask, standing up to examine the canvas on Helena's easel. It is stunning — an argument of color and texture, flames of orange and red fighting tongues of violet and olive. "This is amazing," I tell her. "You should exhibit this somewhere."

"Well, I'll let you know when the Chicago Art Institute is banging down my door," Helena says with a dry grin. "Hey, I meant to ask you, are you going to the Homecoming dance tomorrow night?"

My gaze flicks to Damian. As usual, he's completely wrapped up in his painting. We seem to have arrived at an unspoken agreement not to speak to each other in art class. Not to give the other students even a hint of our knowing each other.

"Yeah. But I don't have a date or anything," I reply. "I told my friend Rachel I'd go just to keep her company while she moons over some guy."

"Ah, I see." Helena's face lights up with a big smile. "Well, I'm glad you're coming. I'll be there with Cam." Cam is her boyfriend. Her very cool, very cute boyfriend, whom I've never met, but I've seen him wait for her outside of art class. He is dark and handsome, just as arty and beautiful as Helena. I am not surprised that they're together. I study Helena's profile. She is gorgeous, with her flowing blonde curls, perfect skin, big blue eyes, and funky style.

"Nice." I smile as the bell rings and we begin gathering up our materials. A part of me is wistful — I wish I could tell her how mixed up I feel about Damian. Or just tell her about Damian and his paintings and his studio in the barn and our afternoons there. I wish I could tell her about what I said to him when I got out of his car yesterday. I'm dying to ask if I've made a hopeless fool of myself. But I just can't bring myself to open up to her about him. Especially not here, not when he's sitting twenty feet away. Oh my gosh.

"I'll see you at the dance!" Helena calls, and glides out of the classroom.

• • •

But before the dance comes the football game. Homecoming. I remember asking my dad why a football game was called Homecoming. What about watching two teams scrabble around on a muddy field suggested coming home? His voice would grow soft with patience and take on this warm timbre when he answered my little-kid questions. "Rabbit," he had explained in a very serious tone, "Homecoming is a celebration for everyone who has ever gone to the school to come home and cheer for the team," which was why most of the residents of Lincoln Grove came out for the LGHS Homecoming game.

My family went to the Homecoming game every year. The four of us would huddle together on the bleachers, surrounded by all of our neighbors and friends. We'd share blankets, and my dad always brought a thermos of hot chocolate, which my mom would pass around in steaming cups to keep us warm. I never paid much attention to the game, but the Homecoming parade and the crowning of the court was wonderful. I loved to watch the marching band, anchored by the enormous sousaphones that wrapped around their players, leading the homemade floats. The band would play familiar marches that were rousing and made us clap our hands and cheer, as convertible muscle cars with the previous years' homecoming courts, the school president, the principal drove past, and the floats constructed by each class would circle slowly around the gravel track that encompassed the football field. Then, once the parade had completed its circuit, the court would be announced, and these girls who looked so glamorous and grown-up, like Barbie dolls, would be called onto the field, presented with red roses and, finally, the sparkling silver crown would be placed on the queen's inevitably poofy blonde head. It was always raucous. It was always so much fun.

This year, our family isn't going. Surprise, surprise. The memory of the four of us sitting, squeezed together, laughing and filled with a warmth in the cold November air squeezes my chest like a vise.

Yet, the day of the game, something leads me out to the garage to my bike, down the street, and into the high school parking lot. I walk my bike over to the chain-link fence surrounding the football field, and I look up into the bleachers. The same faces are there, families tucked beneath wool blankets, Styrofoam cups of hot chocolate in mittened hands, the black-and-red badger pennants waving in the air. Cheerleaders in their black-and-red uniforms, tiny skirts fluttering in the wind, are bouncing around in front of the stands, leading the cheering of the onlookers. Homecoming used to be the time when I most felt like I belonged — to my family, to this town. I've never felt more on the outside than I do today.

Slowly, I back away from the field, jump on my bike and pump my legs, pushing the pedals up and down and around as fast as I can. I race home, and open my sketch pad to a blank page. Then I take a breath and look at the map over my desk. Today, I'll draw Kenya, the tall grasses of the Serengeti Plain, a herd of wildebeests drinking from a river. Escape . . .

• • •

The gym shimmers with flashing strobe lights and gold-and-crimson leaves that dangle from the ceiling on fishing lines. A white vinyl mat painted with more leaves of ocher, yellow, rust, and scarlet has been laid down to protect the basketball court floor from the hundreds of feet.

I pause in the entryway. It feels like I've stepped into a movie. A film about high school. This is one of those soaring music montage scenes, upbeat and uplifting. I gaze around in wonder. This is my first *high school dance*. It is surreal. Maybe more than a movie it feels like a dream.

The guys are barely recognizable. Gone are the messy T-shirts, scruffy blue jeans, and raggedy sneakers. They are all dressed up, some in suits, others wearing button-down shirts with ties and khakis. The transformation of the girls, though, is truly incredible. Like exotic fish, they float through the gym, filmy fins of dresses in all colors, some sparkling with sequins and delicate beads, others in flowing chiffon and clinging satin.

I suck in a breath and turn to Rachel, who is standing beside me looking as excited as I've ever seen her. How does she not feel terrified? I'm pretty sure my own terror must be written plainly all over my face. I am certain I do not fit in here. Even in my green dress, which I still love. But I feel like a fraud, a fake. The dress is too good for me. Too pretty.

I think Rachel senses my anxiety. She reaches over and squeezes my hand. "You look great, Cor. Really."

I squeeze her hand back and whisper, "Thanks, Rach. So do you." I glance down at my dress. The grass green silk swishes daintily around my knees. Maybe it will be all right.

Holding hands, we step farther into the gym. The bass backbeat throbs in my chest, echoing in reverberations through the floor and walls of the gymnasium. Kids are clustered in tight circles, swaying to the music. Some look around themselves self-consciously, checking to see if others are watching them. Others — fewer — look truly enthralled by the music and the dancing. More kids stand in an uneven line ringing the dance floor, looking on wistfully.

There is such beauty in this room — such hope. It's almost tangible. And just a little bit, I feel moved, like the gentle stirring of a bow over the strings of a violin. Every day these kids do everything they can to keep apart, to avoid mixing, but here, on the dance floor, all the colors bleed together, blending like watercolors.

At the same time, though, I watch as the usual groups cling together, still identifiable in formal wear. And that makes me a little bit sad. The picture is so much prettier without the boundaries of geek and jock and loser.

"Want to dance?" Rachel asks.

"Sure," I answer. We link arms and thread our way through the throng of people and onto the dance floor.

"It's so crowded!" I have to shout to be heard over the music. "Look, here's some space." I try to guide Rachel over to a hole in the tangle of bodies.

"No, wait, let's go farther in," Rachel says, tugging me in the opposite direction.

"Why? It's more packed."

"But I can see Josh over there, dancing with Kellie and Macie. Come on, please!" Rachel insists. She tightens her grip on my arm.

"Okay," I sigh, rolling my eyes.

We continue to push our way through the crowd, when suddenly, I have the sense that I am being watched. The noise, the music, and the press of warm bodies seem to fall away. I feel as though I am swimming underwater, following Rachel, but not seeing, the echo of the din muffled and far away. My neck grows itchy and tight, and my steps feel jerky.

Then, I find him. I find Damian's gray eyes across the dance floor, focused on my own, and everything comes back. He smiles and dips his head, and I send him a nod and a grin in return. He came! A million thoughts are rioting in my mind. Did he come for me? Oh my, he looks cute. He's wearing a crisp white shirt, a lavender tie, and khakis. I tear my eyes away, embarrassingly aware that I've been ogling him and staring like a total nut-job. I follow Rachel until we're just outside the circle of Nasties and soccer jocks, including Josh. My heart is racing, and I crane my neck, trying to keep Damian in my line of sight. He's disappeared.

"Ready?" Rachel asks, planting her feet before starting to dance.

I can't sense him watching me now, but I still feel completely self-conscious. If I'm going to be perfectly honest with myself, I must admit, I had hoped, but I had never actually expected him to come to the dance. I am jittery and nervous.

"Come on, Cor, dance with me!" Rachel begs. I realize I've been standing leadenly in the middle of the dance floor, probably looking like a weirdo.

Enough. Just stop thinking, I tell myself.

I close my eyes and let the music in, let it fill me up. My limbs loosen and my feet unstick and I begin to dance. I don't pay any attention to the Nasties, or to the fact that their circle remains closed to Rachel and me. I try not to pay attention to Rachel or to the longing so apparent in her eyes. It's sad, but I'm afraid I might look the same way. Because I am lonely, too. And Damian, let's face it, looks amazing, and I hope — oh, I really do hope — he came to the dance because of me.

Then suddenly, the tempo of the music shifts and the lights dim further. A slow song. I see Rachel's gaze dart over to Josh, then down to the ground. Josh has wrapped his arms around Pearl O'Riley's waist.

"Come on, Rachel," I say gently, and begin to steer her from the dance floor.

"Hey, Cora," a deep, rumbling voice interrupts us. I look up quickly to see Damian blocking our path from the dance floor. It's weird to see him without his customary trench coat; he looks vulnerable, younger, as though he's shed his battle armor.

"Hi," I reply. My voice trembles.

"So, um," Damian begins, scuffing his toe on the vinyl mat, "would you, uh, like to dance?" He looks nervous, I notice. That's curious. Wait, what did he say?

"Oh, um —" I look back at Rachel, whose mouth is hanging wide open. She wraps her fingers around my wrist and squeezes. Like a vise.

"Come on, Cor," Rachel whines. "I have to go to the bathroom."

I freeze. Pathetic, yes, I know. Then I remember the bonfire and the lunch table abandonment, and I defrost real quick. Looking up at Damian I say, "Yes, I'd like to." I turn to Rachel. "Go on to the bathroom without me. I'll see you after, okay?" Without waiting for a response, I follow Damian back into the crush of bodies on the dance floor.

Slowly, we turn to face each other. My stomach flutters nervously. There must be about a hundred butterflies in there. We've sat this close inside the barn, but this feels very different. Carefully, with such care and gentleness, Damian wraps his arms around my waist, and draws me nearer to him. His touch is soft.

He looks very serious. I bring my arms up to his shoulders. His cheeks are dusted with the tiniest hint of stubble, and he smells of something warm and spicy — nutmeg, maybe — and a pine forest. His eyes are moving over the dance floor, but as they settle on me, I feel a stinging heat wash over my face. We've barely started, but my stomach feels like it is dancing, dancing. I can't get used to the warmth of his hands on my back; it feels right. The palms of my hands tingle against the smooth fabric of his shirt. What do we look like to all the other kids at the dance — do we fit together, do we look like a couple? Do Damian and I look graceful together? Are the others even looking at us? Is everyone thinking about Nate and what a pair of freaks we are?

The song is languid and speaks of love and loneliness and loss. Why does love always seem to go with the sad things? Damian and I do not look at each other as we sway, turning in circles, and I can't bring my eyes up to his face. Yet, every piece of me is aware of him, of his closeness. For this moment, I can almost believe that his loneliness has run away.

We're both lonely. Like two empty halves of a seashell.

When the song winds to an end, Damian and I quickly drop our arms and step apart. I don't know where to look, what to say.

"Thanks." Damian speaks hesitantly, smiling a small, mysterious smile down at me.

"You're welcome," I whisper back. "Thank you, too." My heart is squeezing and expanding and jumping and maybe breaking apart just a little bit.

"I think your friend is waiting for you," Damian says, tilting his chin toward the press of kids on the edge of the dance floor. Rachel is there, an impatient look on her face.

"Oh, I should probably go to her," I reply. Damian's face drops, his eyes darkening, and for a moment, I wonder if I've hurt him.

"All right," he says. "I'll see you around."

"See you."

Damian vanishes into the crowd. My heart hurts. I sigh and make my way to Rachel. A thundercloud seems to have descended over her.

"Hi," I say, making my voice sound bright as I come to her side.

"I can't believe you," Rachel practically spits.

"What? What did I do?"

"I can't believe you went out there and danced with that waster, in front of *everybody*. Everyone saw," Rachel hisses.

"I'm sorry?" I say stupidly. "What did you say?" I couldn't have heard her right.

"You heard me. You danced with that loser in front of the whole world."

"What?" I repeat, louder this time, as I realize what Rachel is saying. "Who are you to call Damian a loser? And who cares if everyone saw us dance? He's my friend. What is your problem? Is it that you're jealous?" Rachel flinches, but I press on. "You're just jealous, aren't you? Because Josh didn't ask you to dance, because he was there dancing with Pearl! Is that your problem?"

"You're my problem," Rachel shouts. "*You* are. You walk around school, acting like a giant weirdo, and now you're associating with a freak, and you know what? People are talking about you. They're calling *you* a freak. You're just a freak and a baby, and I don't need to be associated with that." Rachel's eyes glow with anger. "I'm done." She whirls around and marches away, not looking back.

I stand rooted to the spot. What just happened? Rachel . . . Rachel of all people calling me a freak — these awful names? *Rachel?* Well, I don't need her, either. What a monster! I can feel my neck, my ears, my cheeks burning as Rachel's words burn in my mind. *Weirdo. Freak. Done.* Did she really say all those ugly things?

Tears prick the back of my eyes, and I run outside. I pull my cell phone from my purse and, with shaking fingers, dial my mother. "Mom?" I ask, my voice quaking with sobs. "Could you come pick me up?"

As I'm crashing through the halls, blinded by tears, someone calls my name. I keep sprinting down the corridor; faces are blurry, and I hear my name shouted again. I slow to a walk and I realize that Helena is streaking toward me, her corn silk curls flying out behind her. Her face is filled with concern and as she reaches me, she takes my hand in hers. "Cora, are you okay? What happened?" she asks.

I wipe my nose with the back of my hand and swat away the tears dripping down my cheeks. "I'm sorry," I say, not really sure why I'm apologizing, except I hate to think that I'm messing up the dance for anyone else. Especially Helena. "I'm fine. I'm just . . . I'm just going to go home now."

"Why? Cor, what happened to you? Did Damian do something?"

When I whip my head around to glare at her, she stutters, "I'm s-sorry. I just saw you two dancing and thought maybe he'd said something to hurt — Sorry . . ." she finishes lamely.

"Why does everyone hate Damian? It's like the whole school is out to get him!" I snarl.

"Cora, I don't know what you're talking about, but no one is out to get Damian. I just saw you two dancing and thought maybe something had happened between you." Helena's blue eyes are flashing with hurt and frustration.

"Helena, I'm sorry," I sigh. "I just . . . We're friends, and after I danced with him, my *supposed* best friend reamed me out for it."

"Oh," Helena says, her mouth pursed. "What a jerk!"

"Yeah, well . . ." I don't know what to say. Helena puts her arm around my shoulder and draws me into an embrace. Even though she's older, she's shorter than I am and slight, and so it feels like being hugged by a fairy, and in her sea-colored blue dress of filmy organza with iridescent beads sewn onto it, she looks like she could be a water nymph. "Hey, you look really pretty," I tell her as I pull back.

"Thanks," she says, smiling, then peering at me searchingly. "Are you all right?"

"Yes, really, I'm fine. Thank you. Thank you for listening and for — caring."

"Look, I don't know Damian that well," she begins, "but he's always seemed like a nice guy to me. Trouble, maybe, but not a bad guy. You know?" she says. She squeezes my hand then ducks into the girls' room. Turning back to me, she calls, "I have to get back soon; Cam awaits. Have a good night, Cor, and don't be sad!"

Chapter Nine

The viciousness of my exchange with Rachel at the dance plays itself over and over again in my mind. I am lying in bed, blanket pulled to my chin. I threw my beautiful green dress on the floor, where it remains, crumpled like a piece of garbage. Part of me aches to pick up the phone and call her, to make up and take back all the hurtful things I said. But as the cruelty of her part in the fight comes back to me, I get burned up with anger again.

Are people really calling me a freak? Do I look or act like a freak? The word itself sounds scary, sick. *Freak*. It is an ugly word. There's so much malice in it, in people's voices when they speak it.

Freak. The way the mouth puckers, like it's filled with revulsion or loathing, to form the *f*, the disgust that gets spit out with the final hard *k*. I roll the shape of the word around in my mouth, and my eyes narrow with the long *e*.

And a *baby*. Because I don't want to dress up and hang around with the Nasties and wear makeup and hook up? Does this also brand me a freak? If it does, so be it. I'm not ready. For any of it.

I shudder. I've become an object of disdain, of hatred, maybe. Does death mark those it touches this way? Are the real victims of Nate's accident those of us who were left to survive him?

My thoughts turn to Damian, whose life was also turned upside down since Nate's death. He and Nate worked so hard over the past three years to make sure no one knew about their artwork. Why? Why didn't they want anyone to know what they did, what they cared about?

I can't imagine life without my art. It would feel so empty. Barren and cold and terrible, like that Siberian tundra. I reach under my bed and slide out the bundle of Nate's watercolor paintings. Leafing through them, I study the delicate splashes of line and color. I pause when I come to an image of a young woman staring out a window. It is a portrait of Julie. Her profile is rendered with such grace and care. There's something about the edge of her nose, the hint of eyelashes, and a wistfulness in her bearing. Nate captured her humanity, her very humanness, with so much longing and desire and hope. Sometimes I feel I am filled with hope. Had Nate been hopeful? I can't be sure. He was so angry all the time.

Maybe boys just don't manage it as well, don't handle all the pain and worry and need as well as girls do. It's frightening facing the fact that things may or may not work out as you'd like them to. I figure all I can do is hope that life will turn out the way I want it to be, that I will turn out to be who I want to be, that I'll accomplish all that I want to do. That someday I'll reach a point where all the wishing and dreaming and hoping finishes in something grand. And hope is a flimsy thing. So maybe boys don't deal with the unpredictability, the capriciousness of hope as well as girls do.

Oh, I do not want to be trapped in this tiny town, watching tiny football games with the same people year after year, with no chance to see what lies beyond the highway, beyond the county road. Was Nate afraid of this, too? Is Damian scared, as well? Is everybody in the whole world walking around feeling frightened all the time? Full of the sense that life promises so many possibilities, yet we're totally petrified of missing them, at the same time? I suspect that this might be the case.

Nothing would be more dreadful than being stuck in Lincoln Grove for the rest of my life — like my parents. I have to get out. I have to get to London. I stand up, filled up with resolution. My mom has to see. Has to be convinced. But what can I do to change her mind? Is it hopeless? My dad will certainly be of no help — his silence is worse than my mother's shrill anger, her bitterness, her fear.

I need to talk to someone about all of this. I need help. I need to get out of this house. With a deep breath, I reach for my cell phone and again thank Damian silently for programming his number into it. Will he think it's weird that I'm calling him now — after the dance? I begin to dial.

"Hello?" His voice sounds muffled, gruff.

"Damian? Hi, it's me, Cora," I say.

"Hey, what's up?" he answers. He sounds happy to hear from me, I think — or, at least he doesn't sound horrified.

"Hey, um, I wondered if you would meet me at the diner? I just . . ." *Just what?* I have no idea. "I guess I just want to talk to someone. To you." Ah, I am such a dolt! "I'm sorry. I'm just . . ."

"No problem. I can meet you. Twenty minutes?"

"Sounds great," I reply, very relieved. I open my window, look out on the roof and down at the ground below. I've never snuck out this way before, but my mom is still roving around in the kitchen. I hear her opening cabinets and running water in the sink. I think of Nate, how carelessly he pulled himself out through the window. Then, carefully, nervously, I throw one leg over the windowsill and pull my body through the window after it. Have I joined Nate's rebel ranks? Or maybe I'm already way past that point.

Balanced on the roof, I have plenty of room, but my knees are knocking. My whole body is shaking, actually. I teeter down the length of the roof until I come to the gutter. I hook my arms and legs around the pipe and let myself slide to the ground. All together it isn't more than a twelve-foot drop. I land easily and, brushing off the front of my coat and pajama bottoms, I look around, checking to make sure I haven't caught my parents' attention, then I sprint down the driveway, toward the diner.

Twenty-three minutes later, Damian and I are tucked into a booth at the back of the diner on Union Street. The orange-and-yellow vinyl benches are cracked and stained. The smell of cleaning fluids and grease and stale coffee coats the red formica table, the long countertop, the air.

I swirl a straw around in my chocolate shake, watching the milk froth and mix with the ice cream. I glance up quickly and find Damian's steady gray eyes on me. I look down into my shake again. He is drinking coffee: one sugar, no milk. He's so much more grown up than I am.

"So, what's up?" Damian asks casually, curiosity leaking into his voice.

"I'm not sure," I respond. "I'm just having all these thoughts about Nate and my parents and what I want to do. And I don't know what to think." I stop to take a sip of my milk shake.

"Well, what are you thinking exactly?" Damian prods.

The thick shake travels up the straw slowly, and I wince when it finally fills my mouth, the cold sending a shot of dull pain to the center of my forehead. Brainfreeze . . . how appropriate. I shake my head, then, as the pain subsides, I speak quietly. "I'm thinking that I have to get out of here, but I'm too much of a wimp, a coward, to do anything about it."

"Okay, start from the beginning," Damian directs with a half grin.

"The beginning? I don't even know where that is anymore. But I can start here: Remember how Ms. Calico told us about some summer art programs?" I wait for him to nod yes. "Well, she wants to recommend me for one. She gave me the application and everything. They have a class on mapmaking. All expenses are paid except for the travel — meals, housing, everything."

"Sounds good so far," he says questioningly.

"Yeah, well, the catch is the program is in London. And there is no way my parents will ever, *ever* let me go. Not in a million years." A heavy sigh escapes me.

A sigh is like a salty yellow triangle.

"Are you sure? Did you ask?"

"Yes, I asked. But really, does it surprise you? My mom doesn't want to let me out of the house, out of her sight. I'm lucky she hasn't started homeschooling me. Ever since — you know — it's like she's convinced I'm going to do something stupid, something dangerous — something unlike anything I've ever done before in the fourteen years of my life."

"Well, you have gotten in a car with me. She probably wasn't prepared for that one," Damian adds, his grin widening.

"It's just so unfair! Seriously — it's not like we make a run to the liquor store before you drive me home!" I wail. "I'm just so sick of not standing up to her, of taking her crazy rules all the time. Why can't I be strong — like Nate was? He always stood up to her." I twirl the straw some more. "I just want to run away, you know?" I look up at Damian. His gray eyes have narrowed as he considers my words.

Finally, he speaks. "Cora, you're not weak."

"Uh-huh." I smirk, disbelief seeping into my voice.

"Really. Look, ever since school started — ever since Nate died — I've been thinking about this stuff, about all of us, a lot. Cora, you've always been the stronger one," he says vehemently. "You were always stronger than Nate. Think about it — all Nate and I could do was act like royal nightmares, thinking we were so rebellious and cool, and really we were just a pair of jerks. And look how we ended up — dead and a deadbeat."

"What are you talking about?" I ask softly, a scalding heat climbing up my ears, my neck.

"Don't you get it? We put on this ridiculous act because we were afraid that to be smart, to be talented, to like art, to care about anything like grades or college or the future, to be even a little bit responsible or mature wasn't cool. It was easier to be bad, dangerous, to drive really fast, to not listen to anyone. We were just scared. Can't you see?" Damian's voice grows higher, as if he is pleading with me to understand. "And acting like this made us feel free, made our art feel raw . . . real. Pure. No one could tell us what to do, and we were free from all the rules and restrictions, anything that could stifle. But the worse we behaved, the less everyone expected from us. And we didn't know . . ." His voice trails off, and Damian looks down into his coffee cup. "We didn't know that we could be creative without destroying everything around us . . . including ourselves." His brow creases and he won't meet my gaze. "And we couldn't just *be*. You know? We had to be tough, cool. It was easier to be crazy. But we were really just cowards. Phonies putting on this whole big stupid act. And Nate died because of it." Damian stops and slumps back in his seat, shaking his head as though he still can't believe it.

"I — I don't know what to say," I whisper lamely. I feel like someone has picked up the whole restaurant and shaken it like dice in a cup. I'm also shaking. Could Damian be right? Could he possibly be right? I do want the same things as Nate did — to get out, to make art, to do so much. I don't *think* I feel like I have to destroy anything to do it.

Could I be stronger than I thought?

"It's okay. You don't have to say anything," Damian replies bitterly.

"No, it's not okay. I mean, Damian, there's so much you can do. *So much*. You're so talented; those paintings in the barn — why are you hiding them? And the drawings in art class — they're amazing. You should show them to somebody. To everybody."

"Thanks," he says, his voice laced with cynicism, "but everybody — my mom, my teachers, even my friends, well, ex-friends — have pretty much given up on me. I don't think there's any room for me to change. Nobody wants me to. . . . I'm just a misfit, a loser. And that's it. They don't think I'll ever change. *I* don't think I'll ever change. Nobody wants to see the stuff in the barn, Cora, because it's garbage. And nobody gives a crap about garbage that comes from human garbage."

"Damian, stop! Please. Listen to me. You're not garbage. Your art is not garbage. And I'm your friend, and I care. I care a lot. Your work is beautiful and you have changed. Or, you've grown up or something. There is so much you can do," I cry. I can feel my heart breaking.

He smiles ruefully. "I want to *do something* with my life. All Nate and I ever wanted was to do something that would matter. But we screwed up bad. So bad. Nate is dead, and it's my fault. It's over. I'm over. I'll never go to art school. I'll never do anything. Probably work in a garage or something." His eyes glisten and he looks into his coffee cup again. He takes a sip, cupping his hands around the mug as though offering it in prayer. "Cold," he murmurs.

My eyes are filling with tears, too. It's gotten to be a habit, it seems. But Damian looks so small, so lost and scared and weak. Scared. "It's not over. It can't be too late. You're only seventeen." I am desperate. "What about Ms. Calico? She is new. . . . She doesn't know about Nate or — or any of it. You could show her your paintings." When he just shakes his head, defeated, a wave of panic and sorrow engulfs me. "Damian, it's not too late!"

"Anyway," he says, the wry half smile returning, turning the attention away from himself. "What will you do? We have to get you to London."

"I don't know . . . but I know I have to go."

We pay the check and stand up to go. I look at Damian, really look at him. His long black coat hangs like the wings of a raven around him, and his eyes are downcast. But his hands and shoulders are strong, and his eyes are clear, sharp. If only he could see.

Damian drops me off half a block from my house, and, praying I don't meet either of my parents, I silently let myself in the front door and head up the stairs. As I get ready for bed, my mind is racing. I throw myself back against the pillows and try to find sleep, but my eyes do not want to stay closed. Each thought pries them wider apart. What is happening now, here? What is happening to me? Maybe there's a part of me that will never feel at peace again, but there has to be a way to make things better. For me, for Damian. Maybe for my parents. For Rachel, even. I just have to find the right path.

I get out of bed, cross my room, and pull the application papers out of my book bag. I smooth out the wrinkles and creases, and begin filling in the blanks on the page. Like a scientist on the brink of discovery, or a mountain climber nearing the summit, I feel ready to plunge ahead. I pore through my sketch pads and books and begin to plan my portfolio. I wonder if I can use anything I've already done. Since the cartography class they offer is a big part of why I want to go, why Ms. Calico recommended me, I decide to include my maps. Mongolia, Kyrgyzstan, Bhutan, France . . . there are many to choose from. It's so strange to think how these maps used to be all my own. They didn't serve a purpose. Except, maybe to keep me sane. But they certainly weren't for anyone else to see, to use. Now, though, I am going to release them into the world, use them for something — something concrete. *Is this growing up?* I wonder.

I am just putting the finishing touches on a drawing of Sevilla, Spain. A flamenco dancer whirls around in the middle of a plaza. Her layered dress fanning out behind her, flashing eyes and flashing castanets. There, the portfolio is ready. I am ready to submit my application. Oh my gosh.

• • •

On Monday, I can hardly concentrate during any of my classes, I'm so nervous about turning my application over to Ms. Calico. The package feels like it is burning a hole through my bag, scorching my shoulder. Before Ms. Calico can begin making her rounds to all of the students, I tiptoe up to the front of the classroom and whisper that I have my application and portfolio ready to send out.

"May I see it?" she asks. I hand my portfolio to her, and she turns the pages, studying each of the drawings critically. "These are lovely," she tells me. "I think you stand an excellent chance of being accepted." My eyes widen. "I have a letter of recommendation ready — if you'd like to leave this packet with me, I will send out the whole thing after school."

"Oh, that would be amazing," I reply, my heart pounding with excitement. "Thank you."

"I'm really glad your parents agreed to let you do this. I think it will be a wonderful opportunity for you."

I step back uncomfortably. Under no circumstances can Ms. Calico know how messed up my family is, how crazy the whole situation is, how my mom actually said no. "Uh-huh," I mutter stupidly.

Well, it's a start.

Chapter Ten

The holiday season is here. It feels as though the whole house is holding its breath. Today is Thanksgiving, and each of us is locked in his or her own room — my dad in his den, gin and tonic in hand; my mom in her sewing room, doing who knows what; and me — well, I'm in Nate's room, lying flat on his bed. I've been dreading the start of the holidays since September. I knew it would be awful, but I wasn't ready for how lonely I am. How dead this house feels.

Last year, I remember my parents argued with Nate all morning about coming downstairs for dinner. My grandparents were supposed to arrive, but Nate said that he thought holidays were stupid excuses for consumerism and that family time was a fake front.

"A fake front for what?" my dad had asked less than calmly.

"For the fact that we have nothing in common!" Nate had screamed back.

My mother was twisting the beads of her pearl necklace

around her fingers, pulling the string taut against her throat; she'd looked so hurt.

We sat around the table, five of us, my grandparents, parents, and me, caught in a silence as thick as an oil spill and twice as deadly. We waited and waited, the room mute and heavy. We waited for sixty-five minutes. Nate eventually came down for dinner, and ate as much turkey as anyone. He'd refused the pumpkin pie, though, and charged back up to his room after a terse good-bye to my grandparents, completely ignoring me.

Back then, I could tell myself, *He's just a jerk, but someday he'll snap out of it.* That day never came.

Today it's rainy and the rain is a little bit frozen. The whole world looks like a ceaseless wash of gray. As it happens on weekends, I made my own breakfast, got my own lunch. I haven't heard my mom in the kitchen, so I expect dinner will be another microwaved wonder. I can't wait.

Nate, where did you go? I wonder. Where is he now? Is his soul floating around the house? Is he haunting Julie? Did he go to heaven? Does someone who puts the principal's office placard on a stall in the boys' bathroom have a place in heaven?

Are you sorry you won't get to taste Mom's turkey or her pumpkin pie again? Will I get to taste them again? Will we ever snap out of it, heal, come back together as a family? Is this the end of the Bradley family?

It's strange to think about, makes a strange pressure in my chest that feels like it's pushing all the air from my lungs.

When I get back to school on Monday, Helena asks me how my holiday was. I try very hard to keep my face normal, to keep it from crumpling, and myself from collapsing into tears. "It was fine," I tell her.

She and I are sitting at a lunch table with Cam and a few of his friends. Cam is serious and quiet, seemingly the opposite of Helena's effervescence.

Shyly, I ask him how his holiday was, eager to steer the conversation away from me. "It was nice," he replies. "My sister and her husband just had a baby, so everyone was focused on them. Which was fine with me," he adds with a mischievous smile. "The less attention my parents pay me, the better."

"Really?" I ask. Sounds a little bit like how Nate used to talk. Is that a boy thing?

"Yeah, well, with my sister out of the house, all their attention is saved up for me. Every little move I make is fodder for their microscopes."

"I know what you mean," Helena says. "Sometimes, when my parents fight, I'm just relieved they aren't thinking about me."

I sit back, glad to have removed myself from the focus of the conversation, and refreshed by the normalcy of this lunch. Still, I can't help but glance around the cafeteria, until I find Rachel in her now usual spot beside Elizabeth Tillson at the Nasties' table.

"I wonder why parents get like this — so focused, so worried all the time?" Cam wonders aloud, breaking into my thoughts.

"I guess it's because they don't feel like they can keep us safe anymore," I answer, taken aback by my directness.

Helena stares at me closely. "Yeah, I think you're right," she murmurs.

After lunch, she grabs my elbow and asks, "Was that okay? What we were talking about, I mean? I didn't even think —"

"Everything is fine," I reassure her. "It was really nice to sit with you guys. Cam is a good guy."

Helena nods, her eyes glittering. "He is, isn't he?" she says happily.

• • •

Winter break. Sixteen whole days stuck in the house with my parents, and no escape. Damian and his mom are traveling to Missouri to visit his cousins; Helena and her family are going to Indiana to visit her grandparents. And, Rachel . . . well, Rachel and I still aren't speaking. It's the longest fight we've ever had.

Thanksgiving was bad enough, and that was only four days. But now I have more than two weeks of isolation. The snow comes down hard outside, the white flakes dancing on the wind before driving into the ground with an aimless fury, coloring the whole world a dull gray. It's numbing. Too cold to ride my bike, I'm stuck inside, and there's no Christmas tree, no decorations, no hint of holiday cheer. It's the first year we haven't had a Christmas tree or lights strung up along the gables of our upstairs windows. There's a gloomy absence, like a big black hole, swallowing up this house.

On Christmas day, the snow abates for a bit. So, I pull on my puffy ski pants and strap on my clumsy snow boots, and clomp my way over to the Wyatt cornfields. Last time I came by here was in the fall, when everything was tinged a warm golden yellow. In the snow, though, the dried out stalks are bent, leaning wearily like broken old men. In other places, the husks stick up from the snow, like the remnants of a deserted, destroyed city. I set off, trudging between the rows, letting my mittens brush against the dead leaves that rattle at my touch.

When I reach the end of one row, I continue straight on, away from the barn and the farm and the road. I walk until I come to a pile of hay bales and plop myself down. The sun is bright and the air is sharp. In the distance I hear the lowing of cows. It's so peaceful here.

"Merry Christmas," I whisper to myself. "Merry Christmas, Nate."

I think he would have liked sitting here with me in the crisp silence. You can think here. The shutters of this tiny town seem wide open in this field.

When we were little, Nate and I would wake up at dawn on Christmas morning, run downstairs, and peer at the array of presents that had been placed beneath the tree during the night. We'd sit on the living room floor, shake each one of the boxes with our names printed on them, and make lists of what we hoped our presents would be. Nate, his brow wrinkled, would really think about it, then cross his fingers and squeeze his eyes shut like he was praying. When he was nine, Nate asked my mom if every child got Christmas presents. My mother had responded truthfully, saying, "No, not every child celebrates Christmas, and even some of the ones who do aren't as fortunate as we are." Nate had been very distressed by this revelation. He asked if he could give one of his presents to a child who wouldn't get a gift. My mother had chuckled, but she'd looked proud. "That is very generous," she'd told him. "How about you keep all of your presents, and we can go to the store and pick out something to send to a charity?" Nate liked that idea. And the wrinkles in his forehead had smoothed out.

Last Christmas was a different story, though. Nate didn't wake up early and examine the gifts with me. He didn't wake up until afternoon, by which time my parents and I had already exchanged presents without him. His gifts were left under the tree. The three of us were in the kitchen, drinking fresh orange juice, while my dad made waffles. We were laughing and trying our best to ignore the fact that Nate had decided to skip Christmas that year, when he wandered in, groggy and grumpy.

"Nice of you to join us," I'd smirked.

"Whatever, dork," he'd mumbled.

"Nathaniel, you come with me," my father had said menacingly. I could overhear him, when he took Nate into the living room. "You are hurting all of us, especially your mother with this behavior."

"What behavior?" Nate had asked sarcastically.

"You know very well what I'm talking about, and I'm tired of it." My dad's voice was low and harsh.

"I don't know what you're talking about," Nate replied. "I was tired; I overslept."

"Nate, you'd better think about whether you want to be a part of this family. And you'd better think about how your behavior is making everyone else feel. I will not stand for it, and I won't see you hurting your mother this way." Then Dad stalked back into the kitchen. Nate followed sulkily, sat at the table, and ate waffles with us. He didn't join in the laughter, but the atmosphere in the kitchen had changed, and the laughter felt forced anyway. Our last Christmas together. What a sorry memory.

When my fingers and my nose are frozen and I can't feel my toes anymore, I rise from the hay and slowly make my way back toward the farmhouse. The sun is high in the robin's egg sky. *I can't wait for spring,* I think wistfully. *For the return of flowers and leaves and birds.* I miss hearing the call of cardinals and the humming of jays. I miss Nate. Oh lord, how I miss him. Too cold to cry, the force of my loneliness carves out a hollow space in my belly, like a worm gnawing its way through my gut.

I can't go home yet. I walk back through the fields and head east toward the creek. When I come to the willow tree, I slide down into a pillow of snow at its base. I long for the white bird to come back, to fill my emptiness again with the same sense of magic and hope. Because I have to get that feeling of purpose back. I look into the creek; the surface is frozen, but I can see the hint of life beneath it. From where I sit, it almost looks like a painting, muddy browns and whites sliding into each other, from bank to creek bed.

That's it, I tell myself. *It's about the art. I have to remember that.*

The crooked angles of dead branches and the humpbacks of rocks lining the creek remind me of the towering mounds of metal in the Wright barn. Nate's art. I still have that piece of him. Maybe he isn't wholly lost to me. Maybe I can touch him, hold on to him through his art, and through my map.

Once again, I start off, trudging toward my house. I can do this; I just have to focus on the art.

As I creep back into the house, I see that the light underneath the door to my dad's den is still on, but I can't hear the television. Instead, I hear a low keening sound. I move closer to the door, and press my ear to it. A shuddering moan. My father is crying.

I leap back as though I've been stung. What is he doing? He's turned to ice. He doesn't cry. He can't cry. The sounds are guttural, almost animal-like. There is so much sadness in that room. It's overwhelming, and I think I could drown in it.

I wander back to my bedroom. My mother has left a tray containing a TV turkey dinner with the plastic cover still on it, and a feeble Christmas present for me on my bed. Crumpled blue wrapping paper, no box, no ribbon. I tear off the paper, and uncover a sweater, green with little white flowers. I will never wear it, because it will always remind me of this awful Christmas day. I crumple it into a ball and throw it into the back of my closet. This day has been too potent, too heavy with grief, and I feel it heaping all around me, over me. If the dullness of the walls of my room stifled me before, now it seems that the weight of so much sorrow might, instead.

At least I have a project to keep me occupied. It's time to get to work, time to make something of this map.

• • •

Tonight is New Year's Eve. For the past week, I've been working feverishly on the map, sketching and re-sketching the scenes I want to include on the boards in the barn, figuring out how to piece it all together. But now I am going to take a break and watch the countdown to midnight on television.

As I watch the carousers taking part in the festivities in Times Square, a hunger starts to grow in my belly. And I'm plenty full from dinner. I watch couples standing hand in hand, kissing and hugging as they count down the seconds to the New Year.

I want that. I want someone to hold me, to kiss me, to ring in the New Year with me. I close my eyes and imagine what an arm around my waist would feel like, its heavy weight, a comforting warmth. What a pair of lips brushing over mine would feel like. What if that arm and those lips belonged to someone — someone I know? What if they belonged to Damian?

Keeping my eyes closed, I try to picture myself kissing Damian. My ears are burning, and I'm all alone. This is ridiculous. But my heart is racing a little bit, and I can't completely ignore the tingling in my shoulders.

Chapter Eleven

I dream of walking alongside the creek, the trees and rocks, grasses and water lit by the moon with an icy silvery light. It is like walking through a ghost story. All is silent. Then suddenly, the white bird is standing before me, poised on its slender legs. Its neck is curved and sleek, shining feathers tucked tightly against its graceful body. The bird peers at me with an orange eye, head cocked to the side. A sense of wonder, electrifying, charges through my body. The ground seems to tremble and roll beneath my feet, yet the bird remains perfectly still, watching me. I struggle to keep my footing, and when I begin to fall, the bird suddenly stretches out its wings and soars into the air. It circles around me, its wings V-shaped and stark against the starry night sky. My breath runs away from me in a rush, I can't catch it, and I fall to my knees, then I'm falling and falling. . . .

I wake abruptly, my heart throbbing. The bird. Its unwavering gaze stays with me. If a bird could have an expression, this one seemed . . . expectant. Like it was telling me I had work to do. Yes, this bird that looked like the swash of a paintbrush seems ever to be propelling me toward my art, toward Nate's art. It was the bird that made me realize how dearly art matters, that gave me this connection to Nate. Maybe, if I could show the world Nate's sculptures, if I could convince Damian to show his paintings, maybe everyone could see this better side of both of them, and Nate could be remembered as more than a screwup, and Damian could have a second chance. He could go to art school.

• • •

7:52. *Oh my gosh.* My first day back, and I'm late. My neck and back are coated in sweat, my hair is plastered to my cheeks. I was dreaming so hard I slept right through my alarm clock. This morning, the notion of school doesn't feel as unappealing as it usually does. I'm looking forward to art class, to talking to Helena about the kernel of an idea I had during the night. Mostly, though, I'm excited to see Damian again. Just the thought of him makes my stomach feel fluttery and light.

Quickly, I dress and run downstairs. My parents have already left for work. I putter around the kitchen, looking for something quick to eat, when I spot my dad's crystal tumbler in the sink. The sound of his weeping still rings in my ears. Suddenly, I am gripped by an urge to see his den. I grab a strawberry Pop-Tart and race back up the stairs. The door to the den is open slightly. It creaks and groans as I push it open farther. The room is painted brick red and six long bookshelves line each of the walls. A large, worn, brown leather armchair takes primacy over the den like a throne, overshadowing the ornately carved antique wooden desk and a rattily upholstered couch that bears the scars of a long-dead cat's claws. The armchair faces a flat-screen television and a small wooden stool crouches beside it. As I approach the armchair, which still bears the impressions of my father's body, I notice something shiny underneath the stool. I kneel to see what it is. A face-down silver picture frame. I draw it out and pick it up. It's a photograph of my dad and Nate that was taken during a vacation to Disney World when I was seven and Nate was eleven. They're smiling, and Nate's head is thrown back, like he'd been laughing. He holds a stuffed Dumbo in one hand and a puff of cotton candy in the other, and his tongue is bright blue. They both look so young, so happy.

There is a hairline crack in the protective glass, but other than that, the photo and its frame are unblemished. I run my thumb along the crack. It stretches down the middle of the picture, severing Nate from my dad's arms. Does my father trace his fingers over this same crack while he cries? His sorrow lingers in the air, pressing on it, on me, heavily.

I replace the frame, and back out of the room. It's impossible for me to think of my dad with anything but resentment now. There isn't room for pity or for empathy anymore. Not since he left Mom and me to go on without him.

I hoist my backpack onto my shoulder, go out to the garage

and mount my bike. Pumping my legs hard and fast, I pedal away. *Enough.*

• • •

The school day passes and I feel like I've been walking through a cloud. Sounds seem muffled, I barely notice the other kids shuffling past me in the hallways, the teachers rambling in class. I don't pay any attention to the fact that Rachel is still ignoring me, doesn't look my way once. It's like I'm not there. Without Helena around, I take my lunch to the library and eat alone.

At the end of the day, as I step out of the art room, I hear someone calling my name. Slowly, I turn to see Helena standing in the doorway of the studio, waving frantically at me.

"Hey, wait up for a second!" Helena calls.

I pause, still feeling slow, fuzzy. I wait for Helena to jog over to catch up with me.

"Hey, how are you? How were your holidays?" Helena starts, then coughs as she fights to catch her breath. "Are you all right? You seemed kind of out of it in art today."

I stare at her curiously, hearing the words but not quite understanding them. "I'm — what?" Helena's eyes widen as if to say, *See, this is exactly what I'm talking about.* "Oh, I'm fine. Just a little . . . tired," I tell her, trying to snap out of this strange soupy funk. "You know, the holidays were . . . weird. How about you?"

"Are you sure you're okay? You still seem kind of spacey," Helena asks.

"Yeah, I'm sure. I'm okay. Just . . . I'm tired. . . . It was a rough couple of weeks," I try to explain.

"Did something happen? Hey — I know — want to go to the diner? We can share some pie and you can tell me all about it?"

I am thoroughly alert now. I think about what my mom would have to say about this idea, and that decides it for me. "You know what, I'd love that. Let me just tell someone. . . ." We've been walking through the school, and have reached the door to the student parking lot. This morning I was so fixated on seeing Damian again, but then, after entering my father's den, I couldn't even look at him in class. Now, the notion of Helena's company feels safe, soothing. I've needed a friend.

I should let Damian know I won't be coming to the barn today, though, and I crane my neck to look for him. Then I spot the familiar black-cloaked back striding toward the blue El Camino. "Will you wait for me here a sec?" I ask Helena.

As she nods, I begin to sprint toward Damian's car. "Hey, Damian!" I holler, not paying any attention to the many heads that turn in my direction across the parking lot.

Damian hears and turns, too. "Hi," I say as I catch up to him.

"Hi," he replies easily. "Did you have a good holiday?"

"Yeah," I say, my pulse leaping. "You?"

"It was nice," he says, smiling. "Hey, happy New Year."

"Happy New Year," I tell him, remembering how I'd thought about him on New Year's Eve, and feeling my cheeks grow warm. Thank goodness he can't read my mind. "So, I just wanted to let you know, I'm not going to come over to work today."

"Oh, okay," Damian says slowly. "Is anything wrong?"

I catch a glint of worry in his eyes. "No, no, nothing at all. I'm just going to go to the diner with Helena. She, uh, wanted to talk to me about something."

"All right," he says reluctantly.

"But can I come over tomorrow?" I ask, worried that he might be angry, might not want me to come over anymore.

"Sure, no problem." His voice, dull.

"Hey, you're not upset with me, are you?"

"No. It's just that — you're not *not* coming because you're avoiding me or anything, are you?"

"Of course not," I make my voice sound light. "No, I just need to take a day and think about the map and what I want to do with it and everything." *He's worried I was upset with* him?

"Okay. Then I'll see you tomorrow." Damian looks relieved, but with his brow wrinkled, I can tell he isn't fully convinced.

"Cool, thanks." I put my hand on his arm and squeeze gently before turning back to Helena.

As I come back over to Helena's side, she says, "You know, I saw Calico had a canvas of his stretched out on her desk today. He's really good. Like, an amazing painter." She cocks her head and looks at me intently.

"I know," I tell her. "He does these incredible paintings where he sticks objects — you know, like washers and screws and bits of metal — right into the paint. They're unbelievable."

"Really?" Helena asks as we — I'm wheeling my bike along beside me — stroll out of the parking lot and head toward Union Street. "I wonder why he doesn't tell anybody, or show anyone."

"I know. I tried to tell him that he should. He's being stubborn."

We approach the diner, which, with its shiny aluminum exterior and big windows covered in paper snowflakes, looks like something from the 1950s. We settle into one of the booths, and I recall how, just a few weeks ago, sitting across from Damian, I'd felt so sad, helpless, and sorry. But now I feel hopeful, buoyed by some sense of promise. Maybe I can do something, something good and meaningful. After we order hot chocolates and a slice of strawberry rhubarb pie, I begin to tell Helena everything.

"Actually, I was wondering if you could help me. I . . ." My voice trails off as I try to figure out how to form the right words, how to explain what I want to do, how to tell her about Nate.

"Help you with what?" Helena asks eagerly. Her eyes shine with a brilliant curiosity.

Her enthusiasm floats over the booth like birdsong. She has always gotten what I've tried to tell her in the past. Maybe she really can help. There's only one thing to do. Leap.

"Okay, here goes. You know Damian and my brother, Nate, were best friends, right?" I wait for Helena to nod her assent, then continue, "Well, they were both artists, and they set up a studio in this barn across town and made all these sculptures and paintings. And, like I told you, they're amazing. Just amazing." Helena nods again. "So, I've been hanging out at Damian's studio working on a big map — all of those little pieces I've been doing in art class are studies, pieces of the larger map, actually. Anyway, I want, somehow, to show Damian's and Nate's art to everybody. I want everyone to know they're not total screwups. That they have been doing something great all along." I stop and look at Helena, half expecting to see an expression of disgust or disbelief on her face. But I see neither. "Do you think I'm crazy?"

Helena sits back and folds her hands beneath her chin. She shakes her head then looks straight at me. "You're not crazy. You're brilliant. I know what we're going to do. We are going to have a gallery opening, a party!" She claps her hands excitedly and blows a lock of pale hair out of her eyes. "Oh my goodness, this will be incredible; we can ask Ms. Calico and get permission from the principal, Mrs. Brown, to include Nate's art in this year's art show, and his sculptures can be the centerpiece of the show! We'll make a big event out of it and advertise to the whole school. Then everyone will see!" Helena hops around in her seat, her zeal getting the better of her.

"Really? You really think we could do this?" I ask as a bubble of hope rises up in my chest.

"Of course! Why not? All *you* have to do is convince Damian to bring Nate's sculptures, and we'll have to get him to bring his own paintings — they should be there, too. And, actually, you should be able to take Nate's stuff yourself, right?"

"Right . . ."

The catch. I have a feeling that convincing Damian may not be as easy as strawberry rhubarb pie.

• • •

I have no idea how to broach the subject with Damian. After school the next day, I go to the barn with him and stare at his back as he hovers in front of a canvas. He has stepped outside of his workshop and is now playing with a new set of oil paints.

It seems strange that Damian and I have been spending so much time together, yet no one else in our lives — aside from Helena, now — knows. I've never met his mother, and while I know Mrs. Archer works two jobs, I can't help but think that it is strange to spend so much time with Damian and not know this most basic piece of his life. It's strange to think about how I used to hate him, used to think he was a monster. So much has changed.

I crouch in front of the map and stare at it, letting the

colors and textures blur before my eyes. The longer I stare, the more the piece seems to break apart and float lazily in layers, the dried-out stems of grass and wheat that I've glued down for the cornfield suspended on top of the flakes of the oil pastels of the ball field. These places meant something to me once. Meant so much. The anatomy of my childhood, a body marked by the games Nate and I played, by dizzying joy and scraped knees, by tears for lost toys and wild imaginings, by time shared and, now, time lost. Will I ever feel that happy again? That free or heedlessly anchored again?

I trace the painted white-blue swirls of the skating pond. Unbidden, the thought that it is probably cold enough to go skating now flits through my mind. I cock my head and sit up.

I want to see the skating pond.

"Damian?" I call softly.

"Hmm," he answers, turning and wiping his hands on a spotted rag.

"Do you feel like going for a walk?" I ask.

"Sure, I could use a break," he responds easily. "Are you ready to go?"

I nod, then follow Damian as he bounds out the door. The sky has reached that hazy violet-and-blue shimmery brightness that comes midway between a winter's day and dusk.

"Thanks," I say breathlessly as we step out the front door into the chilly air. "Thanks for coming with me."

"No problem," Damian returns, smiling. "Any particular direction?"

I start to head in the direction of the skating pond. We walk beside each other in amiable silence, our paces matched. I have to keep my hands in my pockets — I forgot my gloves — and I watch plumes of breath burst in front of me.

We are led through this world by our breath. There can be no going back. Breath fans out, little beads of life, dissipates, and vanishes. And there can be no going back.

Finally we reach the pond, and sure enough, there are skaters, mostly little kids with their parents, wobbling back and forth across the ice. Damian and I walk over to the snack stand and buy a couple of hot chocolates, then sit down on a bench to watch.

I begin to speak out loud, even though I am pretty sure I sound like a complete weirdo. "I've been thinking about what it means to be 'grown up.' You know, when you can look back and say, I'll never be a little kid again. I'll never again be a small child who is sure of my parents' love, of their protection, who knows that whatever mistakes I make, it doesn't really matter. It's not a big deal. Because the worst I can do is break a vase or track dirt onto the carpet. Or forget a book at school or maybe get a bad grade." I stop and look down at my hands. My fingers twist and knead and turn each other white. "*Then,* then, there's this place called home, and it's the safest space in the world. But when we go off to college or whatever, eventually it won't be home anymore. So, when we're old enough to realize all of these things, we have to make the choice to either mourn the loss of that time, the innocence, the safety and ease of it all. Or we can feel excited to be free, relieved of the weight of this giant safety blanket, and released into the world to explore."

"Unless you already stopped feeling safe a long time before you grew up," Damian interrupts.

"What do you mean?"

"I mean . . . my dad took off when I was a baby. I never knew why, but it shook my whole world to its core. As soon as I was old enough to realize he wasn't coming back, I figured out that I was never safe. If he — my dad — could do that, just walk out and not even look back, anyone could."

I open my mouth, to say what, I have no idea, but Damian cuts me off with a sharp look. "Anyway, I think I'm way past the point of being able to make mistakes without them mattering. I've screwed up everything." His brow is wrinkled, his eyes downcast, portentous and dark as a thundercloud.

"Damian," I start, very, very cautiously, "what if there was a way to fix it?" He looks up quickly, surprised. "*I* know you're not a screwup. What if you could show everyone who you really are? What you've been doing — making?"

He cocks a wary brow at me. "And how would I be able to do all that?"

"We-e-ll, I've been talking with Helena Carson — you know who she is, right? From art class?" He nods. "So, we've been talking about, well, remember the school art show? We want to have, like, a gala opening or something. And I, um, I wanted to show Nate's art. And the map. And I think you should show your paintings."

"What? No. No way." Damian is shaking his head vigorously, gripping his hot cocoa with whitened knuckles. "No way," he repeats.

"Why? Why not?" I press. "What are you scared of? Remember at the coffee shop, you said you wished you weren't such a coward? This is your chance, Damian. Don't you see?

"I mean, I'm totally freaked most of the time. Some days I just live in this snail's shell of memories, wishing I could go back and be a little kid and have it all safe and easy, and other days I feel like I'll die if I don't get out of here, out of my freaking house. And believe me, losing Nate doesn't make the survival instinct in me feel very strong. I'm so scared I'll mess up.

"I've got this image in my head of how I want my life to look, and I have absolutely *no idea* how to get there. And I'm so scared that I'll make some wrong decision — just one — and everything will get messed up and go wrong — for good. I have no idea what I'm supposed to do. But I have to think that doing this, showing Nate's and yours and my art can only help. I truly believe it will help you."

I don't know what else to say to him. We sit there and watch the little kids tottering around the pond on their skates.

They're all bundled up in parkas and hoods and scarves and mittens, like snowmen mummies, so they can barely move their arms or turn their heads. Dads and Moms stagger after them, most of them not looking any more sure-footed than the twerps. And everyone is laughing.

They are all so happy. Perfectly happy.

I remember how my dad used to take Nate and me skating here when we were little. He had this really thick sweater of navy blue wool with white snowflakes knitted in lines across it and around his arms. That sweater always made me feel safe. It was the "Daddy and Rabbit weekend sweater." When he wore it, I knew that he was going to take me to the pond to skate or out into the woods to hike or that we were going to play Monopoly in front of the fireplace in our living room.

One day he brought Nate and me to the pond to skate, and he was wearing the sweater and these big woolly mittens with leather stitched onto the palms. He knelt in the snow at the edge of the pond, clenched those mittens between his teeth, and tied my skates for me. He patted Nate on the top of his head and watched as Nate hurtled out into the middle of the pond. Then Dad held my hand and very gingerly, very carefully, lowered me onto the ice. "Ready, Rabbit?" he asked, his eyes crinkling with that warm smile he used to save for just the two of us. He held my hand as I skated, pretty much holding me up, since I was completely unsteady on my feet. When I toppled over, he grabbed me under the armpits and hoisted me up, all the way up into the air, so he could plant a kiss on my cheek, then he swung me back down onto the ice.

Nate skated in circles around us, sometimes moving so fast his legs blurred, and he came careening toward us, laughing wildly — not with meanness, but with this crazy joy for the speed and crisp air and the knowledge that my dad would scoop him up before he could crash and swing him around and roar with a laughing mock anger.

This is home. An immense sadness, but a sweet one, fills me then. What a beautiful time it was. It's over, *so* over, now. But at least I can remember it. At least I had all that once. Maybe I can't hate it anymore.

I glance at Damian. He is sitting completely still.

We sip our cocoa in silence, when suddenly Damian looks at me. "Maybe you're right," he says. "Maybe you're right, so I'll do it."

I put my cup down. "Really?" I shout, and throw my arms around him.

Then I remember who, where, what, and everything, and am beyond embarrassed.

"Sorry," I mutter. "But thank you. This is so great."

He chuckles softly and turns back to look at the skaters. He rests his chin on his hand on his knee, and shakes his head so slightly. Again, the space between us yawns wider. I wish I knew what filled it.

Chapter Twelve

Now that I know what I'm supposed to do, I can't seem to get myself to stay still long enough to work. Finishing this map is something I have to do, something I *want* to do. It's interesting how there's a sort of breakdown in communication between what I know I want and actually getting my hands to do the work. All these grand ideas, and then, poof, the brain gets lazy and easily distracted.

Tibet is shaped like a crocodile head. I move the cursor up and down on the screen, letting it crawl over the Tibetan Web page. The blinds are shading my windows, keeping out the late afternoon light.

Nate liked Death. Death was in the clothes that he wore and the music he listened to. He would wrap himself in a black sweater and ask Death to ride along with him in his Honda Civic.

And out on the county road, a half mile from the turn that is shaped like a bear's claw, where the bent oak tree stands, it seems Death leaped up from the backseat, grabbed the wheel, found the tree, and took my brother.

Tibetan children are kept busy fetching water, shepherding, and gathering yak dung.

Yak dung, huh? Well, my mom always used to say that busy hands are happy hands. Does that apply to hands picking up yak poo? And if idleness supposedly breeds wickedness, then here is what I can't understand: Nate was busy. He had plenty of stuff to do. The evidence of that is under my bed, rolled into a poster tube, and tucked away in sketch pads. So, why was he so filled with bad thoughts, bad ideas — like driving without headlights, like stealing and vandalizing and defacing?

I will never know, will I? I'll just never understand why Nate did what he did, why he behaved the way he did. His death will stay meaningless and stupid and pointless and a waste. I'll never know.

Anyway, I have to get to work. The map really is nearly done. But the last piece still needs . . . finding. I can't figure out what the last piece is, but there's a hole in the map that stares up at me like some walleyed fish searching for water. That hole needs filling. I flip through my sketches and try to figure out what part of the whole remains undefined, unevinced, undrawn.

I know why I can't concentrate. It's because of Damian. I like him. I do. And I mean *like* like him. I like the guy my parents think killed my brother. What would Freud have to say about that? I kick my legs up onto my desk and clasp my hands behind my head.

Damian has this tiny white scar on the fleshy triangle of his hand, between thumb and forefinger. The scar is shaped like a crescent; he got it burning himself with the soldering gun. And I can't stop picturing it in my head, thinking about taking his hand and touching that scar, caressing it. I can't figure out if Nate would hate this, hate me for liking his best friend. I'm fairly sure that none of this would be okay with him if he were alive. Then again, if Nate were still alive, Damian probably never would have noticed me anyway. But I wonder if, maybe, Nate left Damian behind as another piece of himself for me to find, so I could hold on to him. Even if Nate didn't think of me much when he was alive, I have to believe that wherever he is now, he does think of me, that he misses me. And that he knows how much I miss him. I miss him so much.

None of this stops me, however, from wondering what it would feel like if Damian liked me back. If he kissed me. His mouth is like a seashell, a droplet of water, pink and round and perfect and smooth. A warm buzz fills my stomach when I imagine touching those lips.

Then, a crash from downstairs jolts me from my ruminations. Loud. I run to my door and out into the hallway, then crane my neck trying to peer over the banister and down the stairs. My father is crouched over a pile of — *stuff* in the middle of the floor. The front room closet is open and a landslide of boxes continues to pour forth from it, spilling all around him. Seeing my father outside the depths of the freezer or his den is new. I'm just about to turn around and retreat to my room, when I notice his shoulders shudder and his pale, skinny neck hunch over his knees.

"Dad?" I whisper, tentative, nervous. There is no response. I creep down the stairs so softly, as if I were approaching a wild, frightened animal. In truth, I'm the one who's frightened. "Dad?" I try again.

I come up beside him and kneel down. An old cardboard box, weathered and torn, lies on its side, and all sorts of objects have leaked from inside it: a pair of navy mittens connected by a length of yarn, a tatty softball, a Hawks baseball cap, a dirty, beaten pair of cleats, and a pom-pom of blue and gold — the Hawks colors — streamers. I turn to my father, who still crouches with his head bowed and tucked into his arms. Then I see that a baseball glove has fallen to the floor in front of his feet. Nate's old mitt.

"Dad? Are you okay?" Now I'm getting worried. "What happened?"

He looks up as though surprised to see me there beside him and quickly wipes at his eyes and rubs a hand through his gray, thinning hair.

"Nothing," he replies in a deadened voice. "I'm fine. I just thought I'd get rid of some of these old things. Give them to Goodwill." He sinks back against the wall and slides fully to the floor, limp as a sack of corn. Then he looks at me, really sees me. It may be the first time since The Accident that he does so, and it feels like a knife is cutting deep into my ribs, through the tissue and bone and muscle that might protect my heart. My eyes fill with hot tears that I try to blink back.

"I found this," he says, picking up the glove. "And I just remembered him standing out there in his uniform, playing, and . . . oh . . ." His voice breaks and his eyes are glossy. He presses his forefingers to the corners of his eyes, as though trying to dam the tears. "He was such a good boy." A low sound, almost a growl — but not — a sob, snarls in his chest and rises up into his mouth and escapes, dropping into the space between us and hanging there.

"I know," I say; then I sit down beside him and reach for his hand. "I know he was."

My father lets me hold his hand. He doesn't squeeze mine back, but he lets me sit there with him and put my head on his shoulder, and he sees me. He sees me for the first time in such a long, long time. We sit there and cry together.

I know it's not a breakthrough or a new beginning or the end of the bad period — the freeze-out — but it's something. I curl my fingers around his, feeling the putty-like flesh, warm and soft, against my own. Like the warmest, safest blanket.

Dad's head snaps up as footsteps near. He presses my hand so gently he might not have done it at all, then rises and begins to scoop all of Nate's old things back into the box. My mother appears in the doorway.

"What are you doing?" Her voice comes out in a strangely strangled clanking.

Almost without thinking, I stand and begin to back up to the stairs. My father doesn't look at her, nor does he answer her as he continues sweeping the clutter back into its container.

"Daniel, what are you doing?" My mother's voice rises, taking on that tinny quality it gets when she is about to explode. I can almost smell the cordite. "What are you doing?" Her face grows red and her fists are clenched at her waist. "Put the box back in the closet, Daniel."

My father has finished depositing everything back into the box and now has it tucked in the crook of his arm. Then quietly, he says, "Marie, it's time. It's time to let him go."

"Shut up, Daniel, and put the box down. Right now!" She's really yelling now and tears are streaming down all three of our faces, but it's as though I'm not even in the room. She runs over to him and tries to pry the box away from my dad, and suddenly they are in a tug-of-war match, each grasping a flap of battered cardboard, yanking and heaving and my mother's chest is heaving with sobs, and they glare at each other. Glare as though they hate each other, hate and hate and they pull and glare and pull until the box splits apart with a meek exhalation, *ffrrip*. All of Nate's things arc through the air like a waterfall and fall to the floor in a clatter.

My father stands mutely, gaping; he stares around at all of the things, while my mother swoops down and grabs as much as she can hold in her arms, cradling the baseball mitt like a baby, and runs out the door. I hear the door to her sewing room bang shut. Then silence. My father raises his eyes to mine briefly then turns and shuffles past me up the stairs. His face, his skeleton — it all seems to have collapsed in on itself, and he looks as fragile as a butterfly. The den door squeaks open and closes with a click.

I shake my head, and follow in my father's wake up the steps and slide past the den into my own bedroom. Then, carefully, I put my shoulder to the door and nudge it shut. I lie down on my bed and cry until I think I'll throw up. This was the worst thing I have seen since the night he died.

When I'm cried out, I walk to the bathroom, my eyes and nose and whole body dried out, empty, wasted, like some bug exoskeleton wasting away on a windowsill. After I wash my face, I remain in front of the mirror above the sink. I stare at my reflection, I don't blink. Brown eyes, dull and brown, look back at me. Dark brown hair hanging in heavy waves. My face is pale and my eyes are bloodshot. I can't detect much of a difference between this fourteen-year-old self and the thirteen-year-old one. Same flat chest, skinny arms, collarbone that sticks out sharply, all the way to my shoulders. What a watery picture I make. *Enough.* I have to be stern with myself. Enough with this. I grab my cell phone and start to dial Rachel's number. Quickly, I snap the phone shut. What am I thinking? I shake my head clear, then call Helena.

"Hey, are you busy?" I ask.

"Nope. How about you?" she replies.

"Want to go to the mall?" Maybe chain stores and the lure of shiny objects will erase the whole horrible scene I just witnessed.

"Why not?" Helena says good-naturedly. "Meet me at the entrance in twenty?"

"Sounds like a plan," I tell her, silently thanking whatever power made her free.

Why can't this — life, living — come easier to me? My parents and their insane fragility scare the crap out of me, all of this looming possibility that seems beyond my reach, the idea that I'm not good enough, the notion of being lonely and alone for the rest of my life, and this grief — this crushing, breath-sucking grief. It's too much.

• • •

"I need to have some fun," I tell Helena as we stroll past the fluorescent-lit shops that look like candy-colored daisies lined up in a plastic garden. "I'm so sick of being morose, of everyone treating me like I'm going to break down all the time. Over it. Done."

Secretly, I'm reveling in breaking Rule #5, although I've been breaking Rules #3 and #4 for the past five months. Guilt and elation make a funny cocktail.

"Okay, fun . . ." Helena says thoughtfully, tapping her finger to her lips. "I've got it!" she exclaims, her eyes shiny in the glow of the extra-bright mall lighting. "Come on!"

She takes my hand and pulls me down the polished beige stone tile path, weaving between shoppers and bulky bags and kiosks and baby strollers.

"Where are we going?" I ask, trying to catch my breath and keep up. Helena sprints and darts like an elf.

"You'll see," she says, a wicked grin spreading over her face.

An instant later, Helena comes to an abrupt halt in front of Tricia's Trinkets, a tiny boutique that sells cheap earrings, necklaces, bracelets, and so on. She stops so quickly that I walk right into her with a gasp.

"Sorry," I mutter, catching her arm before she falls over.

"Cora, I have the antidote to your gloominess. We're making jewelry," Helena announces.

"You mean buying it," I correct her.

"No, making it. You know, taking everything apart and redesigning it?"

"Oh," I say to Helena. "That sounds cool."

"Good enough," she says. "Come on, let's buy some stuff. Then we'll take it apart and put it back together even better." She looks so excited, I feel something lift inside of me.

Yeah, fun. Remember how this used to feel? I ask myself.

"Let's go," I say and put my hand through her arm. We step inside, grab a basket, and begin filling it with beaded necklaces and bracelets, modeling feathered earrings for each other, and giggling. Suddenly, I hear a familiar voice and some of the weight bears back down on me.

"These look just like the ones Macie was wearing the other day. They're cute, don't you think?" Rachel's voice resonates through the shop, echoing off mirrors and glittering headbands. My stomach clenches. We still haven't spoken since Homecoming, and that was more than a month ago.

"Totally," Elizabeth Tillson's unmistakable, shrill voice replies. Another Nasties hanger-on.

How can I avoid them? There is nowhere to hide in this stuff-filled, idiotic place. As I'm wheeling around the rack I'm hiding behind, hoping to take cover behind another, I spin right into Rachel's path.

"Oh," she says, a note of surprise catching in her throat. "Um, hi." She clearly has no idea how she's supposed to act.

"Hi," I say back, offering a smile but not much more. I don't know how I'm supposed to act, either.

"What are you doing here?" she asks. "You hate this place." A hood has come down over her eyes. I can't see my old friend. Elizabeth comes to stand just behind her, as though she were coming to be Rachel's second in a duel.

"I'm just, um, picking up some stuff." It's very strange to be speaking in such a strained, awful way like this with Rachel, who's been my best friend for as long as I can remember. Then, Helena comes up beside me. Rachel's eyes switch over to Helena's face and give her a long once-over. It is not friendly.

"Oh. Well, see you around," Rachel says stiffly, then gives me a searching look, the hood rising a millimeter, and I could swear I see the same hint of regret behind her eyes that chisels at my chest. Then she turns and marches away, Elizabeth hovering at her side.

"What a freak." Elizabeth's voice wafts over to us. "I can't believe you were friends with her."

"Ugh, I can't believe you were ever friends with *her*," Helena whispers to me.

"It wasn't always this way. She wasn't always this way," I tell her. It's so strange how so much has changed, how Rachel and I seem to have grown out of each other, grown out of our friendship. Does that always happen? Does it have to happen? Does it mean that all ten years of our history are meaningless? Blown away, like dust?

"Hey, come on." Helena breaks into my thoughts. "Let's pay and go back to my house." She looks at me with big, earnest eyes.

The truth hits me: Helena is my friend. I am not alone, and whatever happens between Rachel and me, Helena is my friend. Maybe I know how to be a friend because of Rachel. I don't know. . . . Now I'm getting corny in a way I don't think I want to carry on pursuing.

• • •

Helena lives on Elm Street, on the other side of the county road, a quick walk from the mall. As she strides down the sidewalk, she bounces on the balls of her feet, a funny, rolling, cheerful gait, and when we arrive, her mother, who also has a mane of blond curls, welcomes us warmly. She is wearing an apron tied around her waist, and the whole house smells deliciously sweet, of cookies or muffins. I'm struck by how normal everything here seems. Like one of those old sitcoms — but not in a bad way.

"Hey, Mom, this is my friend Cora from school," Helena trills as we walk into the kitchen, heading for Helena's father's basement workshop.

"Oh, Cora, it's so nice to meet you!" Her mother plants herself right in Helena's path and beams at us so widely, she looks a bit like a satellite dish. "I'll call you girls when the cookies are ready," she says, still smiling as we duck around her and head for the stairs.

Helena looks at me and rolls her eyes. "Sorry about that," she whispers.

"What do you mean? Your mom seems really nice," I reply.

"Well, she is nice. That's the problem. She's too nice, and she just takes the crap my dad dishes out to her. It's pathetic," Helena sneers, but her voice is soft and sad.

"I guess even when things seem perfect, they never are," I murmur.

"I guess so," Helena responds, shaking her head.

As I'm mulling this over, a flash of inspiration strikes, and I look up as though a bolt of lightning has touched my head. That's it . . . the last piece of the map. I know what it should be.

My home.

We get to the bottom of the stairs where a long workbench of two plywood planks resting across three sawhorses stretches along the far wall. All kinds of tools are hung up on display, and shelves with little containers of nails and screws and bolts and washers fill the back side of the workbench.

"Here we are!" Helena announces. "The shop. Come on, let's empty out all our loot and see what we've got."

We dump the contents of our shopping bags out onto the rough surface and spread all the pieces around.

My eyes catch a fake amethyst pendant. "Ooh, I love this color," I say, and hold up the stone against the leather cord from another necklace.

"Let's get to work," Helena says.

We begin cutting and pulling apart all of the jewelry we bought, separating beads and chains and stones and shells and cords into piles, then rearranging and putting them back together again.

"Who says making your own stuff isn't better than buying designer stuff?" Helena asks out loud, waving a pair of pliers as if punctuating her point. She cuts some lengths of thread and fishing line and hands me a needle and scissors.

"This is amazing," I reply. "Making exactly what I want, how I want it."

"And it's relaxing, too," Helena adds.

"Yes, not exactly retail therapy, but therapeutic all the same." It's true — working with my hands like this, designing, being creative feels invigorating, liberating somehow.

"So, what's up with you and Damian?" Helena asks.

"What do you mean?" I can feel the heat of a blush coloring my cheeks. I can't ever seem to *not* show how I feel. It's becoming pretty annoying.

"*What do you mean?*" Helena repeats, mocking me with a grin. "Come on. I know you like him, and you've been spending a lot of time together. So, what's going on?"

"Nothing is going on," I stammer, my cheeks growing hotter.

"But you do like him, right?"

It feels like all the air in my lungs is spiraling out of me in this bubbling rush, and suddenly, talking like this feels good.

"Yes, I like him!" I shout, louder than I intended. "Satisfied?"

"Yes!" Helena yelps gleefully. "I knew it! So, what are we going to do about it?" Her conspiratorial *we* makes my insides feel even fizzier.

"I don't know. I don't think there's anything I can do. He was my brother's best friend. He was in the car with Nate when he died. It's a little weird, isn't it? I'm sure Damian, let alone everyone else in this tiny town, would think so —

would think I'm totally creepy for even considering liking him that way."

"I think you're looking at this all wrong," Helena begins. "I mean, the fact that Damian was Nate's best friend means that he and you share this special bond, this closeness and connection that he can't have with anyone else. Except, maybe, your parents."

"Who hate him," I break in.

"Right. Well, anyway, what I was saying is that you need to look at this tie between the two of you as a good thing."

I pause and let Helena's words sink in. Maybe she has a point. What if I've been so freaked out by the idea of the very thing that has actually brought Damian and me together?

"So what do I do?" I ask her.

Her brow crinkles up as she contemplates my question. "This I need to think on," she tells me. "But we'll come up with a plan." She pauses. "Hey, whatever happened with the London thing?"

"Oh," I say, feeling suddenly uncomfortable. "I sent off the application. I should hear in the next couple of weeks."

"Your mom finally gave in, huh?" she asks, smiling. "See, I told you! It always works out in the end."

Yeah right, I think. But I nod in pretend agreement and force a grin to my face.

By the time I have to leave, we have gorged ourselves on chocolate chip cookies, and Helena has a new pair of feather-and-beaded earrings. I leave with a leather cuff bracelet with the purple stone and some shells stitched around it and a somewhat hopeful feeling. Helena and I have agreed to meet at the diner tomorrow afternoon to talk about the art show. I'm supposed to call Damian when I get home and ask him to come, too. Helena says that when she sees us together, she'll be able to get a better read on the situation and come up with a strategy. We'll see. The whole idea of, well, any of this makes my stomach turn cartwheels and kick like an angry gymnast.

As I reach my house, I meet the mailman at the foot of the driveway. Accepting the small bundle of letters, I thank him, and walk my bike into the garage. I'm thumbing through the envelopes, mostly bills for my parents and junk mail, when I see a yellow envelope poking up from the bottom of the stack. There's a strange blue stamp with a lady in profile on it.

"What's this?" I mutter aloud.

I slide the envelope to the top and my heart skips a whole lot of beats when I see my name printed on it. And a *London, United Kingdom,* return address. It feels as though a whole garden of butterflies has been released into my gut. Could it be from the art school? Already? It's early. Hungrily, I tear open the envelope and pull out the small sheaf of papers tucked inside.

The letter begins:

Dear Ms. Bradley,

We are pleased to offer you a place in the King's School of Art Summer Program.

Oh my gosh. I got in. I freaking got in! I fall back against my dad's Volkswagen. I can't believe it. I can't believe they thought my drawings were good enough and let me in. My eyes fall down across the rest of the letter. And the engines on the jet I was about to fly to the moon, to London, to wherever, flicker and die as I read the last line:

Kindly include the enclosed permission form signed by a parent or legal guardian with requisite registration materials.

Crash-landing. A signed permission form. How am I supposed to achieve that? It would take nothing less than sheer magic. I wonder if Ms. Calico could sign it for me. No, the note says it must be signed by a parent or legal guardian. Suddenly, I feel like a deflated balloon. The registration forms are due back by March 15. That leaves me about two months to figure this one out. I fold up the letter and place it back inside the envelope, and when I get upstairs to my bedroom, I place the envelope at the bottom of my backpack.

"Rest safely," I whisper. "I'll figure out how to get to London. Promise."

• • •

Helena and I are seated on one side of the red Formica table, across from Damian. He's twisting a straw wrapper around his finger, over and over, and not looking at either of us. I'll admit it, I took care this afternoon as I got ready to come to the diner. I put cream in my hair to flatten the frizzy flyaways, I brushed it until it was glossy and smooth. I dabbed some lip gloss onto my lips and I chose my favorite blue jeans and the ocean blue sweater with the delicate navy embroidery around the neck. I wanted to look good. Here we are, though, and Damian won't even make eye contact. Very glad I went to all that effort.

"So, I thought we should figure out how we're going to pull off this art show party, how to get permission to enter Nate's stuff, and how to advertise it," Helena begins brightly.

Damian is silent, sullen.

"Well, I was thinking you could ask Ms. Calico, Helena," I say, "and I'll ask Mrs. Brown." The principal of LGHS is infamous for saying no to student-organized activities, and she was certainly no fan of my brother's. I'm going to have to figure out a way to appeal to her soft side. If she has one.

"That sounds like a good plan," Helena replies, looking uncertainly at Damian. Still he says nothing. "So, Damian, what do you think?"

"I don't know," he grumbles. "Do whatever you want."

"Well, I would love to know what *you* think," Helena continues, cocking her head like a bird examining a juicy-looking worm. "I mean, you worked with Nate, and besides, your paintings will be such an important part of the show, you should have a voice in this."

Damian looks up and squints, as though he's trying to see inside of Helena. Then he looks at me. "Okay," he starts slowly. "I was thinking that maybe we could ask Ms. Calico if we could do it on February eighth."

"The anniversary," I say softly. Damian nods and looks at me, his gray eyes piercing. I return his nod. "That's it. I'll ask first thing tomorrow."

"Wait, the anniversary of what?" Helena asks, confused.

"Of the day Nate died," I tell her gently.

"Oh . . . I'm sorry," she mumbles.

"No, it's fine," I reassure her.

"Great. Then we'll just have to make posters calling for submissions and advertising the date."

Damian and I both start at Helena's words. "Call for submissions?" I ask.

"Well, yeah. I mean, it's already open to whoever wants to show their art. Don't you think we should *encourage* everyone to submit stuff?" she says.

I stop and think about it. She's right. The whole point of doing this is to give Nate the opportunity to be recognized for what he made. Shouldn't everyone get that chance?

"Cool," Damian says, and I look at him, surprised.

"Yeah, great," I add.

"Okay, it's a plan. See you guys tomorrow!" Helena slides out of the booth and stands up. She winks at me and, shaking her hips, makes her way out of the diner.

Damian shifts in his seat and stirs his coffee.

"Is everything okay?" I ask, peering at him. His forehead is creased with lines and he looks ill at ease.

"Yeah, I'm fine," he answers tersely.

"You sure? You look kind of, I don't know, upset."

Damian drops the spoon into his coffee and sinks back against the vinyl seat. He folds his hands together and picks up his head to meet my eyes. "You know, I'm just kind of nervous."

"You mean about showing your stuff?"

"Yes. And the whole thing with Nate — marking the anniversary, showing his work. People are going to . . . I don't know . . . look at me; I'm the guy who killed his best friend. What right do I have to be showing his art?"

"Damian, you didn't kill him," I say quietly. I don't know how to make this better. I don't know how to take away the hurt and the guilt, how to soothe it. "He was the one behind the wheel. He was the one being reckless. And, he could have killed you, too. Then what?" I can't seem to catch my breath. "Then what?" I repeat, louder. "I never would have found out about his art. And I . . ." my voice trails off.

"And you what?" he asks, looking hard at me.

"And I would never have gotten to know *you*, Damian. And

I don't know how I would have survived this year without you."

"Really?" he asks, his voice heavy with disbelief.

"Yes, really," I reply, feeling embarrassed and, somehow, excited at the same time.

"That's good," Damian says slowly. "Because I don't know how I would have survived without you, either."

"Really?" Now excitement is definitely gaining on my embarrassment.

"Yup." Damian is looking at me intently, his silver eyes glinting. "Hey, want to get out of here?"

"Yes," I say. "Yes, I do."

Chapter Thirteen

My heart is thumping as fast and hard as a jackrabbit runs. We pay our bill and get up together. Damian stands back to let me walk ahead of him, and I can't help but think, *He's a gentleman,* and I can't help but sigh. I'm such a dork. We cross Union Street in silence, cut diagonally across the county road, and begin heading down toward the park, neither of us saying a word.

Damian matches my pace and stays close to me, his arm brushing my shoulder every so often. With each touch, as light as a breath, waves of electricity swim up my arm, through my chest and my belly. His black trench coat can't be nearly warm enough. Icicles hang from branches, clear and jagged, as though all the boughs of all the trees are weeping. I want to take Damian's hand, but something stops me. Once again, I find we are so close, only a hairbreadth stands between us, but it might as well be the Grand Canyon. I wish I knew what he was thinking.

Finally, we reach the snowy, muddy swath of grass that surrounds the playground and leads out to the baseball diamond.

My breath fogs out in front of me in puffs. Damian stares straight ahead, marching forward, ignoring the belching, slippery mud beneath our boots. Unexpectedly, as I take a step, my foot slides in the wet muck and I start to fall down, when something grabs hold of my waist and hauls me back to my feet. I'm pressed against Damian, and he is looking down at me, grinning.

"Careful there," he tells me gently.

"Thanks," I mutter.

His arm is still around my waist, and when I turn away to keep walking, he keeps it there. I want to lean into him, but my whole being feels electrified, and I can't help but keep ramrod straight. I wouldn't be surprised if my hair were standing on end, too. And all I can think is *Oh my gosh oh my gosh oh my gosh*. We continue tramping across the field, Damian's arm warm and heavy around me. Finally, we reach the playground, where the tire swing sways slightly in the frosty breeze.

"I used to come here with Nate," I say quietly.

"I know," Damian answers. "It's in your map. Want to swing?" I nod, and Damian unwraps his arm. In an instant, I miss his warmth. He stretches his long leg over the lip of the tire and hops on. "Come on!" he calls.

I quickly scramble up onto the tire and sit across from him, the cold of the chains whistling through my woolen gloves. Damian kicks his legs back and holds us poised, ready, then lifts his feet, and the tire swings crazily, tilting and spinning in wild circles. Damian is smiling a wide smile that is as unburdened and light as a child's. He throws his head back and laughs a deep belly laugh. The lurching of the swing loosens something inside of me, and I can't help but giggle madly, too.

Finally, as the tire starts to lose its momentum and we begin to slow down, Damian drops his feet and lets them drag us to a halt. We stay in place, knees just brushing.

"So," he says.

"So," I search for something to say, "I have news." I feel buoyed by the wild freedom of the swing, by his closeness, by the memory of his arm around my waist.

"What's your news?" Damian asks, eyeing me keenly, a small grin playing at his lips.

"I got accepted to the summer art school."

"The one in London?"

As I nod yes, Damian lets out a loud whoop. "That's amazing!" he shouts, and reaches across to grab me in a hug.

Oh my gosh, he smells good, like some exotic but comforting spice, nutmeg or cardamom. Slowly, Damian lowers his head to mine and I think my chest might explode, my heart is tap-dancing so quickly.

He's going to kiss me.

I've imagined this and now that it's really happening, I am like a block of wood. I can't move. I can't breathe. I close my eyes just as the lightest feather of a breath, then lips, brush over my lips. His breath is sweet and the taste of coffee barely lingers in his mouth. I feel as though my whole body has turned to liquid, into a river of millions of droplets, rushing apart and then back together.

"You have the softest lips," he whispers as he pulls back to look at me.

"So do you," I murmur. *Oh, was that a stupid thing to say?* I turn my face into his jacket and breathe in his scent.

"Hey, are you okay?" he asks.

I straighten up and nod. "Fine. Better than fine, actually." I feel shy all of a sudden.

"Good," Damian says, a satisfied grin spreading over his face. "So, how about London? When do you leave?"

"I don't think I'll be going, I'm afraid." I sigh and scuff my boots against the ground, letting the tire rock back and forth.

"Your mom?" Damian prods.

"Yeah. I need to get her to sign a permission form. And as we all know, that's about as likely to happen as Mr. Wyatt's horses growing wings," I say sarcastically.

"Well, we need to strategize. There *has* to be a way to get you to London." Damian's brow wrinkles in concentration.

"Unless I can get my dad to sign it in his zombie-like state, it's never going to happen for me. Unless . . ." I have an idea. I'm certain it's a bad one, but it could work.

"Unless what?" Damian asks eagerly.

"Unless I sign the form myself."

"What do you mean?" Damian's confusion is evident, scrawled all across his face, etched into his eyes.

"I mean, I could forge her signature."

"But then what? What happens when it's time to go?"

"Then I just go." A cocky sureness is growing inside me. I could do this. I could do it and get away with it. Just leave and finally slip out from underneath my mother's controlling thumb.

"Cor, I don't know. I don't think —"

"Damian, I don't really see any other options. Do you?"

He looks at me pleadingly, then drops his gaze.

"Look," he mutters, "just promise me you won't do anything rash just yet, okay?"

"Fine, I promise." It is as though a chilly frost has fallen down upon us, hangs in the air between us. In an instant, this discussion has opened up a chasm between us, like a paper cut. Narrow, almost invisible at first, until the blood begins to pump to the surface, and the cut widens, becoming painful.

"I just don't want you to do something stupid," Damian says warningly.

"How is it stupid? If I don't go —" I take a deep breath and look into Damian's eyes. "If I don't go, I will die." I want him to understand; I need someone to help me know what to do.

"I don't want to fight, Cor," Damian says, reaching for my

hand. "Just promise me you'll wait a while. And that you'll talk to me before doing anything irrevocable, okay?"

"I promise you," I reply, squeezing his hand and smiling into his gray eyes. He leans over to kiss me again, and this time I bring my hand to his cheek, which is cold and rough. "I promise," I repeat.

"I'm freezing here," Damian says, pulling back. "Let's walk?"

"Let's walk," I agree.

We disentangle ourselves from the tire swing and begin to walk, muddy snow squirting and squirching beneath our feet, toward the baseball diamond. Damian holds my hand.

"You know, all of this just makes me wonder, what are we supposed to do?" I tell him.

"What do you mean?"

"I mean, am I meant to just eat, sleep, go to school, do what my mother says, work, and then, someday, die? Is that all there is to life? To living? Because something tells me there is more to it than that. More to it than just existing like an animal. Might as well be a cat if we're just supposed to eat, work, sleep, and die."

"Well," Damian starts slowly, "no, I don't think that's all we're meant to do. I mean, I think that's probably part of it. But I think we're put here to do more than just exist. We're meant to *live*. To experience and to create. To sense, to taste, to see things and make new things. To love."

"That's what I think," I tell him. "Life is supposed to be about passion, but how am I supposed to know that, to experience it, if I'm stuck here?" Damian looks down at the ground. Oh, I've put my foot in it. "No, Damian, that's not what I meant. I mean beyond this town, beyond high school. What about when we grow up? My family has always lived in Lincoln Grove. My parents were born here, their parents, too. Not one of them has ever lived anywhere else. How can staying in this one tiny town be living and experiencing life to the fullest?" I ask.

"Well, I would guess that it works differently for everybody," Damian explains. "I would guess that for you and me, *living* has a very different meaning than it does for our parents."

"Maybe. I guess that makes sense. I just think that if I can't get to London, I will shrivel up and then I might as well be dead. You know what I mean?"

"I think I do," Damian says, looking off to the tree line. "Yes, I think I do."

"Damian, could I ask you something?" I am hesitant to go on, but at his questioning nod, I take a breath and continue. "What happened in the car that night?"

Damian sucks in a sharp breath and winces. His eyebrows climb into his forehead and crash down, casting shadows over his eyes.

"We don't have to talk about it if you don't want to," I say quickly.

"No, it's okay," he says, pulling me down beside him on a snowy-damp bench next to the baseball diamond. "It's all right."

"Are you sure?" I ask. Damian nods, then begins to talk.

"Nate, you know, was really ticked off because Julie had just broken up with him. Over the phone. And he called me and said, 'Hey man, I just have to drive, but I don't want to be alone.' And he asked if he could pick me up, and I said sure, and then he was driving so fast, and I started to get scared when he pulled out onto the county road and you know, as he drove out of town, he started flying all over the road, and I kept asking him to slow down, telling him 'Man, just take it easy,' but he wasn't listening. It was like some demon just took over, and then he looked at me and said, 'Here's a new trick,' and he switched off the headlights, and I was shouting at him, telling him to stop the car, to just pull over, but he was somewhere else, and then all I can remember was this horrible rending screeching crashing sound. Like the tree was screaming. Maybe it was me screaming. And then I passed out. That's it."

Damian shakes his head, and his eyes are shining with tears that he wipes away roughly. "I tried to make him stop, and he just . . . he just wouldn't. I replay that night over and over, trying to figure out how I could have made him pull over. How I could have pulled up the emergency brake or grabbed the wheel. Something. *Anything*. But I did nothing, and he's dead because of it." A veil of tears clings to his eyes, and he blinks, trying to shake them loose. I feel my nose and my own eyes leaking.

"Damian, you did everything you could. I know Nate. I know how stubborn and pigheaded he was. I *know.* There's nothing you could have said to convince him to stop. And I just . . ." A sob shudders through me. "I am just so grateful that he didn't kill you, too."

I wrap my arms around Damian's neck and pull his head down to me, and we stay like that, huddled together, crying and breathing each other in, until the sun has nearly set.

"You should get back," Damian says. "Or your mom might get upset."

"You're right." I sigh with remorse.

We begin the long march back through the meadow, hand in hand, and watch as the sky turns a hazy tangerine, streaked with long, scarlet fingers. Damian walks me home, wheeling my bike for me. As we turn onto my street, Damian brushes his lips against my forehead and says good night. Then he heads off in the direction of the diner to pick up his car.

"See you tomorrow?"

"Wouldn't miss it for anything," Damian answers, his voice warm with affection.

I walk up the driveway and notice the curtain at the kitchen window that faces the street move. *Was someone watching us?* Shortly, I open the door into the house, and my mother is standing there in the kitchen, eyes flashing, hands balled into fists at her waist.

"What were you doing, Cora?" she snaps.

"What do you mean?" I ask. I have no idea what she's seen, what she knows.

"I mean, Cora, what were you doing with that boy?" Her tone has grown nasty, and it catches on *boy,* which she spits out like acid.

"You mean what was I doing with Damian Archer?" I sneer.

"Do not even think about getting smart with me, young lady. What were you doing with that *boy*. What on earth were you doing? I want to know right this instant."

"I was taking a walk with him. Is that against one of your many ridiculous rules?"

"Is that boy taking advantage of you?" Now her voice grows higher, tighter.

"Would you stop calling him that boy?" I snap back. "He has a name. It's Damian. And no, he is not taking advantage of me. He is kind and gentle and generous to me." All of the anger that has been building inside of me for the past eleven months is seething like a mass of snakes. "Nothing like you." My mother's head jerks back as though I've slapped her.

"How dare you! How *dare* you!" she hollers. "You don't know the first thing, you hear me? That boy killed Nate. He is good for nothing. How dare you gallivant about with him! How dare you!"

"Damian did not kill Nate!" I shout back at her. "Nate took care of that all by himself. And we're just lucky Nate didn't take Damian with him! Nate was a beautiful artist, and he wanted to live, but it was you and Dad who pushed him and pushed him and made him feel like a failure, like a screwup. It's *your* fault he died! Do *you* hear *me?*" I scream. "It's all *your* fault!"

My mother's face is as white as the snow outside. "You little monster. Don't you tell me it was my fault! Don't you dare. You don't know anything about it, about what it's like to be a parent," she says, her voice quiet and mean. "You couldn't possibly know what it's like to lose a son. You couldn't possibly know!" she roars. Tears are streaming down both of our faces.

"I know you lost a son, Mom. It's impossible to forget it, because you and Dad have turned this house into a cemetery. I lost my brother, Mom! I lost Nate, too! But I want to live!" And I spring from the kitchen and up the stairs. Then I slam my bedroom door behind me, taking no comfort in the way the walls shudder and a picture frame containing a photo of the four of us falls from its perch over my desk.

I feel as though all the breath has been knocked from me. I'm literally shaking. I can't stop trembling, my hands, my legs, all of me. There is so much hate and hurt in here, and I can't live with it anymore. I curl up on my bed, boots and clothes and all and feel my thoughts grow cold and still. I have to get out of here.

• • •

Sometime in the middle of the night I wake up. At first I lie on my back and look for stars outside my window. But the sky is cloudy and I can't see any, just a sliver of moonlight. Then I sit up and turn on the lamp beside my bed. I pull my sketchbook from my backpack and begin flipping through the pages. This map of all that I know, all the places I've known my whole life . . . well, it's small and large at once. There are acres and acres of fields stretching out, yawning for miles to meet an endless sky. There's so much space, but everything feels so close. Here in the middle of this country, where we are locked in by land and more land on all sides, hemmed in by roads and fences and little white and yellow houses with their blue and red shutters and all these people who have lived in this tiny town their whole lives, whose parents and grandparents have lived here all their lives. My parents and grandparents were all born here. No one could belong here more than me.

So why do I feel like I don't fit?

If I run away to some far-off place, will that sever my connection to Lincoln Grove? If someday I don't live here anymore, will I stop belonging altogether? And can it even matter if I don't feel like I belong? Will I ever know the answers to these questions? Something tells me it may be a long time before I figure it out. For now, though, this house doesn't feel much like a home.

Chapter Fourteen

When I ask Mrs. Brown, the principal, if we can feature Nate's art and have a special gala opening at the start of the art show, the crease between her eyes deepens until it's a small canyon. She twists her face into the sternest grimace. But as I explain that it would still be a chance for all the students of LGHS to show their artwork — not just Damian and me and Nate — the frown lines smooth out, and she gives the most imperceptible nod.

"All right," she says. "I'm going to give you permission to do this in Ms. Calico's art studio. But I don't want any funny business. Clean and quiet, you understand, Ms. *Bradley*?"

The emphasis on my last name wasn't lost on me. I got it. No Nathaniel antics. Not that I'd go in for that anyway. It still astonishes me how so many teachers and kids lump me together with my brother.

I report all this to Helena as we huddle in the library during lunch. She just tosses her head. "Witch. Forget about her. At least we got the green light. Now, we paper the place."

"Huh?" I ask, confused.

"Posters. We're going to wallpaper the school with posters. Only the posters have to be art, too. You know, to incite, to excite. It'll be awesome. What are you doing after school? Can you come to my place to plan?"

"Well, I'm pretty sure I'm grounded for life, since my mom caught me with Damian yesterday, so —"

"Wait, *what*!" Helena interrupts with a squeal. The librarian, Ms. Sheldon, glances over and shushes us loudly.

"Easy there, you might break every single pane of glass in a five-mile radius," I tell Helena wryly.

"You are clearly holding something *huge* back, and I don't like it! You'd better tell me everything. And don't even think about leaving one single little detail out."

"Well, I was getting to that, but Mrs. Brown seemed like a priority."

"Lady, it would seem your priorities are not straight. Spit it out!" Helena is anxiously twisting a lock of buttercup hair around her index finger. It's like her whole being is carried away by her excitement and energy and curiosity — about everything, anything. She is electricity.

"Okay, well . . . we kissed."

There, I just say it and sort of enjoy the blazing heat that engulfs my ears and neck and cheeks.

"Seriously?" she shouts, earning her another glare from the librarian.

"Helena, quiet! Yes, seriously," I reply.

"Wait. No. This is most unsatisfactory. Start from the beginning," she instructs me.

"You left us at the diner, and, I don't know, somehow we ended up walking to the park together."

"To the park!" she screeches, then quickly lowers her voice. "What next? What did he say? What did you say?"

"I'll get to it if you give me a chance," I tell her. "We were walking, and I sort of slipped, and he put his arm around me, and he just . . . kept it there. Then we got on the tire swing —"

"The tire swing?" Helena sighs. "That's so romantic!"

"Will you let me finish?" I wait for her to nod. "So, we were swinging, and then he just sort of leaned over and kissed me."

"And it was amazing?" she prods.

"Yes, it was amazing," I reply, and there is nothing I can do to peel off the goofy grin that is plastered to my lips. "He smells so good."

"That's the best, isn't it?" Helena says. "When they smell so good, and you just want to stick your nose against their neck and stay there?"

I nod in agreement. Not that I have much experience. Beyond yesterday, none, actually. But it did feel good to be close to Damian like that, breathing him in.

Helena is staring off into space, and she has her own silly smile stuck to her mouth, and I imagine she is thinking of Cam. I don't tell her all the things Damian and I spoke of; it's not for her to hear or to know. Those words are between Damian and me, and maybe Nate.

"Anyway, when I got home, my mom came after me, because she saw Damian walk me up to our driveway, and she completely flipped out. It was like Antietam. Awful. So, I don't know if I should be traipsing around town after school today."

"Yikes," Helena says.

"Yeah. Thanks," I reply.

"Well, if you're grounded, should I come over to your house?" she asks.

"You're willing to risk it?" I say disbelievingly.

Helena flashes a cocky grin, then bolts as the bell rings. I watch her as she leaves. Everything about her is fluid as a river. Her messy hair, her xylophone voice, the strokes of her paintbrush. Even her camouflage army jacket hangs loose, flowing like ribbons.

While everyone else has treated me like I have a mildly contagious rash, Helena just swept in and nursed me back; she makes me feel normal. And what a wonderful feeling that is.

• • •

We're sitting in my bedroom, Helena at my desk, thumbing through my copy of *The Odyssey*, while I'm stretched out on the floor, sketch pad and pencil in hand.

"So, what do we write?" I ask.

"Something that will make everyone want to come see what's

going on, and everyone who has some kind of artwork stashed in their back pocket want to come show it," Helena says as she flips the atlas to a page showing a map of France. "What if we make a collage of pictures of Paris or famous museums or something like that?" she suggests.

"Sounds like a good idea to me."

We set to work, cutting photos from the unread, unopened *National Geographic* magazines that have been languishing in a wicker basket in our living room, pasting them down onto sheets of poster board, then filling in the white spaces with charcoal sticks, colored pencils, and tempera paints.

"So, how did you meet Cam?" I ask.

"Cam? Well, I don't know. I've always known him. We've been best friends since we were little kids. Like, since first grade. And one day, things just changed."

"Really? I mean . . ." I struggle for the right words. "How did that happen?" So often, when I'm around other kids, I feel at a loss for words, like language just escapes me. Then the wrong thing comes out. I never used to feel this way with Rachel . . . until recently, that is. When I think about how Helena and I came together, I can't help but wonder at how, even from the start, I felt perfectly comfortable around her. She never made me feel like she would judge me, or if I said the wrong thing, she would tease me or be embarrassed by me — or hate me — for it.

"You know, I don't remember how it happened. But one day,

when we were in eighth grade, we were hanging out in my backyard, just sitting under this big old oak tree we have, and he just leaned over and kissed me. And it was perfect." I imagine she is bathing in her memory; her face has turned a light shade of pink, and she's lit up and happy. A carnation.

"It wasn't weird between you two after that?" I ask.

"No. I mean, it was different. Completely different. And not. It was like everything suddenly made sense, you know?" She looks at me earnestly, the dopey glow still lighting her face.

I remember how I felt with Damian at the park, as we sat on the bleachers, our arms around each other. As if, in that short space of a half hour and the few inches of cold metal bleacher between us, all of the shards of this fractured life came hurtling together like the pieces of a kaleidoscope, forming a pattern that actually makes sense. "Maybe," I reply. "Maybe I do know."

"It's like you can get through anything — the ridiculously cruel fights your parents have, the stupid craziness of school —"

"A dead brother," I interrupt.

"Why not?" she asks ironically, a giggle escaping her.

I giggle, too, and then it becomes totally contagious. We are both doubled over with laughter. We lean into each other and laugh until tears are streaming down our cheeks.

Perfect, I think. *Just perfect.*

• • •

Today I feel like I'm floating outside of my body, hovering just on the periphery of life, watching myself feeling so happy. This moment, like a snapshot, will be frozen forever in my memory.

Helena, Damian, and I arrive at school early, a whole hour before the first bell, to tape up the posters that Helena and I painted last night and photocopied in the school office this morning. We are working our way through the corridors, from one end of the school to the other and have a system down — Helena picks a spot, Damian holds the poster in place, Helena rips the masking tape, and I roll each strip into loops and hand them to Damian, who carefully lifts each corner of the poster, places a loop of tape on it, then waves his hand over it, smoothing any creases and bumps.

We work mainly in silence, but every so often, Helena or I will murmur to Damian that the poster he is holding up is crooked, or he complains that his arms are falling asleep if I take too long to pass him a loop of tape. Then he shoots me a crooked grin and hangs his head between his raised arms as if unbearably weary.

"These posters look pretty good," he admits in a teasing voice. "Even if they are starting to feel like they weigh a ton."

ARTISTS! LGHS WANTS YOU TO BRING YOUR DRAWINGS, PAINTINGS, SCULPTURES, AND ANY OTHER WORKS TO A CELEBRATION OF ART AND LIFE.

FEBRUARY 8, 6 O'CLOCK IN THE EVENING

"Maybe you should start working out," I joke.

"Maybe if you weren't so slow —" I elbow Damian in the ribs, then fall against him laughing. He lets the poster he's holding fall and wraps his arms around me. He's so warm and solid. Suddenly *I'm* the carnation. I can't imagine feeling brighter or more beautiful. And I can't believe I could feel more at home anywhere.

"Hey, I hate to break up the lovefest, but the halls are going to start filling up in about ten minutes, so let's get a move on and try to finish. We only have the D hallway left," Helena urges, an impish smile playing over her lips.

"Okay, okay," Damian says with a heavy sigh and a playful shrug of his shoulders. "The lady is a taskmaster."

His silver eyes are dancing with laughter. I have never seen Damian so light of heart. It is contagious and it is wonderful.

We quickly finish papering the last hall just as the first bell rings. Waves of bodies pour into the D hallway as we gather the leftover posters and rolls of tape. We stand back and watch as, one by one, kids notice the posters and stop and stare, as if trying to puzzle out the answer to some complex math problem.

"Think people will show?" Damian asks, looking down at Helena and me.

"I do," Helena says with certainty. "For sure."

"Well, here's hoping," I add. Damian reaches over and

squeezes my hand. My stomach flutters nervously. Excitedly. It's as though a new page is turning over.

• • •

Later that afternoon, Damian and I are in the barn, sitting beside each other, staring at my map. Now that I am several feet away from it, my breath catches as I recall the plain board covered with gray smudges I found just half a year ago. Half a year. Time goes so fast. It's almost a year since —

The map. The pieces of Lincoln Grove spring from the pine surface. The board is shaded over with greens and browns and yellows and blues, from pastel pencils and acrylic paints. The background colors and textures reflect the fields and roads, rivers, woods, creek, and pond. On top of the paints and pastels, I drew in some of the buildings and houses and streets of Lincoln Grove with charcoal and marker. Every single fragment of this town is there, painted and positioned in its proper place.

I've highlighted the spots from my list with all sorts of odds and ends: bits of earth, metal, wood, grass, leaves, cotton wool, and fabric. And I've drawn the scenes atop these materials with markers and paint. The schools are built of piles of pebbles, the baseball diamond a mat of grass, the Wyatt cornfields yellow flannel. I used moss and leaves for the park grounds and creek, a standing tree branch at the bend in the county road, blue mylar from a balloon for the swimming pool, cotton stuffing for the skating pond, and a black button strung from a tripod of paper clips for the tire swing. The details are intricate, and although the distances are not to scale, I can truly see my town in it. It is a living thing.

But, there is a hole in the northwest corner, where my house should rest. It gapes at me. I do not know how to make a house that no longer feels like a home. How do I render that?

Then I know. Seashells. Houses that are no longer homes.

I turn to Damian. "Where can I find seashells?" I ask.

"Seashells?" he repeats. He puts his fingers to his temples as he ponders the question. "There are clams in the pond. Would clamshells work?"

"Yes! You're a genius!" I exclaim, and kiss him roundly on the lips. I pull back quickly, embarrassed by my forwardness.

"I know," Damian answers smugly. He leans in for another kiss. It's become completely natural, this kissing business. Still weird to me. But lovely.

"Fancy a trip to the skating pond?" I ask.

"I hear it's beautiful this time of the year," he replies. "Let's go." Damian extends a hand and pulls me to my feet.

"Beautiful it may be, but do you think we can find clamshells this time of the year? I mean, the pond is frozen over."

"Maybe we should bring shovels, just in case," Damian suggests.

"Where are we going to get shovels?" I grumble.

"Not to fear. I have a place," he replies with a grin. We pile into the El Camino and roar across Union Street, keeping south of the county road. We're passing houses that don't look very dissimilar from mine, but some are slightly run-down. Soon, Damian pulls into a driveway. The house is painted a mustard yellow with green shutters, and although the driveway is cracked with weeds sprouting in many places, the house looks well kept.

"Welcome to my humble abode. Now, you stay here," Damian urges me to stay in the car. But I follow him up the driveway and into the garage anyway.

Clutter. I've never seen so many *things* all in one place. It is practically filled to the ceiling, from wall to wall, with stuff. There are naked lamps without shades; there are lamps with shades that have turned brown and yellow with age; there is a pair of wooden chairs with red upholstered seat bottoms littered with holes and tears where the stuffing climbs out; there is a wilted cardboard box with a baseball bat and a collection of various balls — baseballs, basketball, soccer ball, football, tennis balls; there is a mustard yellow stove that is missing a burner; there is a crowd of vases and flowerpots, many of which are chipped and cracked; there is a dirt bike and a lawn mower and a tool bench and shelves of plastic containers holding nuts and screws and nails and bolts. The back wall is lined with a wooden plank to which hooks are nailed, holding up hammers and mallets and screwdrivers, two kinds of handsaws, and a drill.

My eyes have gone wide; they're probably bugging out of my head like two brown dinner plates. There's hardly space to walk through the clutter, and I look on as Damian twists and dodges, carving a path to a far corner where a snow shovel and a garden shovel are both propped against the wall. He takes both shovels then pulls a spade down from the tool board.

He finally makes his way back to me, shaking his head. "You've witnessed our dirty secret," he says with a grin. "My mom is going to kill me. I keep promising her I'll clean it out, that we'll have a garage sale. It's just that there's always something else — something better to do," he finishes ruefully.

"Maybe we could do it together?" I offer.

"My mom would clobber me if she knew I'd let you in here to see this mess, let alone allowed you to lift a finger to clean any of it."

"I promise you, our basement is almost as bad as this," I tell him, wrapping my arm around his neck. "*Almost,*" I add with a chuckle.

"Come on, let's go," Damian says, digging a finger into my side to tickle me and laughing at my answering shriek.

We climb back into his car. I still marvel at how he holds open the passenger door for me, watching to make sure my fingers, legs, and coat are all safely stowed inside before carefully closing the door.

Once we arrive at the pond, Damian takes the shovels from the back of his truck and I follow him past the ice-skaters and the hot cocoa stand, to the edge of the frozen water at the far end of the pond, where the ice stays thin. He drops the garden shovel and hands me the spade, then, with snow shovel in hand, bends, tucks the trowel into the ground, and lifts up a load of fluffy snow. He drops it behind him then goes in for another shovelful. Once he has cleared a bare patch of soil, I kneel down and begin to scrape at the hard ground with the spade. It's tough going, and, even with wool gloves on my hands, my fingers are turning as stiff as the dirt. I drop the spade and flex my fingers, then start again.

"Here, let me," Damian says, nudging me over and taking the spade from my frozen fingers. I stay next to him and look up to see several ice-skaters eyeing us curiously.

"What a strange pair we must make," I remark.

"What do you mean?" Damian stops digging and drops the spade, turning to look at me. There isn't a glint of a smile in his eyes.

"I just mean that we must look pretty weird, crouched here, digging."

"Oh," he says woodenly, then turns back to work.

What did he think I meant? I wonder.

All of our earlier cheerfulness seems to have been sucked

away, as though someone pulled the plug in a bathtub drain. What's worse is I can't even say what changed. But something happened to create a chill that now hangs in the air between us. The cold seems to pierce my heavy down coat, clawing its way through layers of feathers and wool sweater and cotton shirt, burrowing deep into my skin. And suddenly our hunt for clamshells by the side of an ice-skating pond in the dead of winter feels worse than absurd. It feels childish. Foolish.

Has Damian just been humoring me these past few weeks? Has he grown tired of it, tired of hanging around with a flat-chested fourteen-year-old? A ball, heavy and bitter, lodges in the back of my throat. I look over at Damian. He is scratching at the frozen soil with a strange ferocity. Does he want to break up with me? We aren't even officially dating, so I'm not sure that he would have to.

"We must look ridiculous —" I start, but am cut off by a vicious glare.

"You think we look ridiculous? Are you worried about being seen with the freak of Lincoln Grove?" he snaps.

I feel like I am reeling. His words might as well have been a bat brought down on my head.

"What?" I gasp.

"Oh, come on. You don't want to be seen out here with me. Maybe you're embarrassed by me. I don't know. But don't worry. I'll save you the trouble."

"Have you gone crazy? What are you talking about?" My poor mind is trying so hard to understand, but it's like he's speaking a foreign language. I can't seem to put his words together and make sense of them.

"Crazy?" he snaps. "Yeah, maybe. That would make a whole lot of sense to everyone, wouldn't it? Although everybody might be wondering about you. I mean, what are you doing hanging around with the crazy dude who killed your brother?" He's yelling, and his eyes have gone narrow and look as hard as the frostbitten earth. Some of the ice-skaters have stopped skating and gliding in their circles to watch us.

"Damian, I don't understand!" I sound like I'm pleading with him, but I don't know what I'm begging for. It's as though I need forgiveness, but I haven't done anything. Have I?

"Don't worry. I'll spell it out for you. Really clear." Damian springs to his feet, quick and fluid like a panther. Then he tosses the spade down to the ground, and it rings with a metallic hollowness and the sharpness of gunfire. He throws one leg over the wooden rails blocking access to this end of the pond. He kicks the rusty metal sign nailed to the post. NO SKATING. THIN ICE. He starts to walk toward the center of the ice, his trench coat billowing out behind him like a parachute. My heart has started beating a rapid staccato and I don't think I'll ever catch my breath again. *What is he doing?*

"Damian, come back here! What are you doing?" I scream.

He doesn't waver, continues moving in a straight line toward the center of the ice. I can hear his heavy black combat boots crunching over the frozen surface. My stomach is churning, my brain is churning. Before I am even aware of what I'm doing, I have started after him. All I know is I have to get him back.

The ice is mostly covered with a light dusting of snow, but before I am five steps from the shoreline, my foot suddenly slides out from under me, and the rest of my body follows. I hit the ice hard, and my breath escapes in a grunt.

I am sitting on my bottom when I hear it. The worst sound. A thunderous cracking, like the report of a starter pistol, shakes me to my senses. I look down and see a long seam in the milky ice threading out from under me, snaking toward Damian. The white ripple grows like an arm, reaching, reaching. And it is crossed by a second fissure.

"Cora!" Damian calls. He turns around gingerly and I can read in the horror splashed across his face that things do not look promising. I glance down. The ice has begun to splinter, jagged branches radiating out from under my butt. "Cora," he says, "look at me."

It's impossible to tear my eyes from the doom I see scrawled across the ice. Another gasping, tearing sound clenches at the air. I look up and find Damian on his hands and knees, crawling achingly slowly toward me, weaving around the fissures and cracks.

He comes close to me and reaches for my hand. "Cora, can you slide toward me?"

I shake my head. I am frozen; I think my bottom may be frozen, fixed to the pond's surface. A crowd has formed at the far end of the pond. People point and shout, but I can't focus on what they're saying. We're really a spectacle now.

"Hey, Cora, you can do this. Just look at me, and push off with your hands and slide." Damian is coaxing me in the soft, lulling tone he might use if he were trying to soothe a wild animal. A crease of worry pocks his forehead. He reaches out a hand to me, and slowly, so slowly, I lift my hand, too.

The booming of another gash opening up spurs me into action. I plant my back hand on the ice, feeling the rough unevenness of the fractured surface through my glove. I begin to crab walk, moving deliberately as though in slow motion, toward Damian. My heart is beating an angry, frightened tattoo. This must be how deer feel when the rumbling explosion of a hunter's rifle pursues them. Must move quickly, smoothly.

"That's it, Cor." He is crawling closer, then I feel the steadying warmth of his hand closed around my wrist. Then Damian begins to inch toward the shoreline, towing me after him. As we reach the bank of the pond, another rupture in the smooth, frosty surface follows us to the very edge. Damian quickly shoves me forward, and then I am splayed out on my stomach on the snowy bank. I feel him beside me before I can turn my head to look for him. "I'm sorry," he gasps. "I'm so sorry, Cor."

That's when I realize I am shuddering with great, heaving sobs. I am lying facedown in the snow, and the cold damp is filling my nostrils, and I cough and splutter, and sit up before I drown in snow.

"What were you doing, Damian?" I manage between sobs.

"I — I don't know," he admits, his voice low. I cannot bring my eyes to meet his.

"Were you trying to prove something?" I ask. "Because I don't know what you possibly could have been thinking. Or what you were trying to prove."

"I can't even remember now," Damian mumbles. "I was so upset, and now . . . I just can't remember."

I look hard at him, study the right angle his jawline makes, the teardrop shape of his cheekbones, the line of his nose, the square of his chin. He is handsome, but maybe he isn't for me. Not anymore, not after this. "I don't know if I can do this," I say.

"Cora, I'm sorry. I thought —"

"What? What could you possibly have thought to make you believe that walking out onto that ice was okay?"

"I thought you were ashamed of me, to be seen with me," he replies, a deep blush staining his cheeks.

"What?" I splutter. "That is insane. Where could you possibly have gotten that idea from?"

"I don't know. I guess . . . I guess I just don't understand why you would ever want to be with me. I'm a total screwup," he says. "I mean, look at me. Look at what I just did. Seriously, if you never wanted to speak to me again, I'd understand," he tells me, disgust filling his voice.

"Damian, we're all screwups. Each in our own special, stupid way," I tell him. As I say the words, I realize how true they are. And maybe that's the trick to getting through it, through life: realizing that everybody, including ourselves, is lugging around some kind of screwed-up baggage. Maybe we are put here to help each other carry the loads.

"Do you hate me?" Damian asks, his voice cracking.

"Don't be stupid. How could I hate you? You're the only one who gets me," I answer ruefully. He puts his head down in the snow with a relieved sigh. I do the same, then he turns over onto his back and begins waving his arms and legs back and forth. "A snow angel?" I have not made one for years. I flip over onto my back, too, and move my arms and my legs in and out like a scissor. And there we lie, side by side, two screwup angels in the snow.

• • •

When we are too wet and shivery to lie there any longer, we roll ourselves up and Damian helps me to my feet.

"Thank you," he says softly, then plants a kiss, soft as a snowflake, on my cheek. And we walk back to his car, hand in hand.

Chapter Fifteen

I am about to do something. Something bad. My whole body is trembling. Whether it's with disgust or excitement or fear, I can't tell. The permission forms for London are due soon, by March 15, but I can't wait. I am sitting on my bed, the acceptance and registration papers balanced on my lap. Where I have the pen point pressed, the black ink bleeds deep into the fibers of the paper. I hold the pen there, willing my hand to steady itself. Then quickly I trace the swoops and swirls of my mother's signature. There it is, *Marie Bradley,* outlined in heavy script, and I stare at the thick, familiar-looking letters. I can't see anything else.

Oh my gosh oh my gosh oh my gosh. What did I just do?

I did it. My blood feels like it has frozen in my veins. I signed my mother's name. I forged her signature. Now my hands won't stop shaking. I have never done something like this before. I've never even imagined doing something like this before.

One part of me is horrified, the other part is exhilarated. I feel free, independent — grown up. *She* can't tell me what to do, nor can she stop me from doing what I want to do. When it's time to buy my ticket, I will walk to the bank and get a cashier's check, drawn from the savings account flush with the money my grandparents have sent me over the past fourteen birthdays.

Wow. I can get away with this. I am really going to London. I shiver with excitement. And nausea. This is a lie bigger, so much bigger, than any I've ever told before. I shake my head, as if to clear it of dust. I should feel glad that I did this. Empowered. But, I have to admit, it feels — I feel — kind of awful. My parents will be so sad when they discover I've left. Left without a word and without a warning.

Now, I just need a stamp. *How much is it to send an envelope to London?* I wonder. Silently, I wend my way to the door and into the dark hallway. I need a stamp, and there's only one place to find stamps in this house. My dad's study. I start off down the hall, pausing to listen for any noises, but I don't hear a thing. Maybe they've gone to bed. When I'm in front of my dad's study, I halt and press my ear to the door. Not a sound escapes. Slowly, I turn the knob and nudge the door open.

"Cora?" comes a weak voice.

My heart sinks into my stomach. "Dad?" I whisper hesitantly. What do I do? Should I turn around and return to my room? Do I make up a story for why I need the stamps?

"Come on in, Cor," he says. His voice is so soft, so low, I can barely hear him.

"What's up?" I ask warily, thinking maybe I can make him forget that I am the one breaking into his study.

"What are you up to?" he inquires gently.

"I just . . . I was just looking for a stamp. I wanted to send a letter to — uh — to Auntie Janie," I lie. She's the only sibling of either of my parents who moved out of state.

"Oh, well, stamps are in the top drawer," he says, indicating the oak desk that fills up part of the room. "You know."

"Yeah, um, thanks," I say as I start toward the huge, old, hulking desk.

Quickly, surreptitiously, I peel off a stamp and stick it to the palm of my hand.

"I heard about your little project."

Dad's voice, scratchy, as if from disuse, catches me off guard, makes me catch my breath. Does he suspect that I've forged Mom's signature on the permission form? Does he know what I'm doing? In more than ten months, he hasn't shown an iota of interest or concern for what I'm doing. What is with the questions all of a sudden?

I stare at him. I am sure my mouth is hanging open. "Huh?" I gurgle ungracefully.

"You're having an art show of some sort?"

My heart stops racing, but now my head is spinning. A father who pays attention . . . foreign concept. And how did he find out?

"It's no big deal," I tell him.

"Your mother seemed to think it was," he says. "She told me you had found some artwork by Nate and were going to show it." From the dark recess of his chair in the corner, his eyes seem to gleam in the lamplight as the rest of his face is eaten by shadow.

"Yeah, I guess," I reply tersely. How did my mom learn about it? Did Mrs. Brown call her? Traitor.

Maybe Dad is exasperated with my short answers, but a rumbling sigh comes from his direction, and he doesn't say anything more. I watch as my father brings his hands together as if in prayer, and he rests his chin on the steeple of his fingers. "When?" he asks simply.

"What do you care?" I shoot back at him, then spin around and stagger out the door.

"Cora!" he calls. Loudly. In that *I'm your father, don't get fresh with me* kind of tone that I haven't heard in almost a year. "Come back here."

It isn't a quavering question or a whisper. It's a command, and it has taken me by surprise, so that my feet seem to turn of their own accord and march me back into the study. I stand in the doorway with my hands behind my back, fingers twisting and knotting and kneading themselves anxiously. I cock my head and brace myself, as if waiting for some kind of blow.

"I know I left you alone. I know that I haven't been there, since . . ." His voice trails off. Then he leans forward and clears his throat with a sharp cough that seems to cut through the charged air. "Since Nate died," he continues, "and I'm sorry for that." It is as if he has used up the last of his strength saying this to me, and he falls back into the cushions of his armchair and is enveloped by the evening gloom once more.

I'm reeling, stunned. I had never expected this. An admission. An apology. I don't know what to say to him. One "I'm sorry" is not enough. Will never be enough to make up for all those months of silence. My mouth opens and closes once like a fish, then I leave, closing the door with a quiet click.

Between my mother not speaking to me and my father's renewed interest, I feel like I'm trapped in an insane asylum. Or a fun house, where everything known is suddenly the unknown or the unusual. I wonder what they talk about, Mom and Dad, when they're by themselves. Clearly they do talk. More important, they know about the art show. Will Mom try to stop me? *Ha,* well, she can try.

I never managed to get those clamshells for my map, and there is still a gaping hole in the center. Now this house, this real house, feels even more fractured and foreign. Then I realize, smacking my forehead with a great "Aha!", how to build this.

In Nate's bedroom, there is a tiny mirror with a seashell frame around it that my grandparents had brought back from a trip to Florida many years ago. That's it. I move back up the hall to Nate's room. I open the door; there is no need for hesitation anymore. I know what lies inside, now.

Yet, when I enter the room, a rush of cold air seems to wrap itself around my very bones and marrow; a chill envelopes me.

"Nate?" I whisper. "Are you here?"

I wait.

Nothing.

Wait some more.

Still nothing.

I move over to his bed and perch myself at the edge of the mattress. Another freezing draft slinks into the room like a cat, wrapping itself around my arms and shoulders. I swing my head wildly about, and then I spot, just behind the bed where I'm sitting, a small crack in the window. I reach out my hand and graze the triangular shard with my fingertips. It wiggles. Gently, I prod the loose piece out of the pane. Now there is a hole in the glass, roughly the shape of Michigan. Cold air whistles into the room. I heave a sigh — no ghosts here. The splinter of glass rests heavily on my palm. Carefully, so as not to cut myself, I bring the glass up to my eye and look through it. A cloud of frosty crystals prevents me from seeing clearly, but as I peer through the sparkling haziness of the glass, it's like looking into a dream.

I wonder what my dad is thinking about right now, if he's feeling sorry for himself or sorry for the way he messed up everything. Sorry for me. I wonder if he knows about

London, if my mother told him she'd forbidden me to go. Probably not.

A year ago, he'd have looked at this broken window and roared about how the heat he was paying for was escaping from the house, and how did this window break, *blah blah blah*. Now, I bet he'd just shrug his shoulders and shuffle back to his chair.

I can use this piece of glass. I pocket it and then, rustling through the drawer of Nate's bedside table, I find the mirror with the seashell frame, and slip out of the room.

When I'm back in the safety of my own bedroom, I take a long piece of cardboard out from under my bed — my dad gave it to me once to use as a hard surface when I used to draw on loose sheets of construction paper. Gently, I place the shard of glass and the mirror on the cardboard. Then I set about fiddling with the mirror, trying to pry it loose from its frame. It seems to have been glued together. I grab a palette knife from my desk and wedge it between the mirror and the frame and begin to pull it apart. In the wiggling process, seashells start dropping off the frame, because the glue is old and dried out, I guess, onto the cardboard. *Maybe,* I think, *I can just pull off all the shells instead*. They come off easily, and soon I have a pile of tiny shells. Then, I bring my tennis racket out of my closet and rest the butt of the handle on the mirror and press. The mirror pops and shatters into a dozen jagged pieces. I shift the racket over to the piece of glass from the window and do the same.

Using tweezers to pick them up, I begin to glue the pieces of glass and slivers of mirror and seashells to each other, until I have cobbled together what looks like a miniscule house. There is a peaked roof and even a little chimney. The base of the house is glued to the cardboard, and so I cut away the excess cardboard, leaving a small square beneath the house as a base. I can mount this onto my map. The final, missing piece.

I clean up, taking care to pick up any extraneous shards of glass, then wipe my hands on my jeans and grab the now-stamped envelope with the permission form off my desk, and head out to the mailbox. As I pass through the garage and slowly weave my way between my parents' cars, I remember Damian telling me, all those weeks ago, when the acceptance letter first arrived, not to do this, not to do something stupid that I would regret. To talk to him about it first. But I know that if I don't mail this letter right now, I'll lose my courage. I'll wimp out. Besides, it's Friday night, and I can't even see my boyfriend (if that's what he is), which just goes to show that I'm a prisoner, and this is the only course of action open to me.

So, I suck in a deep breath and jog down the length of the driveway to the mailbox. It's Friday night, so Joe, the mailman, should pick this up early tomorrow afternoon. I open the mailbox, pop the envelope inside, and lift the red flag. That's it. Done is done.

• • •

When morning comes, I feel like I am going to bounce off the walls of my bedroom. I jump out of bed and look out my window to the mailbox. The flag is still up. I check my clock. It's only 8:30; Joe won't get here for at least another four or five hours. I sigh and flop back down on my bed. Then a terrible thought occurs to me. What if my parents have to mail something — a letter or a bill?

I dig out my slippers from underneath the disheveled piles of drawings and books and discarded clothing, and run downstairs. There are no envelopes in the BILLS AND LETTERS AND THINGS pouch in the kitchen. I think I'm safe.

"Are you looking for something, Cora?" My mother's deadened voice startles me.

"Oh, Mom, hi." I fumble for something to say. "Um, no, just wanted a glass of juice," I tell her.

"Okay," she replies, "help yourself."

I pull a glass down from the cupboard and pour myself some orange juice. Before, we used to have fresh-squeezed juice on the weekends. My dad would pick up oranges from the grocery store on his way home from work Friday evenings, then my mom would squeeze the juice when she got up. It was the first thing she'd do, after switching on the coffee machine. But that tradition went out with The Accident, too.

I bring my glass over to the table and study my mom, sitting there in her ratty pink terry-cloth bathrobe. She looks exhausted. There are dark circles under her eyes, and her hair hangs in strings around her face. She is clutching her coffee mug as though it were a lifeline.

"Are you — are you okay, Mom?" I ask.

"No, Cor," she says, looking at me earnestly, "I don't think I am." She picks up her mug and pushes out her chair, then gets up and wanders into her sewing room.

I feel a tug in my chest, a tiny burning pull. I am doing something bad by lying to her. I just don't see any other way.

Chapter Sixteen

February 8. One year has passed since The Accident. I don't know how a whole year got by me. On one hand, it feels like just yesterday that Nate was calling me a dork as he breezed out of the house. On the other, it's as though we three remaining Bradleys got tangled up in a pool of quicksand, were left hanging in some kind of suspended animation, just trying to keep breathing — and time got stuck in there with us.

What's changed? Well, there is the obvious stuff, like Nate is dead, and I miss him. My parents act like zombie prisonmasters. I started high school and have been kissed — a few times — by Nate's best friend. And Rachel and I aren't speaking to each other, but I have a new friend.

Then, there are the more subtle changes. Like when I think about Nate, I no longer concentrate on the fact that he either ignored me or tormented me. I remember how he used to help me catch minnows in the creek and hold my hand when we crossed the street to go to the pool. I remember his laugh and the way his nose scrunched up when he smiled. I remember how intent he looked when he stood out in the baseball field, and how he would daydream with his eyes open, sucking on his lower lip. I remember how looking into his eyes felt, somehow, like looking into my own. I suppose another difference is that I know about Nate's art now, and I am so proud of him. And I'm making my own art, and I feel good about it.

My parents used to trust me, they used to pay attention to me. Now, I am treated like a broken thing to be guarded. But they're broken. When I think about what I've done, forging my mother's signature, I guess they'll never trust me again. The thought makes me feel sick to my stomach.

One thing that's stayed the same: I don't want to be a screwup.

If Nate were alive, I wonder if he would still be acting so crazy. I wonder if I would have found out about his art, or if he'd have continued to guard that secret. Well, today is the day his secret is released into the world. My heart flutters excitedly. This is it.

I get ready for school, carefully packing a change of clothes and some makeup into my backpack. Damian said he'd leave early this morning to pick up all of the artwork in the Wright barn and bring it over to school in his El Camino. Helena and Cam were supposed to meet him there, too, to help bring out all the pieces and load them into the back of the truck. I'm aching to know what happened, that everything went okay.

As I step into the school today, I can't help but remember my first day, how I felt like a fish swimming upstream, against the flow of all the other kids, of how cold, how alienating this building felt. But this school has come to be as much mine as anyone else's, and it feels comfortable. I make my way to the art room, where I find Helena, Cam, and Damian huddled in a corner of the room, popping the bubbles in giant sheets of bubble wrap, laughing. Nate's sculptures are strewn across every flat surface in the classroom, Damian's paintings are resting on easels. And there's my map, balanced on its stone-and-metal base.

"Cora!" Helena drops her bubble-wrap sheet and prances over to me and throws her arm around my neck. "Look, we did it!" she proclaims happily.

"Wow! Thank you, guys, for doing all this. I'm sorry I couldn't come help. But you know, the jailer wouldn't let me out of her sight."

"Don't worry about it," Cam chimes in. "It was no problem. And, hey, I like your map. It's really cool," he adds, brushing his floppy brown hair out of his eyes. A dimple winks in his cheek as he tosses me a shy smile.

"Thanks," I reply, feeling a warm glow heat my cheeks. I like this feeling of us being a foursome. "So, did anyone else drop off any pieces to be in the show?" I ask.

"Not yet," Damian says. He comes over and puts a hand on my shoulder. "Hey, how are you doing today?"

I smile, grateful for his thoughtfulness. "I'm fine. How about you?"

"I'm okay, too. Hey, look, I think we have our first participant." Damian thrusts his chin in the direction of the door. "Hey, Dana," he greets her.

I turn, and recognize a girl from the junior class.

"Cora, this is Dana. She's in my English class," Damian introduces her. "Dana, this is Cora, my girlfriend, and Helena, and Cam."

Wait. What? His girlfriend? Oh my gosh.

I realize that Damian is staring at me, and for a second time this morning I am blushing. He smiles at me, his gray eyes silvery in the bright sunlight pouring through the windows. And I smile back at him.

"Hi, Dana," I manage to reply. "We're still trying to figure out how to set up everything —" I stop talking as a stream of people start to file into the art room. There must be at least two dozen kids here from various classes, all carrying paintings, sketches, prints, collages, sculptures, mobiles, and other assorted works.

Helena comes over to Damian and me with her hand over her mouth. "Can you believe this? Most of these kids don't even take art! It's all our posters," she whisper-screams. "Pretty soon there won't be room for all of this stuff. It's amazing!"

"It is amazing," I agree.

I never would have guessed that all of these people were artists. I survey the crowd of kids dropping off their works. It seems every clique is represented; there are kids from the basketball and soccer teams, there are goths and emos, and skaters and calculator nerds, cheerleaders and hip-hop wannabes. It's like a high school rainbow.

Some more kids trickle in, leave their pieces and walk out again. The first bell will ring any minute. One last silhouette appears in the doorway, hesitates there. Suddenly, Damian is by my side. He squeezes my hand and nudges me toward the door. As I move toward it, the figure steps forward into the room.

"Rachel?" I ask, wincing at the note of shock in my voice.

"Hi," she says uncertainly.

"Hey, what are you doing here?" I ask. "Do you have something to submit?"

"No," she answers with a gruff chuckle. "I don't have an artistic bone in my body. You know." I nod in agreement with a small smile. "I just wanted to come by and see if you needed help."

"Oh," I say, surprised. "Thanks, but I don't think we do."

Her eyes meet mine. They are wide and full of apprehension and growing moist.

"Please don't cry," I whisper. "Because then I'll cry, too." Too late, a tear has already slipped down my cheek.

"Okay, well, then, I guess I'll go." She turns to leave, then twists around again. "Look, I'm sorry, Cor," Rachel says. "I'm sorry for everything. For not being there for you, for being such a jerk." A rush of — I am not sure what — affection, warmth, relief washes over me.

"Oh, Rach, it's okay. I'm sorry, too." We both sniffle and smile wavery, watery smiles, then step out into the hallway. We sit on the sill of one of the tall windows across from the art room. "I was so angry after Nate died, and I just held on to that anger for months," I tell her. "And I think I took a lot of that anger out on you. So, I'm truly sorry for that." Rachel wipes her nose with her sleeve then digs through her bag for tissues, offering me one.

"I just didn't know how to react," she says. "How to talk to you or be with you. And I wanted this year to be different. I just wanted to think about boys and clothes. And somewhere between not knowing how to talk to you and not wanting to think about what had happened to you, I became this giant jerk," she says. "I'm sorry for that."

"Peace?" I ask.

"Peace," she replies.

"Hey, do you want a sneak preview of the show?" I propose.

"Well," Rachel begins uncomfortably, "I already promised Lizzie — Elizabeth — that I'd meet her before homeroom. But I will definitely be there after school."

I guess things are not going to go back to the way they used to be, but as I look at my old friend and think about my new friends in the art room, I realize it's okay. "All right, I'll see you later then," I tell her.

When I return to the art studio, Helena, Cam, and Damian are lining up tables and stools around the periphery of the room, and Ms. Calico, whom I didn't even see slip inside, is directing them and helping to clear tabletops and easels.

"Unfortunately, we won't be able to hang the paintings — we're just not equipped for that — but we can rest them on these easels," she announces. "And if you guys can come at lunchtime, we can clear out the center of the room, so there's space for people to walk through the exhibit and stop in front of each of the pieces."

I'm shifting some easels to stand against the wall by the door, when I sense that someone is waiting to enter the classroom. I look up and my breath catches as I recognize who the latecomer is: Macie Jax, Nasty #3, Queen Bee.

"Hi," she mumbles.

"Um, hi," I respond. Very smooth. Just giving the Nasties more fuel to use against me.

"I brought — I brought something for the art show," Macie stammers.

I think my jaw just scraped the floor. Quickly, I close my mouth and try to *not* act like a total idiot. "Oh, wow. That's great," I say. "You can bring it in and just set it down somewhere."

Macie gingerly sets one foot inside the art room, almost as though she were afraid of walking into a snake pit. She looks around, taking in all of the artwork we've amassed for the show, and she seems to regain her bravura and walks boldly the rest of the way. She lays her piece, a collage of papier mâché and found objects, which, I have to admit, is pretty brilliant, on a table with her index card on top of it. Then she gives a small wave and exits the room.

Whoa, I think. A Nasty in the art show. This is unexpected. But kind of cool, actually. The four of us finish moving the furniture just as the bell rings, then walk down the art hallway together.

"It's going to be awesome," Cam says.

Damian and I look at each other, and he winks. I think my stomach has sprouted a whole garden of insects, I'm so nervous all of a sudden.

"Just six hours to go," Helena sings sweetly. "See you guys at lunchtime!"

"See you at lunch," we all echo, then scatter, each of us heading in a different direction.

• • •

Mercifully, my classes pass uneventfully. It feels good to smile at Rachel and say hi as we pass on our way out of homeroom. And I don't believe any of my teachers or classmates are aware of the significance of the date today. No one mentions Nate to me, and for this, I am grateful.

At lunchtime, as Helena, Cam, Damian, and I help Ms. Calico rearrange the room and hide extraneous pieces of furniture in the storage closet, Helena corners me and says, "I wasn't sure how to ask you this earlier, but I wanted you to know that I am here for you if you want to talk. You know, since it's the anniversary and everything." She looks at me intently then pulls me into a loose embrace.

"Thank you," I tell her. "Really, it means a lot. I'm fine, though." Helena shoots me a questioning glance. "I mean, I feel kind of weird about my family, you know, not talking to them, not bringing them to this, but I'm really okay with it." I add.

For the first time I am conscious of the fact that I do feel strange about not marking this day with my parents, and sad that they won't be here this afternoon to see Nate's art, to see my map, to share this with me. I wish things could be different.

Helena squeezes my arm and heads over to help Cam with a long table, which they place in the middle of the room, flanked by several easels.

"What are you guys doing?" I ask, coming to where they are sliding the table, trying to center it just so. "I thought we were leaving the center clear."

"Well, we thought Nate's pieces could go here, in the

middle," Helena explains. "Only if it's okay with you, though. If you don't want us to —"

"No, no, it's fine," I say. "It's really nice, actually. Thanks."

"I think we're done." Damian comes up behind me and slings an arm around my shoulders.

"So, I guess this is it. See you guys here right after school?" I ask as we walk out of the classroom.

There's nothing to do but wait now. Just two and a half more hours. I wonder what the show will be like, what it will bring.

Chapter Seventeen

Ms. Calico brought in bottles of soda and bowls of pretzels and platters of brownies and cookies. She strung up vines of twinkling white Christmas lights around the perimeter of the room. It looks so festive and beautiful. All of the pieces of art that more than thirty of us students of Lincoln Grove High created look terrific. It feels like a real gallery in here.

People have started to file into the room; everyone who has artwork on exhibit is here. We are standing around nervously, twitchy and awkward, trying not to look at our own pieces, complimenting one another. Ms. Calico leans her hip against the table where Nate's sculptures are balanced. Easels holding his watercolor paintings and pencil drawings flank either side of the table. She beckons to me to join her, and when I do, she says, without looking at me, "Your brother was extremely talented. He had such an exciting and original sensibility. It's rare, you know, to have two such talented siblings in one family. Your parents must be very proud."

If she only knew. "Sure," I reply. "Thanks."

Ms. Calico raises an eyebrow then walks over to the corner where my map stands. "And this is just spectacular," she declares. "*I'm* proud of you. And I'm so glad you're going to London. You should be receiving more formal training than I can provide."

I wince as I think about what I've done, forging the signature on the form. I am fairly certain I have messed up everything. But I can't think about that now. I let my eyes run over the map, across the warm greens and cool browns, the blues and yellows and grays — the palette I once found so stifling. Now, standing on the metal-and-stone base Nate had constructed, the board has become a three-dimensional, topographical, touchable, living thing.

"It looks amazing." Damian's voice is in my ear. "The whole thing, but your map is . . . it came out perfectly. Congratulations." I turn to smile up at him, and his gaze is so full of warmth. "I think Nate would love it," he tells me. "I think Nate does love it."

"Do you believe he knows what's going on?" I ask.

"I guess I do," Damian answers thoughtfully. "And I think he'd be happy about it."

"I hope so," I reply. As I turn to look at the table of Nate's pieces, I notice that the room has filled even more. I see Helena in the far corner of the room; she is standing with an older couple. I recognize her mom. Helena is chattering brightly, and Cam is standing at her side, his arm around her waist. However unhappy her parents may be, at least they can come here together and stand in the same vicinity as Cam and be here for Helena and *look* normal — and proud. A flash of self-pity grips me, but I shake it off. There's no room here for that tonight.

"Cora?" Damian sounds uncertain.

"What is it?"

"You'd better turn around," he says, his voice tight. "Your parents just walked in the door."

"What?" I gasp and whirl around to see that, indeed, my parents have just entered the classroom and are craning their necks, searching for me, I guess. "What do I do?" I ask Damian frantically.

"You'd better go to them," he responds. Then the warm pressure of his arm withdraws, and I am alone.

Slowly, I trudge over to the entrance of the classroom and reluctantly lift my eyes to meet those of my mom and dad. Where I expected to find glowering pits of fire, though, I find something wholly different and unexpected. My mother's eyes are filled with tears, and the lines around her brow are creased, but not in an angry way, in a softer, sadder kind of way. And my father, too.

"Did you think we wouldn't come?" she asks me quietly.

My tongue is stuck, robbed of language. I grope for an answer but only nod my head.

My mom's chin trembles, as though she is fighting to keep

herself from crying. "Mrs. Brown called to ask me if I knew about this. Imagine my surprise," she says with a rueful grin. "Well, we're here now. Would you show us around?"

I can tell that there's a pretty good chance that I'll burst into tears, too. I take a deep breath and make a concerted effort to keep it together. I look around for Damian. He's standing in the far corner alone, the only one of the artists who isn't accompanied by parents or a crowd of friends. A dark, brooding look shadows his face. My stomach gives a nervous twitch, but I turn back to my parents and tell them to follow me. I lead them into the center of the room, so they can stand in front of the collection of Nate's sculptures and paintings.

The room is really crowded now, bustling with students and parents and some teachers clustered in small groups around each of the pieces. No one notices the three of us as we gather before Nate's work. Both of my parents are gaping in surprise.

They had no idea.

My mother crumples up like a paper doll, chest collapsing in on itself, her shoulders shaking, hand over her mouth. "My beautiful boy," she cries. "He could have been —"

"Mom," I murmur, not sure what to do.

My father steps in front of me and puts his arm around her, drawing her in to his chest. "Shh, Marie." Tears glisten in the corners of his eyes, too, and for the first time in a year, I catch a glimpse of the man he used to be through the gray pall that painted and stained and changed him, that kept him so far apart from us all these months.

I stand there, just looking at them, an outsider. They fit together. And I am locked out, only a watcher. How I long to be a part of them again, for the three of us to fit together once more.

"Daddy," I whimper. And he reaches out his hand to me, and I step in and huddle with my mother in the safe embrace of my father's arms.

"He was a good boy," my father whispers, then lifts his head from the cloud of my mother's and my hair. "Marie, look, look at this." My father disentangles himself and moves closer to one of Nate's easels. It is the drawing of the mother and son. "It's you and Nate."

My mother wipes her eyes and moves over to my dad. She bends to look at the painting. "Yes, it is," she says softly. A small smile crosses her lips. She reaches out a hand as if to caress the painting, then thinks better of it and pulls her hand back. Instead, her fingertips fall onto my hair, and she begins to stroke my head. "Thank you for doing this, Cora. Thank you for giving this gift to us, even if we didn't know we needed it."

"I'm so glad you guys came," I reply, brushing the tears from my own face.

"Come, Cora, what else is there to see? Do you have anything on display here?" my father asks.

"I do," I say, pressing my hands to my cheeks, which I can feel are flushed. "I'll show you." My mother takes my hand and they both follow me over to where my map stands atop the base Nate built.

"Oh my goodness," my mom murmurs. "This is incredible."

"Cora, you did this?" my father asks disbelievingly.

"Yes," I answer. "Well, Nate built the base. I made the map. What do you think?"

"It's amazing, it's just . . . It's our town," my father says, and turns to me, using his nickname for me for the first time since The Accident. "Rabbit, I'm so proud of you."

Then, the memory of what I did comes rushing back, and I think I'm going to throw up.

"Oh, no," I moan.

"What? What is it?" my mother asks.

"I did something," I begin. "Something awful."

"Whatever it is, we can talk about it," she says calmly.

"No, I did something terrible. I'm so sorry," I bawl. "Mom, I forged your signature on the permission form for the London art program. I'm so, so sorry!"

"Cora, I know," my mom answers.

The thickness in the back of my throat starts to rise, and I really begin to worry I might be sick.

"What? What do you mean? How do you know?"

"You didn't put enough postage on the envelope. It came

back last week. I found it, and I saw that you'd forged my signature."

"Augghh," comes a strangled sound from my throat. "I'm so sorry." The floor, the ceiling, the whole world is spinning, lurching madly. I have messed up so profoundly, I don't know how I'll ever fix it.

My mother continues, "I've been hard on you, Cor. I know it. But I was so scared that if I let you have too much — any — freedom, I would lose you like I lost Nate. I was so frightened, because, I . . . I failed as a mother. I failed Nate, and I was so scared that I would —" She doesn't finish. If only I could somehow staunch the flow of those terrible words and thoughts, and replace all of the fear and blame and guilt with the knowledge of how much I love and need her and my dad.

Then my mom straightens and glances at my father, who nods. "I'm really glad you told us about the form before I had to bring it up. It helps me feel like we can trust you again."

I start to open my mouth, as a spark of hope ignites in me. She waves me to be quiet. "I am not saying you can or cannot go. We will discuss this at home."

"We have much to talk about," my father says, "including what you've been doing with Damian Archer. But this isn't the place." The nausea returns slightly.

"Damian is here," I tell them.

"We know," my father replies. "We'd like to talk to him."

The nausea abates slightly. What a roller coaster of a day. I turn to look for Damian, but can't spot him anywhere. *He wouldn't leave, would he?* I wonder.

"I don't see him. Maybe he stepped outside."

"Cora," Helena's voice interrupts, steering me away from my search for Damian. "You should make a speech," she says, "before it's too late and people start to go home. Ms. Calico will introduce you."

"Really?" I ask, surprised. "I didn't prepare anything."

"You should. You should explain about Nate and everything."

My heart starts to beat faster. I wish I could find Damian. "Okay," I agree shakily. Helena darts off to find our teacher, not waiting for me to ready myself.

"Good evening, everybody," Ms. Calico calls out. Gradually, the room begins to settle, as everyone turns to look at her. "As you know, each year Lincoln Grove High has held an art show, open to all of its student artists. This year's show is special, however. We've made this a gala opening night to honor the life and work of Nathaniel Bradley, who was a student at Lincoln Grove High. This wouldn't have happened without one person, an exceptional artist in her own right, whose map of Lincoln Grove is also on display tonight. Please give a hand for Cora Bradley!"

I can't catch my breath. Everybody is clapping and staring at me expectantly, and there are a lot of eyes out there. I glance at my parents, who are both smiling at me encouragingly.

"Thanks, everyone," I begin. "Thanks for coming and thank you to all the artists who have pieces on display here. Each and every one is phenomenal." I survey the room and am amazed by how full it is, by how filled it is with different people from every walk of life. "This is an important date for me. It's the first anniversary of my brother Nate's death. Some of you may have known Nate. He passed away one year ago today in a car accident." The room is silent. "And in the months since he died, I learned that he was an artist. I never knew this while he was alive. He kept his art hidden, a secret from almost everyone." I look around for Damian again, but there is no sign of him. "Damian Archer, Nate's best friend — *my* friend — helped me find some of his artwork. We thought the best way to remember him and to celebrate him would be to include his work in the show. It makes me really happy to see his artwork here alongside everyone else's, and it makes me even happier that there are so many of you here tonight who I don't ordinarily see hanging around the art room." I smile as some of the kids start to chuckle. "Congratulations, everybody. And thank you." I take a step back, and the room erupts into applause. People who are my friends and who aren't, people I've never spoken to once, are looking at me with shining eyes and clapping as hard as they can.

I don't doubt that tomorrow everything will go back to the way it has always been, but for one night, to come together like this feels like a miracle. "Thank you, Nate," I whisper.

I feel a tap on my shoulder and turn to find Rachel standing before me. "Hi," I say.

"Hey," she replies, then turns to my parents. "Hello, Mrs. Bradley. Hello, Mr. Bradley."

My mom and dad greet Rachel, then wander off to look at the rest of the art.

"This is really great, Cor," Rachel says. "I'm so happy for you."

"Thanks," I return. "I am just so happy it all worked out okay."

Another voice interrupts. "It really did."

Julie Castor, Nate's ex-girlfriend, has come up beside me. Her green eyes are thickly lined and her blonde hair hangs limply around her face. "Hey," she says. "I just — I just wanted to thank you for doing this. I knew about Nate, his art. And one of the things that I just couldn't deal with was how he hid it. How he acted like such a total —" she stops.

"Jerk?" I fill in.

"Yes," Julie looks at me gratefully. "And all the time he had this amazing talent and wouldn't do anything about it. It drove me crazy."

"I can imagine," I tell her.

"Well," she says, "I'm glad you finally got his stuff out in the open. It should be."

"Yeah," I say. How strange and wonderful this evening has been.

Once more, I try to find Damian, and as the crowd thins, and people begin filing out of the room, I realize that he's gone. He left without saying good-bye.

I reach my parents and tell them that I want to go home. Ms. Calico stops us on the way out, and says to my parents, "You must be so proud. Cora has so much potential. I'm so pleased you're allowing her to explore it in London this summer."

My mouth goes dry and I look at my mother. She smiles cryptically, and says, "Well, we're very grateful to you for encouraging her. And for allowing her to include Nate's artwork in the show. Thank you." They shake hands all around, and as we walk through the school building, I hope Damian will materialize. He doesn't, and my parents shepherd me to the car.

Once we're all seat-belted in and on our way home, I speak up from the backseat, "So, what happened?"

"When I found the envelope," my mother begins, "I realized that we were on the verge of losing you, too. Or, that somehow, somewhere along the way, I already had lost you. Then your father and I had a very long and frank talk. It wasn't easy, and the discussion we're going to have won't be easy, either. But if this family is going to stay together, it is necessary."

I sink back in my seat and mull over my mother's words. I don't expect our family and all our problems will be fixed by tomorrow, but I expect things will be better.

Chapter Eighteen

The stink of greasy pizza fills the house. There was a long night of talking and explaining and crying and pizza. My parents and I got to know each other again, and we reached a point of understanding, I think. They lifted the 4:00 P.M. curfew, they told me I could see Damian, and they said they would discuss whether I could go to London and decide before March 15, when the permission form is due. It's not like before Nate died, it never will be; there will always be a hole in our family. But now, it feels like all three of us have come inside, together, from the cold.

I am in bed and my face feels tight from dried tears. I take out my cell phone and dial Damian's number. I can't wait to tell him what happened. How everything changed in one night, and that I'm allowed to see him, and we don't have to hide or sneak anymore.

The phone doesn't ring; it goes straight to voice mail. I try again. Same result. I dial a third time and receive the voice mail once again. *What is going on?* I start to feel nervous.

I turn out my light and try willing myself to sleep. It doesn't work. Why did he leave the art show early? Did something happen to him? Is he upset? Did he decide that the whole thing was a mistake? He called me his girlfriend this morning, though. Could he regret that? I toss around in my sheets. I won't know anything until I see him in school tomorrow.

• • •

When I arrive at school, I immediately spy his blue El Camino in the parking lot. He's here, so he must be okay, I think with relief. After I chain up my bike, I run into the building, fighting through the slow-moving crowd of students toward Damian's locker. No sign of him. I duck my head into his homeroom and spy him crumpled into a desk in the corner of the classroom, his ever-present black trench coat wrapped around him. Like a shroud, I think.

"Damian!" I cry.

Dully, he looks up at me. I wave my hand, hoping he'll smile and leap to his feet, run to the classroom door, and swallow me in a hug. He doesn't stir from his seat. I feel unsteady, uncertain. I'm not sure how I fit now. I start to enter the classroom. All I know is that I have to understand why Damian won't speak to me. I have to know why he left the show early last night and why he will barely even look at me. What happened.

Yet, two steps in, a booming voice rings out, "Miss, I don't know what you're doing in here, but you'd better have a note from the principal saying you've been promoted to the junior class and you're supposed to be in my classroom now." The very tall, very infamously mean Mr. Cross has risen from his desk at the front of the room and is glaring at me crossly. How appropriate. I dart a pleading look in Damian's direction, then bow my head, and mumble an apology and back out of the room.

I hear the footsteps behind me before Mr. Cross's thunderous voice calls, "Mr. Archer, I suggest you return to your seat."

"What is it, Cora?" Damian is standing before me, his eyes dull and wary.

"Damian," I say, and I raise my hand to touch his cheek, but Damian takes a step back.

"What is it?" he repeats.

"I — you left early last night. Without saying good-bye. What happened?"

"Nothing happened. I just didn't feel like hanging around any longer."

"But why? I was looking for you. And you didn't even say good-bye." I sound pathetic. I know I do. Plaintive and wimpy and lame. I can't help it. I am so confused. "Did I do something?" I ask.

"You didn't do anything," he says. "Nothing happened. I just didn't — I don't —" Damian stops and stares at a point above my head.

"What?" I press.

"Cora, I don't think we should be together."

It's as though someone has released all the fury of a raging sea on me. I am knocked down and battered. "Why not?" I can barely whisper.

He takes a deep breath and lets out a loud sigh, as if he is about to explain. Then he seems to think better of it and says, "Look, I've got to go. See you around."

And before I can say a word, Damian has spun around on the heel of his boot and marched back into the classroom. I stand still as a statue. Frozen like petrified wood. I don't understand, tears pricking at my eyes. None of this makes any sense.

The bell rings. Now, not only have I been summarily dumped in the hallway outside of Mr. Cross's classroom, but I'm late. I begin to jog toward my homeroom and all the while trying to puzzle out the reasoning behind Damian's behavior.

At lunch I sit with Helena and Cam and describe our exchange in the hallway.

"What do you think?" I ask.

Helena says, "Maybe he was upset that his parents didn't come to see his artwork."

"No, that doesn't seem like Damian, and besides, he knew his mom had to work," I respond.

"Well, maybe he was intimidated by your parents," Helena guesses. She turns to Cam. "Don't you think that could be why he's acting so weird, if he thinks Cora's parents still hate him?"

Cam appears to consider her suggestion, running his fingers through his hair, then shakes his head. "Why don't you just go talk to him and stop guessing?"

"Huh. That's a good idea," I say, picking at a loose thread on my sleeve. I crane my neck, hoping to spot him in the cafeteria. There's Rachel, perched at the end of the Nasty table, Elizabeth by her side. A sense of regret, of loss rips at me, but I am glad Rachel has Elizabeth. As I look around, I notice that many of the kids who were at the art gallery show last night are here in the cafeteria. Each returned to his or her usual group of friends. *Maybe nothing good lasts,* I think.

Enough. I'm going to find Damian today and I'm going to figure this out.

After school, I look for him again, but he must have slipped out early. The most obvious place to look for him now is at his house. I haven't ridden my bike there before, and it's quite a ways away, but I take a deep breath and resolve to find him.

I'm coasting down the county road, when I spot the El Camino, unmistakable with its racing stripe, pulled off to the side by the park. I quickly turn my bike into the park grounds parking lot and leave it on the sidewalk. Then I begin trudging through the snowy field, regretting not wearing my waterproof boots, following another pair of footprints toward the playground. There, I find Damian seated on the tire swing, the chain twisting and untwisting in rapid circles.

"Hey," I say, out of breath from tramping through the snow.

Damian jumps, visibly startled. "What are you doing here?" he asks. He doesn't look at me, his eyes are downcast, and his cheek muscle twitches.

"I wanted to talk to you," I reply. All the hurt I feel is pouring out in my voice, and I hate it. I hate that my emotions are so obvious.

"What about?"

"Damian, come off it. What is going on with you? What is your problem?" I stomp around the tire swing until I am directly in front of him, and he has to look at me. "One minute you say I'm your girlfriend, and then eight hours later you leave the show and stop talking to me? Come on. I deserve to know what happened," I snap. This anger feels good, a refreshing change from sadness.

Damian exhales loudly, then motions for me to sit on the swing across from him. Cautiously, I climb onto the tire and keep very still, so my knees won't brush his.

"You're right," he says softly. "But I don't know how to tell you."

"Just say it, Damian. Because I'm hurting so badly right now, I don't know how to breathe."

His face crumples, and for an instant I think he might cry. But he straightens and grips the chains so tightly, his knuckles turn white. "I didn't mean to hurt you," he murmurs. "I just . . ."

"Just what?" I prod.

"I just saw you with your parents and didn't want to get in the way. You should be with them. You guys should be talking and working things out. And I know how they feel about me. I can't get in the way of you guys making up."

"That's it?" I ask, astonished.

"Yeah, I guess so," he replies bitterly.

"Oh, Damian, you idiot." I begin to laugh.

"Look," he starts angrily, and stands, swinging one leg over the rim of the tire.

"No, I'm sorry. I didn't mean to call you an idiot. It's just — look, I forged my mom's signature on the London form, and they found out. You were totally right. I shouldn't have done it, but in the end, it helped all of us to see that our family was broken. And we need to fix it, and make it better," I explain.

"Great," Damian says. "I'm happy for you. I really am." He extracts his other leg from the tire and begins to head back in the direction of the parking lot.

"Would you wait a second, please?" I shout at him. Slowly, almost unwillingly, Damian turns around. "What I was trying to say was that my mom finding out that I forged her signature made her realize that she'd been unfair. Completely psychotic, actually. To me, and to you, too. We want to try to work things out, to make our family right again. And I want you to be a part of this. They want you there, too."

Damian is staring at me uncertainly now, as if he doesn't know what to believe. "I don't — I don't understand. They don't hate me anymore?"

"Well, I don't think they actually ever hated you. I think they are confused and you can't just turn feelings on and off, but they realize they were wrong. And they want to try to make it up to you. And to me. Would you give us a chance?" I ask.

"A chance," Damian repeats softly.

I nod and feel a flutter of hope in my chest. "Please?"

He walks toward me, and I rise, trying to step out of the tire, but my legs get tangled and I trip, falling forward over the tire.

Damian runs over and catches me. "You do this a lot," he whispers fondly.

"I need you here to catch me," I say.

"Okay."

"Okay?" I ask.

"Okay." And Damian leans down and plants a gentle kiss on my lips.

• • •

I wish I could say we all lived happily ever after. I can't. But I can say we lived. Our love for Nate lives, and he's left us this piece of himself in his art; it was his gift to us. We know him now through his art, and I can take comfort in that.

I guess the thing about high school is, it's the moment when

you start to cross from being a kid to being an adult, and this journey to know yourself begins. Nate's journey ended too early, and I thought I had to run away to some far-off land to start mine. But, for now, it seems to me that I have enough to explore right here. There's a whole continent to discover in myself, and I know that it's love — love for my parents, my friends, my brother, and my art — that will guide me. Love will be my map.

Acknowledgments

I am so grateful to everyone who had a hand in bringing *A Map of the Known World* into being — from those who actually worked on the book to those who supported me as I wrote it.

This book would not be possible without two people: Meredith Kaffel, my very wise and patient agent, who is very much responsible for drawing Cora out of me and helping me to shape her world; and Aimee Friedman, my insightful and brilliant editor, who helped me to craft this story with her astute pen. To both of you, your unflagging enthusiasm and deft eyes, your fortitude and love and nourishment mean the world to me and make me far less neurotic. Thank you both so much.

Additionally, I must thank my wonderful family at Scholastic, all of whom have given so generously of their time, talents, and friendship to me over the years, including: Becky Amsel, Stephanie Anderson, Tara Bermingham, Duryan Bhagat-Clark, Anamika Bhatnagar, Alan Boyko, Susan Jeffers Casel, Margaret Coffee, Jody Corbett, Billy DiMichele, Kathleen Donohoe, Brandi Dougherty, Sheila Marie Everett, Nancy Feldman, Sue Flynn, Jacquelyn Fortier, Leslie Garych, Jacky Harper, Dianne

Hess, Jazan Higgins, Roz Hilden, Annette Hughes, Cecily Kaiser, Marijka Kostiw, Carolyn Longest, Grace Maccarone, Nick Martin, Ed Masessa, John Mason, Siobhan McGowan, Charisse Meloto, Suzanne Murphy, Brenda Murray, Nikki Mutch, Stephanie Nooney, Arlene Robillard, Dick Robinson, Mark Seidenfeld, Lizette Serrano, Joy Simpkins, Alan Smagler, Jill Smith, Janet Speakman, Tracy van Straaten, Adrienne Vrettos, Elizabeth Whiting, Dawn Zahorik, and so many others.

Also at Scholastic, I'd like to extend my gratitude to Karyn Browne, a kindred spirit; Rachel Coun, for her immense generosity, support, and friendship; David Saylor, a marvelous teacher and guide; Ellie Berger, whose faith in me has meant so much; Elizabeth Parisi, whom I thank for her beautiful design and for her friendship; David Levithan, an incomparable friend who has supported and encouraged me for so many years; and Ken Geist, who has been a mentor in every sense of the word and a dear friend.

I would also like to thank Charlotte Sheedy; Joe and the folks at Vintage; Kristin Dumont; Tamar Hermesh; Margaret Jones; Joan Konner and Al Perlmutter; Edric Mesmer; Eric Mortensen; Jackie Parker; Alison Pollet; Andrea and Steve Popofsky; Rhoda Sherbell and my friends at the Art Students League of New York; Jerry Weiss; Sarah Gelt; Molly D. Leibovitz; my parents, Nancy and Lionel Sandell; Sharon Sandell; Sarah Trabucchi — dearest friend, thank you for reading this manuscript over and over and over; and Liel — how can I ever repay you for all the pushing, reading, editing, supporting, and loving me? I'll be forever grateful.

About the Author

Lisa Ann Sandell is the author of *Song of the Sparrow,* which was a Book Sense Summer 2007 Pick, as well as *The Weight of the Sky,* which was named one of the New York Public Library's Books for the Teen Age. Music and art have always been an important part of Lisa's life; she studies sculpture and drawing and plays several instruments. Lisa works as a children's book editor in New York City. You can visit her at her Web site: www.lisaannsandell.com.